TEMPTATION

Praise for Kris Bryant

Falling

"This is a story you don't want to pass on. A fabulous read that you will have a hard time putting down. Maybe don't read it as you board your plane though. This is an easy 5 stars!"—*Romantic Reader Blog*

"Bryant delivers a story that is equal parts touching, compassionate, and uplifting."—*Lesbian Review*

"This was a nice, romantic read. There is enough romantic tension to keep the plot moving, and I enjoyed the supporting characters' and their romance as much as the main plot."—*Kissing Backwards*

Listen

"Ms. Bryant describes this soundscape with some exquisite metaphors, it's true what they say that music is everywhere. The whole book is beautifully written and makes the reader's heart to go out with people suffering from anxiety or any sort of mental health issue."—*Lez Review Books*

"I was absolutely captivated by this book from start to finish. The two leads were adorable and I really connected with them and rooted for them…This is one of the best books I've read recently—I cannot praise it enough!"—*Melina Bickard, Librarian, Waterloo Library (UK)*

"The main character's anxiety issues were well written and the romance is sweet and leaves you with a warm feeling at the end. Highly recommended reading."—*Kat Adams, Bookseller (QBD Books, Australia)*

"This book floored me. I've read it three times since the book appeared on my Kindle…I just love it so much. I'm actually sitting here wondering how I'm going to convey my sheer awe factor but I will try my best. Kris Bryant won Les Rêveur book of the year 2018 and seriously this is a contender for 2019."—*Les Rêveur*

Against All Odds

"This story tugged at my heartstrings, and it hit all the right notes for me because these wonderful authors allowed me to peep into the hearts and minds of the characters. The vivid descriptions of Peyton, Tory, and the perpetrator's personalities allowed me to have a deeper understanding of what makes them tick, and I was able to form a clear picture of them in my mind."—*The Lesbian Review*

"*Against All Odds* is equal parts thriller and romance; the balance between action and love, fast and slow pace makes this novel a very entertaining read."—*Lez Review Books*

Lammy Finalist *Jolt*

Jolt "is a magnificent love story. Two women hurt by their previous lovers and each in their own way trying to make sense out of life and times. When they meet at a gay- and lesbian-friendly summer camp, they both feel as if lightning has struck. This is so beautifully involving, I have already reread it twice. Amazing!"—*Rainbow Book Reviews*

Goldie Winner *Breakthrough*

"Looking for a fun and funny light read with hella cute animal antics and a smoking hot butch ranger? Look no further...In this well-written first-person narrative, Kris Bryant's characters are well developed, and their push/pull romance hits all the right beats, making it a delightful read just in time for beach reading."—*Writing While Distracted*

"It's hilariously funny, romantic, and oh so sexy...But it is the romance between Kennedy and Brynn that stole my heart. The passion and emotion in the love scenes surpassed anything Kris Bryant has written before. I loved it."—*Kitty Kat's Book Review Blog*

"Kris Bryant has written several enjoyable contemporary romances, and *Breakthrough* is no exception. It's interesting and clearly well-researched, giving us information about Alaska and issues like poaching and conservation in a way that's engaging and never comes across as an info dump. She also delivers her best character work to date, going deeper with Kennedy and Brynn than we've seen in previous stories. If you're a fan of Kris Bryant, you won't want to miss this book, and if you're a fan of romance in general, you'll want to pick it up, too."—*Lambda Literary*

Forget Me Not

"Told in the first person, from Grace's point of view, we are privy to Grace's inner musings and her vulnerabilities…Bryant crafts clever wording to infuse Grace with a sharp-witted personality, which clearly covers her insecurities…This story is filled with loving familial interactions, caring friends, romantic interludes, and tantalizing sex scenes. The dialogue, both among the characters and within Grace's head, is refreshing, original, and sometimes comical. *Forget Me Not* is a fresh perspective on a romantic theme, and an entertaining read."—*Lambda Literary Review*

Whirlwind Romance

"Ms. Bryant's descriptions were written with such passion and colorful detail that you could feel the tension and the excitement along with the characters."—*Inked Rainbow Reviews*

Taste

"*Taste* is a student/teacher romance set in a culinary school. If the premise makes you wonder whether this book will make you want to eat something tasty, the answer is: yes."—*The Lesbian Review*

Touch

"The sexual chemistry in this book is off the hook. Kris Bryant writes my favorite sex scenes in lesbian romantic fiction."—*Les Rêveur*

By the Author

Jolt

Whirlwind Romance

Just Say Yes: The Proposal

Taste

Forget Me Not

Touch

Breakthrough

Shameless
(writing as Brit Ryder)

Against All Odds
(with Maggie Cummings and M. Ullrich)

Listen

Falling

Tinsel

Temptation

Visit us at www.boldstrokesbooks.com

TEMPTATION

by
Kris Bryant

2020

TEMPTATION
© 2020 BY KRIS BRYANT. ALL RIGHTS RESERVED.

ISBN 13: 978-1-63555-508-0

THIS TRADE PAPERBACK ORIGINAL IS PUBLISHED BY
BOLD STROKES BOOKS, INC.
P.O. BOX 249
VALLEY FALLS, NY 12185

FIRST EDITION: JANUARY 2020

THIS IS A WORK OF FICTION. NAMES, CHARACTERS, PLACES, AND INCIDENTS ARE THE PRODUCT OF THE AUTHOR'S IMAGINATION OR ARE USED FICTITIOUSLY. ANY RESEMBLANCE TO ACTUAL PERSONS, LIVING OR DEAD, BUSINESS ESTABLISHMENTS, EVENTS, OR LOCALES IS ENTIRELY COINCIDENTAL.

THIS BOOK, OR PARTS THEREOF, MAY NOT BE REPRODUCED IN ANY FORM WITHOUT PERMISSION.

CREDITS
EDITORS: ASHLEY TILLMAN AND SHELLEY THRASHER
PRODUCTION DESIGN: STACIA SEAMAN
COVER DESIGN BY DEB B.

Acknowledgments

After writing some pretty heavy books, I decided it was time to write something a little more playful. When you're writing a book, you are in that book for a long time, on and off the page. You are thinking about it when you wake up, when you fall asleep, driving to work, even when you're with your friends. After writing about a mass shooting, a person struggling with anxiety, and a survivor of a plane crash, I decided to write something flirty and fun.

Thank you, Rad, Sandy, and the BSB team for continuing to publish my books. I love our family and I appreciate all the effort that goes into making all of our books top shelf.

Ashley deserves all the credit. She points out things that I miss and hands me tissue when she cuts 15,000 words and tells me to buck up because it was for the betterment of the story. She's the best content editor, and I'll fight anyone who disputes that. Shelley Thrasher did a drive-by jump-in as copy editor and did a fantastic job. A fresh pair of eyes on a story really helps, so I love the guest appearance and look forward to working with her in the future.

A shout out to KB Draper for our writing dates to keep me on track. Where would I be without Saturday-morning coffee and pastries? Thank you, Fiona and Jenn, for your support and love. It's great to be able to talk to you both about anything and everything I need to get off my chest—book related or not. Melissa Brayden is my go-to wine connoisseur and consultant on all important things, and Georgia Beers keeps me and my ego in check. Nikki, Elle (Sugar), and Paula—I count down the days until the next book event where we can get together and do what we do best. I love you all and I thank you for always being there for me.

And Deb. Not only is she an amazing artist and designs my book covers, she catches my many, many mistakes before the book goes to print. Thank you for taking care of Molly and me when I'm deep in a story and I forget about the little things.

Thank you, readers, for picking up my books and giving them a chance. I love receiving emails, reviews, and am so happy when you tweet or post about my books. It makes the fairy tale real.

You know who you are

Chapter One

I noticed her before we even got out of the car. She was standing away from the other parents with her arms crossed and her weight shifted to one hip. Unlike the rest of the soccer moms in their jeans or shorts, she was wearing a designer suit that showed off her curves and demanded attention. She looked bothered to be there, and I immediately thought all the things I shouldn't have—she's a horrible mother who doesn't support her kid, and her kid knows she doesn't want to be there. And wow, she's got great legs.

"I'm going to need some help." Emma's tone was duly noted. She'd gotten comfortable with me after two days, and by the third, she was bossing me around. It was only for two more days, so I let her get away with being a jerk. I didn't care. I needed the money, and Robin and Henry Minks needed a babysitter for the week.

"Hang on. I'll be right there." I pushed open the door and hustled to the back seat, where she regally sat on her booster seat.

"It's about time."

"Don't be rude. It's not nice," I said.

"You work for us. I can tell you what I want."

I ignored her and helped unclasp her booster seat. She refused help after I unbuckled her, and I had to stifle a giggle when she tripped getting out of the car.

"You did that on purpose." She glared at me and plopped on the grass to put on her cleats.

Pissed that I wouldn't let her put on her cleats at home, she'd made a great effort to kick the passenger seat a lot during our short drive to the soccer fields. I didn't care. My car, given to me by my Nana

• 13 •

the week before, was a piece of crap, and tiny six-year-old feet weren't going to damage it more. "I did not. Pick up your stuff and head to your team." She grabbed her ball and marched to the coach. I watched her go and shook my head the entire time. Just when I thought I wanted kids, Emma reminded me why it was a good idea to wait.

"She's a handful. So angelic, yet a tiny demon hides inside," a woman said. I turned to find a pleasant-looking woman with short-brown, stylish hair standing a few feet away. She brushed her hair back and smiled at me. "Hi, I'm Alex. My kid plays on the team with Emma and about fifteen other entitled children."

I laughed. I wasn't expecting such an honest introduction. "Hi, I'm Cassie. Caregiver to Emma this week."

"I was wondering who they were going to rope into watching her while Robin was in DC. Henry wasn't about to take time off. Where did they find you?" Alex seemed genuinely interested, even though the way she phrased her question seemed condescending.

"Care and Companions. This is my first job with them. Emma was so quiet when we first met."

"It's the quiet ones you have to worry about."

I liked Alex immediately. She was laid-back but quick.

"She's just a kid. She'll learn soon enough that being bossy isn't always the best idea. You know, more flies with honey," I said.

We stood there in slightly awkward silence until practice began. Alex pointed out the bleachers for us to sit down, but I wanted to head back to the car. I needed to read a few chapters of my environmental-technologies textbook before my next class, yet I didn't want to be rude, so I followed her to the third row. The woman in the suit was sitting on the bottom bleacher on the edge, as if she needed a quick escape. Her white-blond hair was loose, stylish, and fell just below her shoulders. Even though I hadn't seen her face, I knew she was beautiful. She sat confidently, alone, yet seemingly unfazed. When a boy dribbled the ball successfully in front of her, she sat up straighter and softly clapped. The white-blond hair was a dead giveaway that he was her son. I was intrigued by her standoffish behavior and wondered why she wasn't sitting with the other soccer moms.

"Noah really is a sweet kid." Alex bumped my elbow and pointed to the kid who held the suit's attention. "But he's probably the only one. What kind of snacks did you bring the kids?"

Panic burned throughout me. I was supposed to bring snacks? What the fuck? What snacks? Henry didn't say a thing to me. "Uh, none. I didn't know we were supposed to. Nobody told me anything."

Alex looked at her watch. "Well, we don't have a lot of time left, so let's see what we can round up. I'll text the moms."

I watched several heads shake as they read Alex's text. When the suit looked at me, I froze. She was more beautiful than I expected. Her light blue eyes were expressive, her lips red and full. I was nervous not just because she was beautiful, but she was confident and her gaze never wavered once her eyes met mine. I held my breath for no other reason than I simply forgot how to breathe. She stood and motioned for me to follow. Without hesitation, I stood, wove my way around the other moms sitting on the bleachers, and met her near a very nice, very clean Mercedes SUV.

"Hi. I'm Cassie and apparently have committed the heinous crime of not bringing snacks today." I was nervous and had absolutely no game.

She stared at me for a few moments, then opened the back of her SUV to reveal canvas bags filled with goodies. "I understand you are filling in for Robin. I have juice boxes and oranges that you can pass out after practice. I always have spares on hand for the parents who forget." Her voice held a slight note of judgment.

"In all fairness, I didn't forget. I was never told. Plus, I'm not a parent." I shrugged, trying to convey that I didn't care what she thought about me, but I did. I was always self-conscious around pretty women, especially today with my hair pulled back in a ponytail and very little makeup on. I was babysitting. Who knew I would run into a hot mom? "But thank you. I can repay you Friday."

She shrugged. "Don't worry about it." She handed me the two bags and walked away to claim her seat on the first row, away from everyone else.

I wanted to know her story. I wanted to know why she didn't sit with the other moms, why she was dressed like she was closing multi-million-dollar deals, and why she wasn't wearing a ring on her left hand. I heaved the bags up to Alex and plopped down. Shit. I forgot to ask the suit's name.

"Wow. Good for you. Brook Wellington doesn't talk to a lot of people here."

Wellington. It was a well-known high-society name. "She seems nice. And she helped me out of a bind."

"I've never spoken to her, and our kids have been on this soccer team for two years now," Alex said.

"You're kidding. That doesn't even make sense."

"I mean, I've heard her talk to the group as a whole, but we've never actually had a one-on-one conversation."

I stared at Brook. Her eyes never left her son. When he scored during their practice scrimmage, he turned to find her in the crowd, his face beaming with pride. She pumped her fist in the air, and it looked like they did a distant high five. I smiled. Brook Wellington might be an ice queen with this crowd, but I saw her unguarded, softer side with her son.

"I'm just thankful she had snacks. She just saved me from breaking a dozen hearts."

"She's saved us quite a few times. Always prepared."

When practice ended, the kids circled me like vultures, hungrily picking at the bags. Alex reminded the children of the manners they had abandoned and lined them up like soldiers. I handed each one a juice box and an orange and received more eye rolls than thank yous, but I didn't blame them. Where were the fruit roll-ups? What about chocolate-chip cookies or tiny bags of Doritos? It was bad enough that Emma ate only organic and had zero processed sugar in her diet, but every single kid in this neighborhood, too? That seemed unfair. When snacks were divvied up, I found Brook at her car and handed her the empty canvas bags.

"Thank you so much for saving me back there."

Brook gave me a curt, dismissive nod and told Noah to buckle up in his booster. Once he was secure, she walked to the driver's seat and climbed in. I had no idea why I was still in their space, other than I wanted to stay connected with her.

"I can replenish your supply at the next practice."

"Don't worry about it." Her blue eyes were so piercing I had a hard time breaking eye contact. Most incredibly attractive women made me fidget from nervous energy and fumble around like an idiot. "Have a good night." She drove off slowly, and I stood there watching until Emma growled something rude at me.

"What?" I turned to find her bouncing her soccer ball against my bumper. Although it grated on my nerves, I smiled sweetly at her. Her face scrunched up right before she huffed and gave me the biggest eye roll I'd ever seen a small child make.

"We need to leave. I'm hungry."

Just two more days. "Okay. Let's go home and eat some yummy kale and quinoa."

Saying that made me shudder. Tonight's menu was roasted quinoa with vegetables and avocado. It wasn't as if the food tasted bad; it just wasn't kid food. Emma probably never had a fish stick dipped in ketchup or macaroni and cheese made with powdered cheese from a box. I knew those weren't healthy foods, but they were delicious.

"I don't like the orange you brought." She emphasized that statement by throwing the orange on the floor of the back seat.

I sighed. Working for the Minks family was a lot more than I had bargained for. Henry had neglected to tell me it was their turn to bring snacks. To be fair, he probably didn't know either. He had to text Robin to find out what practice field they were on and text me the answer. "Noah's mom helped out your family by donating the juice boxes and oranges." I rolled my eyes at my own childish antics. I'd sunk to her level. "When we get home, I'll cut you up an apple with peanut butter. How's that?"

"Okay."

It was six fifteen. I had just enough time to fix dinner, feed her, put her in the tub, and tuck her into bed before Henry came home. He appreciated my help even if Emma made it extremely difficult. This was Emma lashing out at a stranger. Her mom must have had it ten times worse.

"Do you have any homework?" I punched in the temporary code to the front door.

She pushed past me to get inside first and gave me another award-winning eye roll. "I'm six. School just started, and we don't have homework yet."

"Get cleaned up and I'll cut up a snack. You can keep me entertained while I cook." I busied myself with the ingredients and put the quinoa on the stovetop to boil. She slipped into the chair and watched me work. "Do you help your parents cook?"

"No. They don't want me near the stove. Or the oven. Sometimes I can use the microwave, but only when they're around."

"That's a good plan. It hurts when you get burned. You have to be careful when you cook."

Emma crunched on her apple slices and a dab of natural peanut butter that I had to stir forever just to get it smooth enough to spoon out.

"I think I want to be a chef when I grow up." Her voice was firm and sure.

"I think that's a wonderful idea. You eat a lot of grown-up type food, so I think you have the taste for it." I decided not to tell her I wanted to be a nun when I was her age. I diced tomatoes and an avocado and slid her over a small plate.

"Yum. I like these."

"See? I didn't like avocados until I was an adult, so you're one step ahead of me."

"What did you eat?" If nothing else, Emma was inquisitive if something piqued her interest.

"When I was a kid? Um, hot dogs, macaroni and cheese, chicken nuggets, corn, grilled cheese, stuff like that." I fluffed the quinoa with a fork and seasoned it. I liked cooking. I just rarely had the time anymore.

"Sometimes the school lunches are fun."

"Fun how?"

I fixed her a plate. She blew across the quinoa to cool it. I'd never seen a kid eat healthy food with such gusto.

"Sometimes we have pizza with red sauce and cheese."

"How else do you eat pizza if it's not cheesy and covered in red pizza sauce?"

She looked puzzled. "Pizza has white sauce and vegetables."

"Oh, sweet child. Pizza has cheese, pepperoni, sausage, and all kinds of other delicious things." I helped myself to some of the quinoa. While it wasn't bad, it wasn't life-changing either. The lime juice I drizzled on top really brought out its earthy flavor. But I still wasn't convinced it was good.

"Can we make a pizza tomorrow? Or get one?"

I backpedaled. I didn't want to be responsible for destroying this child's palate and healthy habits.

"Your mom has a menu plan that I have to follow. But I tell you what. You don't have soccer practice until Friday. Why don't we make some oatmeal cookies tomorrow?" Surely, there was a recipe that was somewhat healthy and low sugar.

Her eyes lit up, and a smile spread over her face. In that moment, Emma was genuinely adorable.

"Yes. Let's do it. Can I help make them?"

I scoffed at her. "It's going to be all you. You have to measure, mix, and bake them. Are you up for the challenge?"

And just like that, we became friends. She didn't fight me when it was bedtime. I was reading her a bedtime story when Henry got home.

"I'm sorry I'm late tonight. I'll be sure to tell the service to add an extra hour," Henry said. He looked exhausted.

I thanked him, got my first hug from Emma, and headed out to my car. Babysitting wasn't too bad. You just had to find a way to communicate with the kid. I was kind of sad that this easy money wasn't going to continue after Friday, but I had a feeling I would see this family again.

Chapter Two

I remember Brook Wellington. Yes, of course." I was elbow deep in laundry and playing Uno with Nana, my new roommate. If she hadn't taken me in, I don't know where I would have gone. She'd missed bingo last week because she gave me her almost-dead 1994 Acura, and her friend who normally took her had cataract surgery earlier in the week so she couldn't drive them. Nana was being way too nice to me.

"She's looking for a live-in nanny for her son Noah. Is that something you're interested in?"

My heart thumped twice as fast as normal. Who could forget Brook Wellington? I sat down to process the request. "Live-in? I can't be a full-time nanny because I go to school."

"I told her you had late morning and early afternoon classes, and she said Noah's in school then anyway. She's looking for five days a week, from seven in the morning until seven at night, with time off during the late morning and early afternoon for your classes."

That sounded very restrictive. Rebecca must have sensed my hesitation. "But the pay is great and comes with health insurance. You'll have the weekends off, and a small studio apartment above the garage is included."

"I don't think I understand. I've seen Brook with her son. She's very attentive. Why does she need a nanny?"

"Ms. Wellington has a busy career, and her hours are all over the place. She needs stability for Noah. And, Cassie? She asked for you specifically."

I sat down. I tried not to read too much into why Brook asked for me. We spent a total of two minutes together. I wanted a job, yes, but being a full-time nanny was a huge commitment. And that also meant that I would see Brook every day. Not that I was scared of her, but I didn't want to crush on her either. I hadn't had a girlfriend in at least six months, and I was susceptible to doing stupid things like falling for beautiful, powerful women.

"When does she want this to happen?"

"As soon as possible."

"But why me? I mean you obviously have a ton of qualified nannies. I've babysat, but I've never been a nanny before." I'd only been employed by the agency for a few weeks. This seemed like a big leap.

"Let me send you over the job specifications. You can review them and call me back. How does that sound?" Rebecca's voice insinuated that she wasn't going to let me say no right away. Within two minutes, I had the guidelines for the job. Make sure Noah gets to and from the school, handle any issues during the day with him at school, fix snacks for him, simple stuff. Brook had a staff that cleaned and a chef that cooked the evening meals. The killer was the one-year contract. Could I commit to one year?

Two months ago, when my parents threatened to cut me off after I dropped out of med school and enrolled in a master's program, I didn't take the veiled threat to heart. It wasn't until the school started pressuring me for tuition payments and my monthly stipend didn't show up in my bank account that I knew they were serious.

When I took a year off after high school to travel across Europe with two of my friends, my parents weren't happy. But I promised to go to med school like they both did, so they backed off. It was only after completing a year of medical school that I admitted I had no desire to become a doctor. To say they didn't approve was an understatement.

Brook had sweetened the deal by having a signing bonus. An opportunity to move out of Nana's house would have been enough. It had been only two weeks, and I was already going crazy. But the bonus pushed me over the edge. I called Rebecca.

"Okay, I'm in."

"Perfect. Let me call Brook and tell her the news. When can you start?"

I wanted to have a few days to get organized, but really it was a stall tactic. School was my only commitment. "I guess I can meet her tomorrow and review expectations, but I should be able to start after we meet." I gripped the phone tighter, anxious about such a big commitment, nervous about Brook Wellington. What if she was a tyrant? What if she'd been through several nannies and simply recognized fresh meat on the market? I wrote down the address and promised to be there at seven in the morning.

"What was that about?" Nana asked when I returned to the kitchen.

"So, I'm a nanny now."

"For Emma? I thought she was a devil child."

"No. For one of the other soccer moms. Brook Wellington. I think she's one of the Wellingtons from the news and all the banks and stuff."

Nana clasped her hands together. "Oh, honey, that's wonderful news. You're so good with kids. And the Wellingtons are a good family to have in your back pocket."

"I barely spoke to her, so it scares me that she requested me personally. The good news is that she has an apartment I can live in. Not like in their house, but a studio above the garage is part of the deal. I'll check it out first before I leave you."

"I'm sure it'll be fine. And if it's shit, you come back here."

There was the Nana I knew and loved. Spunky with just enough kick to make me smile. "I'm sure it'll be fine."

Not only was the studio fine, it was way nicer than the apartment I had once shared with my roommate Lacy. Brook Wellington's idea of studio was more like my idea of a condominium. Brook's garage housed five cars, so the space above it was a solid fifteen hundred square feet. It had an open floor plan with a full bath, full kitchen, and several closets for my clothes. I was in the moment I saw the storage space.

"I know it's not much, but it's private, and it's close to the university."

It was hard not to gape at Brook. This fully furnished apartment was a dream come true. I ran my hand over the taupe couch with bright accent pillows. "This is perfect for what I need." My voice was steady, even though I wanted to break into a song and dance at my good fortune.

She gave me a curt nod, her signature move. "And you can change the code once you move in. The instructions are inside on the kitchen counter."

I gave her a full look-over on our way back to the main house. Her black suit was tailored to perfection, accentuating every beautiful curve of her body, and the raspberry-colored blouse made the lightness of her blue eyes pop even more. Her hair was pulled back in a twisted topknot, stylish yet professional. Brook Wellington was the kind of woman who pinged my radar and checked all the boxes I looked for in the perfect woman. I wondered about her age and figured she had to be either late twenties or early thirties, given that Noah, her Mini-Me, was six. If I had to guess, I would say twenty-eight. I felt like a complete failure, being already twenty-four and just starting my graduate degree. She had a few tiny crinkles around her eyes that I noticed when she smiled at Noah, but for the most part, I had no idea how old she was. I made a mental note to google her later.

"Do you have any questions for me?" She sat at her desk and reached for her cup of coffee.

I slid into a leather guest chair and waited. The silence in the room made her look up at me. I wanted her full, undivided attention during this interview. I didn't want any mistakes or misunderstandings of what was expected of me and what I expected in return. A tiny smile tugged at the corner of her mouth. I couldn't tell if my silence amused her or she respected me for it.

"Yes, I have a lot of questions. I've never nannied before, so I need to know what's expected of me." I held up my hand when she pulled out the same list the agency had handed me. "I know what's on the list, but I want to hear it from you. That way there are no misunderstandings."

"My number-one priority is Noah and his well-being. A lot of my meetings run late, and rather than send everybody to go pick him up and pray that they get him in time, I'd rather have one person I trust to get him to and from places safely and timely." She sat back in her chair.

I leaned forward. "Does he attend after-school care, or would he catch the bus home, or do I need to collect him? I don't mind, but I will need a copy of his schedule so I know when to pick him up, and I'll need a booster seat."

"You won't need a booster seat. You'll have access to the Range Rover when you're taking him places, including to and from school."

"I'm sorry. What?" I was clueless.

"The Range Rover. It's yours to drive when you're taking Noah places. The agency said your driving record was clean. I trust that's accurate?"

Something told me she already knew the answer. "Just a parking ticket at school last semester." I tried not to get excited about reliable transportation. That was my biggest concern. "Does Noah have food allergies or restrictions?" I thought about Emma's dinners and hoped Brook allowed him some sugary liberties.

"No allergies. I try to keep his diet healthy, but I'm not a stickler about it. We can come up with a list of foods and snacks that I approve of."

I smiled for the first time. She wasn't going to be cranky if I slipped him a piece of chocolate or a cookie.

"What does Noah like to do besides soccer? Does he have any extracurricular activities?"

"Good question. He has violin lessons on Mondays and Thursdays from four to four forty-five. Soccer is on Tuesdays, Wednesdays, and Fridays from five to six, but we have only a few more weeks left. And I'll make sure you have snacks on the day we're responsible for them." Heat blossomed on my cheeks when she gave a slight hint of a smile. "I'll leave you his soccer schedule, too."

"What's after soccer? Anything?"

"Thankfully, no. Just violin."

"Is he allowed to play games?"

She looked puzzled. "Like video games?"

I nodded but wasn't going to press. Video games were a slippery topic with parents.

"He has an iPad with a few games, but he doesn't have a gaming system yet. I'm going to hold off on that as long as I can."

"I understand." I had all the systems but hadn't played them in a few weeks. Getting a job was more important than slaying beasts in fantasy worlds. I watched as Brook jotted several notes in her notebook during the interview. She was a lefty but didn't curve her hand like most left handers. Her nails were perfectly filed and painted red. "Why did you ask for me, Ms. Wellington?"

Brook's blue eyes met mine.

"Call me Brook. I picked you because I saw how patient you were with Emma and how you fit right in with the other moms. That means you aren't afraid to ask for help. Emma is a handful, and you didn't let her walk all over you. At Noah's fourth and fifth birthday parties, she was a pure terror, so I know you're good with kids. I spoke with Robin and Henry Minks, and they only had good things to say about you."

"I will say Emma tried my patience. But by the end of it, she really was an angel. We just needed to find common ground and start from there."

Brook cocked her head at me almost in disbelief. I shrugged. "Well, Cassie, what do you think? Are you up for the job?"

"I'm not going to be perfect, but yes. I'm up for it." I took a deep breath. This was a big commitment. The paperwork was straightforward. If I wanted to quit, Brook required a two-week notice. If she fired me, I would get paid up until that moment. "When do you want me to start?"

"As soon as you can. The studio is ready whenever you want to move in, or you can commute until the weekend. You can park your car on the concrete pad beside the garage."

I snorted. "I think I'll park on the street."

She stopped writing and looked up at me. Those eyes. I'd never seen eyes so blue before. I leaned back because her intense stare was both mesmerizing and unnerving.

"What's wrong with your car?"

"It leaks oil, and I don't want to stain your driveway."

The single nod again. "We'll figure something out." She looked at her watch and stood. "I'd like for you to go with me to Noah's school so I can get you added to the list and you can meet his teacher."

I stood when she did. "Sounds good. What time does school start?"

"I get him there before eight. There's a before-care where he gets half an hour to play with the other kids in his class. School doesn't officially start until eight thirty."

Why did I need to be at work at seven if school didn't start until eight thirty? As if she could read my mind or my facial expressions, Brook answered my question.

"I need to start getting to work earlier than I have been. I'll need you to make sure Noah gets up, eats breakfast, and either goes to school for before-care or hangs out here at the house until school starts. It all depends on your schedule and his mood."

Brook slung her messenger bag over her shoulder and motioned for me to follow her. Noah was sitting at the kitchen table eating a bowl of cereal and watching cartoons on his iPad. "Hey, kiddo. I want you to meet Cassie. She's going to help us out around here like we talked about. Say hello."

"Hi." He went back to eating his cereal, his focus on whatever video he was watching on YouTube Kids. Brook reached out and gently pulled the iPad out of his grasp.

"I'm going to need you to do better, please."

His brow furrowed in quick anger, but he didn't say anything. He took another bite, and we waited until he swallowed. His voice was quiet, but each word was distinct. "Hi. I'm Noah. Nice to meet you."

I crouched down to his level. "Hi, Noah. Nice to meet you, too. Looks like we're going to be spending a lot of time together. I can already tell we have a lot in common."

"What do you mean? We just met." He gave me the same head tilt Brook did.

"I like Cheerios, too. And I like *Peppa Pig*. And I go to school, too."

He looked at me and shook his head. "You're too old to go to school."

"Noah. Don't be rude." Brook raised a stern eyebrow at him. He looked at his bowl.

"It's okay. I go to college in town. I like school a lot. I like to learn new things and talk to my friends there. Do you like going to school early?"

He shrugged. "Sometimes."

"Okay, well, you let me know every morning if you want to go. We can make a sign, so when I get here in the morning, I can look at it and see if we're going in early or hanging out together instead."

"What do you mean sign?"

I hadn't planned that far in advance. "We can make it out of construction paper, definitely glitter, maybe some colorful string to hang it up somewhere, and crayons. Do you have crayons?"

He nodded, a glimmer of excitement in his eyes. He was still wary of me, but warming up quickly.

I pretended to be deep in thought, trying to think of things we needed, but I was really studying him and his body language. He leaned slightly away from me and more to the side where Brook stood, but he also leaned forward toward me as we spoke. "How about glue? Do you have glue?"

He nodded again, but this time with a smile.

"How about a hamster? Do you have a hamster or a lizard?"

He laughed that sweet-young-child giggle. "Why do we need a hamster or a lizard?"

"Well, who's going to flip the sign every morning? I thought maybe your pet hamster or lizard could come down here while you got dressed and flip the sign to whatever you wanted. I would totally make him breakfast for being so helpful."

Noah laughed harder. "I don't have a pet. I'll just do it."

I shrugged. "I guess that would work, too."

"Okay. We need to get moving. Noah, put your bowl in the sink and go brush your teeth. Two minutes. Let's go."

"Mom." His voice held a note of embarrassment.

Brook ruffled his hair when he darted by. "You're really good with him. He's hard to crack because he's so shy." Brook smiled at me. Not a fake one, but a genuine smile that I felt deep inside. The kind that made my knees weak.

"He's sweet. I'm looking forward to getting to know him."

We stood in awkward silence until Brook's phone rang. She excused herself and answered the call in the adjoining dining room. To give her privacy, I walked to the floor-to-ceiling windows and stared out at the backyard. It was magnificent. A flat stone patio gave way to a pool with a waterfall. A wrought-iron fence surrounded the pool for safety, but the rest of the yard was wide open and spacious. I was sad I wouldn't get to use the pool. Even though school had just started, the season was changing rapidly from summer to fall.

"I just can't bring myself to close down the pool." Brook startled me with her nearness. I put my hand on my heart.

"It's beautiful. Your house, this estate. Perfect for raising children."

"A child. Only one. That's it for me," she said.

I was dying to know if she was married or dating someone. Her left hand was free of any jewelry. Her right hand sported a silver band on her middle finger, which meant absolutely nothing other than she liked simplicity. I knew in time I would find out about her, but I was curious.

"He's okay being an only child? Has he ever talked about siblings?"

I barely heard the stifled sharp intake, but it was enough to know I'd crossed the line. "Or maybe a hamster or a lizard really is the best idea." I backpedaled to not piss off my boss on what was technically my first day.

She forced a small laugh. "At some point I know we're going to have to get a pet, but I'd like to wait a few more years."

I waved both hands at her in complete surrender. "I totally understand. You're a busy woman, and he's a busy little man."

Noah walked in with his backpack slung over his tiny shoulder. "I'm ready when you are."

"I'm ready when you are," Brook said.

They both turned to me. "I'm ready as well." Apparently, that was their morning ritual that I was now a part of.

"Do you want to drive so you can get used to the car?" Brook dangled the fob in front of me on our way to the garage.

"Oh, no. It's okay. I'm sure the school will be crazy. I'd rather see you drive us there and learn the rules first."

Brook's heels clicked loudly on the hardwood floors. My eyes traveled the length of her legs, down to the source of the repetitive *tap tap* that echoed around us. Her shoes were sexy as fuck and added three inches to her height, which now equaled my own. I was a sucker for a woman in high heels.

"I'll never be able to sneak up on anyone in this house."

Guilt washed over me when our eyes met. I knew she had busted me staring at her legs.

"The shoes. They are disturbingly loud." She pointed to her feet as if my attention wasn't already there.

"The high ceilings make all noises echo. I have a feeling I'm going to get lost here." That gave me an excuse to break eye contact and pretend to look around. It was a large space for just two people. Well, the two I knew about.

"Oops. Careful there, buddy." Brook reached down to steady Noah as he tripped up against her, pushing her into me for just a moment.

"Sorry, Mom."

Brook adjusted his backpack for him, and I took a small step to my right to distance myself from her. She unnerved me. Rich, powerful, attractive, successful—the list went on and on. All the attributes I admired and also wanted for myself. When she opened the door to the garage, it took everything in me to not gape. She had a sleek two-seater sports car with a hard top, a luxury sedan, the SUV I remember seeing at soccer practice, a motorcycle, and the Range Rover she had mentioned. She indicated I should jump into the passenger seat. Noah opened the back door of the Rover and crawled into his booster.

"Do you have your seat belt on?" Brook asked. We both turned to look at him, our faces only inches apart. The spice of her cologne was a pleasant surprise. I expected Brook to smell like flowers and vanilla. The hint of sandalwood and cedar wasn't overpowering, but it was enough to notice.

"I'm buckled."

"Okay, let's head out. Cassie, it's push-button start. I'll give you a fob when we get back. The garage opener is here, and the code to get in is fourteen fourteen."

"Fourteen fourteen. Got it." I gave her the signature one-nod affirmation. A small smile appeared on the right side of her mouth. I think I amused her.

Chapter Three

Hessick Academy, less than ten minutes away, was tucked on acreage that couldn't be seen from the street. I didn't even know the school existed. The driveway was flanked by large sycamore trees and flowering shrubs. The school itself towered at the end of a circular drive. I imagined my new nanny salary rivaled Hessick's tuition. Brook pulled into a parking lot beside the school's main building.

"This looks like a private-college campus," I said.

"It is large, but it's kindergarten through middle school. Thankfully, Noah has to worry only about finding his homeroom class and the gym. His teacher, Ms. Trina, is very nice and is great with the kids." Brook slipped out of the car and opened the back door for Noah to climb out.

I reached for his backpack, surprised at how heavy it was. "How many books do you have in here? This thing weighs a ton." I made a production of trying to heave it over my shoulder and got a smile out of both of them.

"I'll take it." Noah reached out, and I helped him into it.

According to the plaque by the door, Hessick Academy was built in the 1880s and looked as charming as one would expect. The inside, however, was a completely different story. Security cameras and automatically locking doors prevented anyone from just barging right in. Brook walked to a window marked Administration and flashed her credentials.

"Good morning, Mary. I need to get my assistant registered here so she can pick up and drop off Noah. Also, I want to see Trina Moore for a moment, if you could call her." Brook was direct, to the point, and gave off an aura that denying her wasn't an option. Mary nodded and buzzed us in.

"And you are?" Mary looked at me expectantly.

"Cassandra Miller. I go by Cassie." I smiled, hoping to get one in return, but dour Mary turned back to her computer screen and actually pressed her lips together in a frown.

"Look right here." She pointed to a circle on the back of her monitor.

"Why?"

"I need to take your picture for your identification card."

I flashed Mary a brilliant smile that was snarkier than I intended, but it got my point across. I heard a small laugh that morphed into a cough from Brook. Mary shook her head at me and busied herself getting my credentials in order.

A woman about my age with long brown hair opened the security door and smiled at us. "Ms. Wellington, Noah, good morning."

It certainly was for me. She was super cute. Was this Noah's teacher? Damn kid was surrounded by beautiful women. "Hi. I'm Cassie."

"Cassie's helping me with Noah, so she'll be your point of contact if he gets sick or is behind in a subject."

Trina nodded and reached out for my hand. "It's nice to meet you, Cassie."

She was so genuine and downright gorgeous that I almost forgot about Brook standing next to me.

"It's nice to meet you, too."

"Let's head to the classroom, shall we?"

Noah led the way, and Trina filled me in on the school's policies and classroom etiquette. Brook lagged a few paces behind us, scrolling on her phone. The tap tap of her heels weren't as pronounced, but I was still aware of her. When we reached Noah's homeroom and Trina gave us the tour, I was surprised the class had only ten students.

"Cassie, look at Leonardo." Noah pointed to a large aquarium with a box turtle resting on a flat rock.

"Noah's pretty animated today." Trina looked at Brook. Brook gave her the single nod but offered no other information. Trina turned back to me. "Normally, Noah is pretty quiet. He must really like you."

I stood a little taller with pride. "I'd better meet Leonardo." I followed Noah and dramatically gasped.

"Oh my gosh, that's Leonardo the Teenage Mutant Ninja Turtle, right?"

"How did you know that? It's supposed to be a secret. People aren't supposed to know he's here." Noah looked up at me, wide-eyed.

"Oh, no. His secret is safe with me. I won't say a word." I pinched the air in front of my lips and twisted my hand, indicating they were locked.

"Here. Let me show you where I sit." He hesitantly took my hand and walked me to a short but long desk that he shared with another classmate. A cubbyhole was attached on either side. He shoved his backpack into the space.

"Who sits next to you?"

"Tom." His smile fell a little. "He's not very nice."

I felt protective of Noah already, even though we'd just met an hour ago. "Is he mean to you?"

"He's just mean to all the kids in the class. His dad plays football, so he thinks he's important."

I snorted. The Wellington money was probably a lot more than an NFL player's. "Don't let him bother you. I'm sure he's just doing it for attention. And besides, just because his dad is a football player doesn't make him more important than anyone else in your class."

Noah sighed and sat. He pulled out an iPad from his table. Wow, first grade really had changed since I was in school. We didn't have tablets until high school, and even then we had to check them out of the library.

I squatted so I could look him square in the eye. "Do you want me to pick you up today, or do you want to play with your friends?"

"Can you pick me up right after school?"

"Definitely. I'm going to talk to your teacher now, but I will see you this afternoon." I stood and tapped his shoulder playfully. "Have a good day."

"Here's my email address and my phone number if you have any questions. You can email me or text me any time. Noah's such a great kid." Trina handed me a business card that contained all her contact information. Her fingers brushed mine, and I smiled when a tiny flicker of desire warmed the pit of my stomach.

"Thank you so much. Noah wants to be picked up as soon as school's out today. What time can I get him?"

"Three thirty. If you email me, I'll send you the schedule and other important information."

She had a tiny scar in the corner of her mouth that disappeared when she smiled. Her skin was smooth, and the hint of a tan line peeked out from the collar of her blouse. She was attractive in a girl-next-door way, from the sweet, simple style of her hair to her practical, yet fashionable shoes. She couldn't have been a teacher for more than a few years.

"Definitely," I said. Out of the corner of my eye, I noticed Brook glance at her watch. The kids were filing into the classroom, and I knew we had to go. "Thanks for your help. I'll email you later."

"I have a copy of everything you need as well," Brook said.

"It was good that I met Noah's teacher, though. I have a good feeling about her."

That single nod again. "I want you to drive us home." Brook slipped into the passenger side.

"So you can evaluate my driving?" I winked at her. What the hell was I doing? Brook was my boss. That meant she was off-limits. I scooted the seat back to fit my long legs and adjusted the mirrors. "What are the rules for dropping off and picking up kids? Are there rules?"

Brook flipped the mirror down to look at her makeup. I waited as she wiped a tiny fleck off of her cheek that probably wasn't even there. She tucked a strand of hair that had fallen out of her twist. I was staring, but she clearly didn't care. When she flipped the mirror back up, she turned to me, and those brilliant blue eyes were so piercing, I felt as if she could see right inside me and read my thoughts and feelings. I turned away and started the car.

"I'll email you the school's handbook. All the information can be found in it. You'll have to drive slowly around here. And be careful. The accelerator and the brakes are super sensitive."

I eased into the line of traffic leaving the school. I barely heard or felt the smooth rev of the engine, but smiled at its quick pickup. I missed driving luxury. Twenty-five years ago, Nana's Acura was probably a dream car, but time, a few fender benders, and poor upkeep made it iffy transportation.

"If you hit this button and say 'home,' the GPS will direct you back to the house."

"Yes. I had a similar one in my Lexus." A Lexus SUV that my parents repossessed. I cringed, realizing I'd given away too much information.

"Any time you're on the clock. so to speak, you can drive this. Grocery shopping, chores, errands. I don't drive it much."

"I see that. It barely has any mileage on it." The odometer read two thousand and thirty-four miles. This car was brand-new. We pulled up to the gate, and it opened automatically. "Wait a minute. I didn't even punch in the code." I looked at Brook in surprise.

"It's programmed with the gate. All the cars are. I just wanted you to know the code in case you want to park inside instead of out on the street."

"I'll keep it across the street for now, but I'll get a new car soon. Monster is really my grandma's." I needed to stop talking. I was telling Brook my sad story on the first day. My life was better told over the course of several months and a dozen bottles of wine. Plus, my problems were small in the scheme of things.

Brook showed me all the alarm systems, how to arm them, disarm them, and handed me all Noah's schedules. "I have to get to the office, and you probably need to get to class, but call me if you have a problem."

Even though I didn't have to be at school for another hour and a half, I felt weird being there alone, so I headed across the street to my car. It finally started on the third try, after serious praying and gently stroking the dash. One of the first things I intended to do was buy reliable transportation.

"Excuse me, miss?" I yelped in surprise at the knock on the window by my head. I scowled at the security guard and lowered the window.

"Yes?"

"Can I help you with something?" He leaned closer so his face was even with mine.

"I'm here to pick up a student. Noah Wellington. I know I'm early, but I thought I could wait for him here until school lets out. Do some homework, you know." I flashed him my credentials even though he didn't ask to see them.

"You're going to have to either go inside and wait, or come back in twenty minutes." He looked at his watch to confirm the time.

"Look, it's my first day. I don't really know all the rules yet."

"There's a nice air-conditioned foyer with comfortable couches. You could get a lot done in there."

The car was so quiet I almost forgot to turn it off. I grabbed my laptop and scratch pad and followed him.

"I'm Al. Maddie, Pete, and I are the campus monitors at Hessick."

"Hi. I'm Cassie. I'm Noah Wellington's nanny." I cringed at the description. *Caregiver* sounded like I was looking after an old man. There really wasn't another way to put it.

"Noah's a good kid. Introvert, keeps to himself most days."

"You know all the students here, Al?" He struck me as the kind of guy who liked it when people called him by his name.

He shuffled his belt around his waistline as if preparing to say something very important. "I try to. Our school has a strict enrollment policy, and we keep the classes small for more one-on-one interaction." He sounded like a brochure. I found it endearing how he was so proud to be a part of Hessick. "Here. Let me get the door for you." He jogged up the stairs, the keys on his belt clanking against one another in repetition with every step he took, and swiped his key card to get us inside.

"Thanks for your help. I really appreciate it." I emphasized *really* because I meant it. I showed Mary my credentials, and she pretended not to know me even though I'd just interacted with her that morning. I was the only one in the waiting area, but Al assured me that would change soon. Fifteen minutes later, five women disturbed my peace with their laughter and clicking heels. I looked up and made eye contact with two of the five. One smiled at me. The other did not. Everyone else pretended I didn't exist. I sat up straighter and focused on the words in front of me, but I knew the pack was watching me. A few hushed whispers, a sprinkle of giggles, and finally one of them walked over to me.

"Hi. I'm Amanda. Do you work for Brook Wellington?"

She couldn't have sounded snottier if she tried. Thanks to my Nana's sarcastic wit, I had the perfect response.

"No." I looked at my laptop and ignored her as if the entire exchange didn't happen. She stood there for a solid ten seconds and stared at me. "Did you need something else?"

"Ah, no. No."

Probably not the best way to make new friends, but Amanda had *bitch* written all over her face. I was aware of the games of bored, rich girls. Amanda was about thirty and had more makeup on than she needed. Her outfit was top-of-the-line but casual. I was curious if she worked, but not enough to strike up a conversation. When the bell rang, I closed my laptop and waited for Noah. I saw him before he saw me. He was quietly making his way to the front to check out. I met him at the desk and showed Mary my credentials again after she asked.

"Hi. Did you have a good day?" I turned to Noah and straightened out his backpack. He was smaller than most of his classmates.

He shrugged. "It was okay."

"Want me to take your bag?"

"I got it."

He was tough, but I was determined to make him warm up to me. "Well, then, will you carry my stuff?"

"Why would I do that?" Noah sounded genuinely perplexed.

"To be nice. To help me out."

"But you don't need help. Your hands are free," he said.

"I'm just playing around."

A hint of a smile appeared on his lips.

"Guess who I met today?" I exaggerated my voice and drew out each word to bait him into further conversation.

"Ms. Trina. And Leonardo."

"True. But I also met Al, the security guy. He's nice. He knows you." I walked Noah in front of me until we reached the steps. "We're parked right over there." He reached for my hand to walk down the stairs, and I melted. He was so trusting. I gently held his small fingers against mine and pretended it didn't mean everything. When we got to the Range Rover, he climbed in. I helped him buckle up, and we carefully made our way down the drive. "So, we have violin practice today."

"Yeah. I need to get my violin and change my clothes."

Noah's uniform was khaki pants, a white polo shirt, and brown boat shoes. The school colors were navy and red, so those were also

TEMPTATION

appropriate shirt colors, according to the pamphlet I'd read that morning. White surprised me because children were notoriously messy and awkward around anything that could possibly spill on their clothes. Noah's shirt was untainted.

To my surprise, Noah's violin teacher, Ms. Natalie Rowman, made house calls. While I was racing around trying to find an address for Natalie and refraining from panic-texting Brook, the front gate chimed, and a video of a person at the gate popped up on the video monitor in the kitchen. I had no idea what to do.

"Noah? Can you come here, please?"

I hit the button that said *answer* at the bottom of the video and wondered if she could see me, too. "Yes? Hello?"

"This is Natalie Rowman. I'm here for Noah's lesson."

Well, fuck me. All this stressing for nothing. "Sure. I'll buzz you in." I hit the button marked *open* and watched Natalie park and walk to the front door.

"Hi. You must be Cassie. I'm Natalie. Brook let me know you're helping her with Noah."

How anyone managed to work with all these beautiful women was beyond me. I smiled at her before inviting her inside.

"Hi, Natalie. Welcome to day one of me trying to figure this all out."

Her small laugh was sweet. She was charming with her hazel eyes and slight overbite that she hid behind her full lips. Natalie was probably in her early thirties, with brown hair pulled back in a single twisted braid that reached the middle of her back. Her blouse was fashionable and freshly pressed. Her black pants fit her perfectly, and she had the body to pull it all off.

"I'm sure you'll get the hang of it." Natalie was ten minutes early, which she apologized for.

I sat at the kitchen counter while we waited for Noah. "How long have you been teaching Noah?"

"Oh, gosh. About a year now."

"Is he good?" I thought back to my piano lessons and guitar lessons from ages five until ten, when I got into sports instead. I'd hated playing an instrument.

"Well, you'll hear him in just a little while. We practice in the library. It's the quietest place in the house and has the best acoustics." She carefully put her messenger bag on the counter and rifled through its contents until she pulled out sheet music.

I felt like I was in the way, but I wanted to make sure Noah was ready for the lesson and had everything he needed. Brook had never told me the plan other than he had violin lessons Mondays and Thursdays. I wanted to know more about Natalie because I wanted more insight into Noah's world.

"Hi, Miss Natalie."

"Hello, Mr. Noah. Have you been practicing?"

He ducked his head. "A little bit."

"Well, let's go find out." Natalie followed him into the library.

I pulled out my tablet to read for my next class. We were learning about soil management and how to best utilize what was available in a region to grow crops or plants. Both were important for survival. I would read a page, stop and listen to Noah and Natalie, go back and reread the same thing, stop and listen again. I decided to move to the living room, where it was quieter and where I could hopefully concentrate better. Three pages later, I gave up. I could pick this up after work. I had to concentrate on dinner. What time did kids eat?

I poked around in the oversized refrigerator. Fresh fruit, fresh vegetables, organic this and that. It was fully stocked for two people. The pantry to the right of the refrigerator was also full of healthy foods. I smiled when I saw the sugary cereals and cookies tucked in the back, where Noah couldn't see them unless he used a stepladder. At least Brook wasn't a processed-sugar hater like Henry and Robin Minks.

"Cassie?"

My eyes widened at being caught rummaging through Brook's pantry. "Yes?" I tried to sound like I was there for a reason and walked out carrying a jar of natural peanut butter and a roll of aluminum foil.

Natalie looked at my haul and back at me. She cocked her head like she was trying to figure out what I was doing.

"Oh, I'm a scientist." Like that meant anything. "A chemist, really." Still did nothing to explain my weirdness.

"Okay, well, we're done here. Please tell Brook that Noah is doing well, but I want him to practice more than he has been."

"He sounds really good for six years old. I mean, I was a horrible music student, but my parents pushed me until I couldn't do it anymore."

She placed her bag on the counter to tuck the sheets of music back inside. "What did you play?"

"Piano and guitar. By ten, I begged to do something else, so I got into soccer and softball. Now I wish I'd stuck with music."

"Why's that?" She leaned against the counter, giving me her complete attention. It unnerved me. She was so quiet, so confident.

"I love music more than sports. It's hard to make big decisions when you're young."

She shrugged. "It's never too late to get back into it. I'd be more than happy to give you private lessons, too."

I tried not to notice the soft sigh that escaped her lips or the fact that she was leaning toward me. I wasn't an expert in body language, but if I were to take a guess, Natalie was interested in me. My ego inflated, and I bit the inside of my cheeks to prevent myself from giving her the cheesy smile that instantly made me uncool. "Maybe so. Let's see how all of this plays out and what kind of free time I have after taking care of Noah and going to school."

"You're going to school, too?"

"I'm going for my master's in environmental sciences and eventually my doctorate. I dropped out of med school, much to the disappointment of my parents."

"Oh, I'm sure you aren't a disappointment to them."

I kept the bitter retort back and nodded instead. Natalie didn't need to know about my almost nonexistent relationship with my parents. "At least I'm doing something I want to, you know?"

"Good for you for taking a chance."

We stood there smiling at one another until Noah walked in. "Miss Natalie. You're still here."

"Out of the mouth of babes."

I laughed. "It was nice to meet you, Natalie. We'll see you Thursday." I walked her to the front door.

"I'm looking forward to it."

Chapter Four

"I'm sorry, but I'm not just going to let you take him." I was facing off with a woman who had somehow gotten past the gate and was demanding Noah. I squeezed the door handle tightly so this woman wouldn't be able to tell that I was nervous.

"He's my son. It's Wednesday. I pick him up on Wednesday nights. If you ask him, he'll tell you." She tried to lean past me, but I stood in front of her.

"It's not going to happen."

"I'm going to call Brook and tell her this is unacceptable." The woman stepped away from the front door and angrily dug in her purse for her phone. If she weren't such a bitch, I would have found her attractive. First impressions were everything, though, and people who were ugly on the inside made any attractive physical qualities instantly unattractive to me.

"You're lucky I'm not calling the cops." I spoke with more conviction than I felt. I was still shaking.

"Look, I don't know who this flavor of the month is, but she's not letting me have Noah," she said into her phone.

My mind was spinning. First of all, if this lady was Noah's other mom, that meant Brook was a lesbian, or at least had been in a relationship with a woman at one point. Secondly, why the fuck hadn't anybody told me about her? Brook would have mentioned it if this woman regularly picked up Noah. And why hadn't Noah said anything? Wouldn't he be excited to see his other mother?

"Do you want to talk to her? He has to be at soccer in thirty minutes, and I have errands to run before I drop him off. I don't have time for this." She disconnected the call and stared at me.

I folded my arms and waited. I would win this stare-down contest. I was a college student who sat in the longest, most boring classes in the world. I could handle this. My phone buzzed. I broke eye contact to see who was calling.

"Hello, Brook."

"I should have told you about Lauren. She's Noah's other mom and has him on Wednesdays and every other weekend. She hasn't seen him for three weeks, so I honestly didn't expect her to show up." Her voice was even and didn't hint at the stress levels of Lauren's voice.

"Are you okay with me letting him go with her?"

"Yes. That's fine. She'll have him for the rest of the night. Thank you for looking out for him."

"Okay. I'll get him ready, but I'm not letting her in to wait. She can sit in her fancy car." I swore I heard Brook chuckle through the phone.

"Thank you, Cassie." She disconnected the call.

"All right. I'll send him out in a while." I stepped back and firmly shut the door with the palm of my hand; our eyes held until the door broke the stare. What a complete douche canoe. "Noah! Your—" I stopped because I didn't know what he called her. "Your other mom is here."

"Mama's here? Really?"

I stopped him from running out the door. "Hold up, buddy. Get your soccer stuff together because I don't want you to be late for practice. Then I'll hand you over." I silently added *to the Kraken* because this woman was a total bitch. I understood the situation and would be upset, too, if somebody didn't let me have my kid, but calling me the flavor of the month to Brook was degrading to both of us.

"Bye, Cassie. I'll see you tomorrow."

And out he darted. He hugged Lauren, crawled into the back seat, and waved to me. I closed the door after I watched them leave the gate. Well, that was interesting. I'd learned a lot in the last ten minutes. Brook had a child with Lauren, but they were no longer together. Brook dated women. Lauren was unreliable and their parting was not amicable. My mind swirled. Wow. My boss was hot, rich, presumably single, and a lesbian. Life just kept getting more interesting around here.

With my newfound free time, I decided to move in some more of my things. Maybe tonight would be my first night in the apartment. I stripped the bedding, threw it in the stackable washer, and headed to Nana's. I picked up sandwiches on the way, hoping Nana hadn't eaten yet.

"You're home early." She greeted me at the door with a bat.

"New security system, Nana?" I looked pointedly at the bat and raised an eyebrow at her.

"I wasn't expecting you for another two hours."

"Yeah, change of plans. Apparently, Noah's other mother has custody of him on Wednesday nights, but she's sporadic in her visits, so nobody thought to tell me. It was crazy. She was crazy. I wouldn't let her in, so she called me a few things, yelled, and finally called Brook, who called me back to let me know it was okay."

"Wait. What? Brook is a lesbian?"

Nana and I had similar minds.

"I know, right? Surprised me, too. And I think Noah's violin teacher is, as well. Who knew Rhode Island was the mecca of hot lesbians?"

When I came out to my parents in high school, they ignored me for a long time. Nana hugged me and we baked a cake together when she found out. It was exactly what I needed—comfort and love during such an emotional confession. She wasn't surprised, but I suffered a fracture in my relationship with my parents. My mother chalked it up to a phase, and my father refused to accept it.

"The last thing you want to do is sleep with your boss," Nana said.

"Well, it's not really the last thing I want to do, but I know what you're saying."

Nana gave me a stern look. "You focus on school and not your libido."

"Nana, stop. We aren't going to talk about my sex life." I put my hands over my ears and sang to block out whatever words of wisdom she was trying to get across. When her mouth closed, I put my hands down. "Seriously, there are a zillion women out there. You don't have to worry about me and Brook. I will remain professional." I gave her the Brook Wellington single nod.

She pointed her finger at me sternly. "I will always worry about you."

"And I will always love you for it. Let's eat. I want to move some stuff over to the studio before I have to sit down to study. I think I'll stay there tonight. Is that okay?"

Nana bit into her sandwich and nodded. "You should. Then by the weekend, you can show me the place."

Thank God there was a separate gate. I could sneak Nana in without attention. Not that I didn't want Nana to see where I was living, but I didn't want Brook to think I intended to have a lot of traffic. "Definitely. I can pick you up after church if you want."

"Perfect. Then we can go to lunch. You're making good money. You can buy your Nana a delicious meal."

I held up my half of the sub. "What the heck is this then? You know Tony's has the best chicken parmesan in the world."

"I want a sit-down lunch. With cloth napkins."

I still had a hundred from the Minks job. I got paid every other Friday with Brook, but I was only three days into the job. I had to make the hundred work for gas and food for the next nine days and didn't want to dip into my signing bonus because that was the car fund. I felt Nana's hand on mine.

"I'll buy lunch. You can take me to dinner when you get paid."

I breathed a sigh of relief. "That sounds better. And I plan to get a car next month. A small, reliable one so you can have yours back. Thank you so much for letting me use it."

"No rush. I'm sure it's just a matter of time before they take away my license."

I tapped her hand. "Stop it. You'll be driving for at least another ten years." More like five, but I was optimistic for her sake. "Okay. I'm going to take a load over, and I'll swing by tomorrow. Do you need anything?"

"Go. Get your stuff done. I'm planning to watch movies for the rest of the evening."

She kissed my cheek and cleaned up our dishes. I ambitiously loaded the car and headed over to my new place.

I pulled up to the Wellington gate and punched in the numbers. No way was I going to drag boxes and bags up the hill and through the side gate. That would take forever. Nana had given me some cardboard and told me to slip it under the front half of the car to prevent it from dripping oil on Brook's driveway. I wasn't planning to be there long, but I wasn't going to take any chances either. I parked and jumped out immediately, then whipped out the cardboard and shimmied under the car, catching the first drip of oil on it.

"Yes," I said victoriously.

"Yes, what?"

I turned my head to the side and found a pair of running shoes and shapely legs standing next to the car. I'd stared at those legs for an hour weeks ago at a soccer practice. I crawled out from beneath the car and stood. Brook Wellington in running shorts and a long-sleeved T-shirt was an amazing sight. I pulled down my own T-shirt and smoothed back my ponytail. I was not expecting to see her and knew I was a complete wreck.

"Hi."

"Hi."

She looked young with her face void of makeup and flushed from exercise. Her hair was pulled back away from her face and held tight by a hair tie, but it looked surprisingly curly. "Do you need some help?"

"No, thanks. I've got it."

"Well, I'm going to help you anyway because I want to talk to you."

I was unnerved because I wasn't expecting to see her, which made no sense because she lived there, but I must have given her a look because she backed up.

"We can always talk in the morning."

"No. It's okay. I'm sorry. I'm just stressed about the driveway."

"Cassie, cars leak oil. It's okay. This driveway gets cleaned."

I almost rolled my eyes at her. Her first car probably came with a driver. What did she know about oil stains and how difficult they were to get out of concrete?

She raised her hand. "Hold up. I'll be right back." She disappeared to the side of the garage and opened one of the doors. "Pull up inside."

I shook my head. "Absolutely not. I'm going to park it across the street as soon as I finish unloading."

"Come here." She crooked her finger at me. I obliged. "This is an industrial-absorbing garage mat that soaks up water, oil…anything really. It's safer inside the garage than outside of it."

"Really?"

"Yes, now park it inside before you stain my driveway."

I swore she winked at me, but I couldn't be certain. Her voice was so strong and not at all playful. I jumped into my car and parked it over the mat. The motorcycle that had once stood in this spot was in front of the sedan.

"You can recycle the cardboard over there." She pointed to a blue container in the corner of the garage.

I unloaded my car, keeping the grunts to a minimum when lifting the heavy stuff. Did I really need to pack all the pans in one box?

"You have a lot of things. Well, a lot of clothes," Brook said. She was stretching on the stairs and watching my every move. My peripheral vision picked up how limber she was and how effortlessly she touched her toes.

"This isn't even half of what I own."

She raised an eyebrow. "Well, if you run out of space, there's a cabinet over there where you can store boxes and things."

"Oh, I checked out the closets in the apartment, and there's plenty of room. Thank you, though." I didn't want to sound ungrateful because I wasn't.

I had eight boxes and five bags of clothes to take upstairs and was mortified that my clothes were in garbage bags. Brook didn't say a word. She grabbed two bags and followed me up the wrought-iron steps.

"I changed the code," I said and gave up trying to hold bags and a box and type in the numbers at the same time. I slid the box down until it landed with a thud by my feet.

"I'm glad." The nod.

I opened the door. "You can just put those over against the wall. I'll get the rest."

"Come on. Only a few more trips and then you're done."

I followed her because I was sure she intended to help me whether I wanted her to or not. I carried the heavy box of pots and pans, while she carried two more bags. By the fourth and final trip, I was sweating. I closed the door behind her and dropped to the floor.

"You probably ran five miles and then helped me lift heavy stuff."

"More like eight miles," she said.

"Holy shit. I work for Wonder Woman." No response. Awkward.

• 45 •

We weren't friends, and I had to remind myself that not only were we not friends, but she was my boss. I moved to the chair.

"I want to talk about Lauren."

I sat up straighter and gave her my full attention. "Okay."

"I should have told you about her. I did a pretty horrible job of preparing you for my life, for your job, and I'm sorry for that." Her eyes held an apologetic note.

"I have a feeling this is a learn-as-you-go job, but thank you." Manners. Always show your manners. I could almost hear Nana in my head.

"Lauren is unreliable. She's supposed to pick Noah up every Wednesday night and have him from four thirty until eight. That rarely happens, and it didn't occur to me to warn you. Thank you for not just handing him over."

"At the very least, I would check with you. Even if Noah said he knew someone."

"Thank you again. I actually got a kick at how quickly you got under Lauren's skin."

I wanted to play this professionally, even though I was dying to reenact my moment with Lauren. I remained quiet while Brook continued.

"The weekends won't be an issue. She's supposed to get Noah on Friday nights, but she never picks him up until Saturday mornings. You'll only have to deal with her on Wednesdays. Hopefully it will go smoothly from here on out, but don't plan on her being here every week."

Brook stood, indicating she was leaving. I stood, too, and grabbed my keys. "Do a lot of people have the gate-access code? I just need to know what and who to expect."

"I should change that. Lauren doesn't need to have it. She can be buzzed in like everyone else. I'll text you a list of the approved people." She paused in the doorway and turned to face me. I stepped back at her intensity. Her stare ignited a spark in the pit of my stomach, and I reflexively put my hand under my rib cage to stifle it. The longer Brook stared, the hotter it burned. I wanted her to stay because I wanted to know more about her. I had a feeling this was going to be the only open line of communication we would have for a long time. "Stay parked in the garage. I don't want your car towed if one of the neighbors complains."

And just like that, Brook trotted down the stairs and jogged into the main house. Every question I had vanished. I didn't like not knowing a lot of things, but I couldn't ask about all the things I really wanted to know.

Chapter Five

I drove around town, enjoying my new-to-me ride and parked in front of Jake's Pub twenty minutes early so I could learn the radio, sync my Bluetooth, and program addresses into the GPS.

"What the fuck? Is this your new car?" Lacy popped up out of nowhere, scaring the shit out of me.

"Asshole. You scared me." It was good to see her face. I missed her.

She walked to the passenger side and slipped in. "This is really nice."

"Meet Stormy. She's no Lexus, but she's fun to drive and all mine."

Lacy knew how difficult my separation from the posh life had been. My new Civic didn't have the bells and whistles that I was used to, but Lacy was kind and pointed out only the good things about the car. She flipped up the center section and hit a little button on the side that I'd missed, and a tiny compartment opened.

"Look. You have a secret compartment right here to stash whatever you need to. Weed, oxy, cocaine, or the winning lottery ticket."

"The K-9s will find any stash, silly girl. This will be my secret cash stash." I slid out of the car and waited for her to exit so I could lock it.

"How's the new job? I haven't really talked to you the last few weeks. And when the fuck do I get to come visit?" She put on a British accent. "You know I'm dying to see the massive Wellington estate."

I rolled my eyes. "You know I can't give you a tour of the main house. The studio is incredible though. What are you doing after this? I think Brook and Noah are out. I can show you my apartment at least."

"Perfect. Now tell me all about your boss. She is one of the Wellingtons, right? I mean the import business, the banks. Those Wellingtons?"

"Yep. I think they even have a few organic grocery stores."

"What about the kid? Is he spoiled as hell?"

We placed our lunch orders, and then I leaned forward in the booth, my voice just a bit above a whisper. "It's the easiest fucking job I've ever had." I leaned back, folded my arms, and nodded. "Seriously, the kid is amazing. He's super sweet, quiet, and doesn't need help with anything really. He's kind of a loner, so I pick him up every day right after school because I don't want him to ever feel lonely."

"He sounds adorable. Tell me about Brook. What's she like?"

I watched Lacy stir sweetener into her iced tea and waited until she was done. "I can't figure her out. She's so hot and cold."

"Oh, she's hot with you? Do tell." Lacy bent forward in anticipation of juicy gossip that I didn't have to dish out.

"No. I don't mean hot like that. I mean, she's super professional, but then a sliver of normalcy slips out, and she quickly tries to cover it up." I ripped off a piece of bread from the basket. "And she's nice, but she's obviously trying to keep her distance."

"Maybe she thinks you'll play the role of hot nanny." She wagged her eyebrows at me and winked.

"Here's the best part. She's a lesbian." I dropped that bomb and reached for my water.

"Shut. The. Fuck. Up." She delivered each word loudly.

I turned to see who'd heard us and breathed a sigh of relief when nobody seemed interested in our conversation.

"The ex-wife showed up demanding Noah, and I wouldn't give him to her."

"How do you not call me immediately when these things happen?"

Lacy was right. I'd really fallen down on our friendship. "I'm sorry. I should do a better job of telling you what's going on. I know there's no excuse, but school and babysitting are exhausting me. For a six-year-old, he stays busy. Thank God soccer's over."

"Tell me about the ex. Is she as gorgeous as your boss? Rich, too? I need to know things," Lacy said.

For a brief moment, I regretted telling her anything. Lacy was a friend, but I didn't want to jeopardize my relationship with Brook. Even though I didn't sign anything about confidentiality other than Noah and posting photos, warning bells were dinging in my head.

"I didn't say much to her, but she seems terrible. She's definitely pretty, if you like the rich-bitch look."

"So, you're saying you were attracted to her?" Lacy gave me an exaggerated toothy grin.

"I can't get past the ugliness of the moment. She will forever be ugly."

"But if you saw her at a bar, you would talk to her?"

"Eh, maybe. You know how I am about brunettes."

"You're ridiculous. Not every brunette is a jerk."

"Just the ones I date."

"If you want to call that dating." She gave me another toothy grin.

"Let's talk about school. I love my classes, but I have a ton of research to do every night. I can't study with Noah because he's too young to have homework yet, so I hang out with him until dinner."

"Do you eat with the family?"

"Sometimes I eat with Noah. They have a personal chef who cooks dinner."

When our food came and I took the first bite of the cheeseburger, I sighed with utter contentment. I hadn't eaten greasy food in a few weeks. I never had dinner with Noah if Brook was home, but more times than not, she coasted in right at seven, so I ate with him. I complimented Patrick the chef daily. I hated when Brook got home early and I had to slink away to eat canned soup or a peanut-butter-and-jelly sandwich in my studio. I was getting used to lean proteins, deliciously prepared carbs, and even a sweet low-calorie dessert.

"So, tell me about your new roommate. I guess you're doing well since you played tennis this morning?" I managed to keep the jealousy out of my voice.

"Jenn's pretty cool. She's a health nut and is constantly pushing me to go on bike rides or play tennis. It's starting to cool down outside, so I'd much rather go to the gym. You know I hate being cold." Lacy dug into her burger with as much gusto as I did mine.

"You miss my bad influence of loafing and unhealthy foods."

She nodded. "Truly and completely. Although I do feel better."

I tossed my napkin at her. "We're too young to worry about being healthy. And hurry up so I can show you my place and you can be jealous." I flagged the waitress over, paid for lunch, and waited for Lacy to follow me to the Wellington estate. I parked on the street and motioned for her to park behind me. I didn't want her to follow me up the drive.

"You have to park out on the street?" Lacy was already on the defensive.

"No, but I'm not sure what the rules are for guest parking, so I just stopped out here to be safe." I walked up the path to the side gate, entered the code, and opened the door for Lacy.

"Wow. This is amazing." Lacy stood in the driveway, hands on her hips, and did a slow three sixty, soaking in the beauty.

I was nervous that Brook would see Lacy and wouldn't be okay with me having guests. We hadn't discussed visitors, but I knew she wouldn't be okay with cars littering the driveway.

"Come on. I'm up these stairs."

"Holy shit, Cass. This is really nice. And it came completely furnished? What did you do with your furniture?"

"Donated it to the thrift store in town. Check it out. State-of-the-art appliances and tons of closet space."

"If it doesn't work out with you, I'm applying for the job."

"Oh, I'm the perfect employee. I'm not going to screw this up."

"This is better than our apartment."

I smiled with pride that I was somehow responsible for this good fortune. "It's definitely bigger. And I love the open floor space."

"Where's your bed? Where do you sleep? Does the couch fold out?"

"It does, but see that wall back there? That's not really the end of the apartment. That's the wall that hides my bed, so I do have some privacy if I have people over. You know how I hate making my bed." I never made my bed unless I washed the bedding, which I probably needed to do more often.

"What's in this room?" Lacy opened the door to the washer and dryer and hot-water heater. She shut the door and continued snooping. "This is the coolest place ever. Always be Noah's nanny. Even when he moves away to college, like Oxford or some other obscenely expensive place."

"Let's take this year by year, shall we?"

"And by that time, Brook will need a nursemaid or something. You can be her caregiver then."

"Shut up. She's only thirty-eight." When I'd googled her age, my jaw dropped. Brook Wellington looked twenty-eight. She took better care of herself than anyone I knew. I only ever saw a few lines around her eyes on the rare occasion she smiled.

"How long have you been working for her now?"

"Just under two months. Noah and I are in a good pattern. I get along with his teacher, and now the school doesn't think I'm trying to steal the children when I drive up." I handed her a Diet Coke and pointed to the front of the studio after the tour, indicating we would hang out in the living-room area. She put the drink on the coffee table and sprawled on the plush couch.

"This is the best possible scenario after your parents cut you off. Have you talked to them lately?"

My heart clenched. "No. Not in almost four months. I'm actually going to give Nana my phone and get my own. I don't want anything from them." I knew I was being childish, but I hated that they still had control over me. I wanted a complete break and would work my way back to them, my way, on my terms.

"I don't blame you there. They probably have your phone bugged. Definitely traced. They're tracking you. Oh, I wonder what they think seeing it here at the Wellington estate?"

"I'm sure Nana told them. It's not like I'm hiding it. I mean, I'm not posting it on social media, but it's not a secret either."

"Are you going over there for Christmas? I mean, I know it's not for a few months. You know you're more than welcome to come with us." Lacy's family always went to Aspen during the week between Christmas and New Year's.

"I honestly don't know what my holiday plans are. I should probably find that out." I typed myself a note in my phone.

We spent the afternoon binge-watching a cheesy television show, and after about four hours of not moving at all, Lacy dragged herself off the couch.

"I need to go. I have way too much stuff to do, as much as I'd love to hang out and do nothing the rest of the day." I followed her out and down the path to the side gate. She turned and gave me a hug. "This is a great deal. I'm glad it all worked out for you. You seem happy and relaxed, and honestly, a lot more grown-up than before. I'm proud of you."

At that exact moment, Brook Wellington slowed to pull into the driveway. Noah rolled down the window and waved from his booster.

"Hi, Cassie. Who's that?"

Feeling guilty for absolutely nothing, I glanced at Brook, who lifted her sunglasses, I guess to get a better look at us. I wanted to die. Lacy was still in my arms, and I was wearing sweats and a faded sweatshirt.

"Hi, Noah." My voice was surprisingly calm. "This is my best friend Lacy. We've known each other for years."

Lacy leaned down to get a better look. "Hi, Noah. It's nice to meet you." Her voice changed when she spoke to Brook. "Hello. I was just leaving."

"Hello, Lacy. There's no reason to rush. Have a good day." Brook slipped the sunglasses back on her nose, rolled up Noah's window, and drove through the now-open gate.

"That's your boss? Holy shit."

"Right? She's gorgeous. And probably super pissed at me for whatever reason." I'm sure it was because I was outside the estate looking like I just cleaned out the garage. The neighborhood knew Brook had hired a nanny. I was sure I was the topic of many households. At least the parents at the school weren't as curious about me as they were in the beginning.

"Yeah. She doesn't look thirty-eight at all. All blond and beautiful. You are in big trouble, my friend. Big trouble."

I heard her laughing as she drove away. Lacy was right. I was going to have to keep my distance from Brook, because she was everything I wanted and everything I couldn't have.

Chapter Six

I'd prefer it if your friends park inside the gate. I don't want any unnecessary attention. I'm sure you understand.

I sat up when I read Brook's text. Fuck.

I'm sorry. I'll keep that in mind for future guests, but really only Lacy and my grandmother will ever see my apartment. Oh, and I got a car today, so I can park it in the driveway. I promise it doesn't leak. I added the fingers-crossed emoji for a personal touch.

Then you can park inside the garage. I'll leave the opener on the counter Monday.

Thank you.

Well, that didn't leave me feeling warm and fuzzy. I'd gotten a text earlier from Lacy saying how cute Brook and Noah were. I thought she was going to say more, but she dropped the subject. I would have liked to talk about it since the only other person who knew I was working for Brook was Nana. And she wasn't as much fun. She was more about the actual job and less about my gorgeous boss.

I tossed my textbook onto the couch. I just wasn't feeling it today. It was Sunday, and even though I had a test coming up, I wasn't in the mood. Six weeks into the semester, and I was already behind. I needed to spend some time on campus, but I was still nervous about not being at Noah's school at three thirty. He was such a sweet kid, and every day

I was learning more and more about him. He was bright, imaginative, and even though I maintained a healthy distance, I couldn't help but get emotionally involved.

I'd run into Lauren twice. When her code at the gate didn't work a few weeks earlier, she gave me an earful after I had to buzz her up the driveway. I simply smiled at her, nodded more than I should have, and buckled Noah into his booster seat safely. He waved when they pulled away, and I smirked at Lauren. My loyalty was to Brook, but I was definitely interested in Lauren's story. Did she walk away from this fortune, or did Brook kick her to the curb? Was there someone else? For either of them?

I had so many questions and couldn't find anything on the internet. Brook was extremely private. I pulled up only a few photos of Noah, and most of those were family photos arranged by the Wellingtons. Brook wasn't on social media at all. I didn't blame her. There was nothing worse than getting sucked down the Instagram hole for hours at a time looking at this movie star or that singer's life in photos. Plus, Brook didn't strike me as the kind who had the time to do that.

My phone dinged again, and I cringed, thinking it was Brook, but it was actually Trina, Noah's teacher. I sat up.

Do you have time to help us with the fall festival? It's in two Saturdays.

Even though my weekends were free, I usually holed up to study.

Sure. What do you need me to do?

Well, most likely run a booth and help with signs. This week in art class we're making signs, so if you have time, stay and make a few signs with us.

Sounds like fun. Count me in.

The weather usually made a harsh change around Halloween, but it was still enjoyable mid-October. A quilted flannel shirt, long underwear, jeans, boots, and a scarf was my normal go-to wardrobe this time of year, but I thought I might have to class it up a bit. I didn't feel comfortable wearing leggings to pick up Noah, even though I changed into them for school. Sometimes I got dirty in lab, and I didn't want to ruin my nice clothes. I doubted the Wellingtons would appreciate the ultra-casual look of leggings associated with their unblemished name.

Thanks. We can talk about details tomorrow. See you then!

Trina was nice. And cute. Was she single? But it was a very bad idea to try to date Noah's teacher. That was against most corporate rules. Don't date people in your department or even within the company. If things went badly, I would have to see and talk to her every day until Noah hit second grade. And I doubted Brook would be a cheerleader for us.

I turned on the television to drown out my thoughts and picked my textbook back up. I liked print books rather than ebooks, even though they were more expensive. Something about having an actual book in my lap kept me grounded. With my tablet, it was too easy to hit a tab and surf the internet and lose valuable study time to ten thousand videos of kittens playing or dogs reacting to their military owners returning home after a tour overseas.

I didn't remember falling asleep, but nine hours later the kink in my neck told me I should have tried to drag myself to the bed when I woke up long enough, responsible enough, to set my alarm. I stretched and took a hot shower, which helped, but didn't quite get me to a hundred percent. I poured a cup of hot tea. I slipped on gray wool pants and a thin black sweater. I pulled my hair back into a twist, applied enough makeup to be noticed, and headed over to the house. I was a few minutes early, but I didn't think that would matter.

"Good morning, Cassie."

"Good morning, Brook."

She gave me a look-over, not discreet about it at all. "You seem very tall today."

I tried not to smile. "The one good thing about autumn. I can wear boots with heels. It always puts me in a good mood." Without shoes on, I was five foot nine inches. With these boots, I was just under six feet tall.

It was her turn to try not to smile. She bit her bottom lip and nodded. "Noah was feeling a little bit under the weather last night. He still wants to go to school, but if he starts feeling weak, you might get a call. If you have tests today, just let me know, and I can make other arrangements."

"I'm fine. We shouldn't have a problem." I smoothed the front of my sweater, because keeping eye contact with Brook was unnerving. She must have sensed my unease because she quickly poured coffee in her travel mug, nodded, and headed out the door. I let out a sigh. She was intense. Did she know I was attracted to her?

"I don't want to go to school early today. Can we sit and watch TV?" Noah walked into the kitchen, his shirt untucked and no socks or shoes in sight.

"After you eat a little bit for breakfast and put socks on. How are you feeling? Your mom said you had a rough night."

He wiggled onto a chair at the kitchen table. "I feel okay. Can we have pancakes today?"

Fuck, really? Pancakes? Why couldn't it be simple like cereal, oatmeal, or toast? "Let me dig around in the pantry. Remember, I'm not Patrick. I can't whip something up out of nothing."

He smiled. "I know. If we don't have the stuff, we can have eggs. You can make those, right?"

"I made you eggs just last week. You already know I can. And I'm pretty sure you ate your eggs and then tried to steal mine."

That earned a soft laugh. "I did not. I asked if you were done."

"I'd just sat down at the table. Of course, I wasn't done." I'd ended up giving him half of my scrambled eggs that morning. Noah was warming up to me nicely, and I wanted to keep developing our relationship, even if that meant I had to eat fruit for breakfast instead of bacon and eggs from time to time. I checked the pantry. Patrick didn't have pancake mix hidden in there, but I thought maybe Brook used it on the weekends. I eyed the stash of sugary cereal but decided it wasn't mine to spoil him with. "Sorry, buddy. Looks like you get scrambled eggs instead. How about you go find something on television, after you put on your socks, and I'll bring breakfast into the living room."

"Really? We can eat on the couch?"

Oops. That was probably a mistake. "Only because you had a rough night, and this will have to be our secret." I knew it was futile to swear him to secrecy. I just hoped this wasn't enough to have Brook talk to me about it. Our communication had been minimal at best. And as much as I wanted to get to know her better, it was for the wrong reasons. I'd been working for her for almost two months and knew as much about her now as I did when I first started.

To say Brook was private was an understatement. I knew she liked her coffee black, she rarely wore the same outfit twice, and she liked to speed. I didn't know if she was dating, what kind of music she liked, or what she did in her very sparse spare time. The clock dinged, telling me it was seven thirty and I needed to get moving. I had a plate of cheesy scrambled eggs and a slice of toast on Noah's lap in fifteen minutes. "What are we watching?"

"*Pokémon*."

"You're welcome." I plopped next to him with my own plate of eggs and toast.

"Thank you." He was polite, even if I had to remind him on occasion.

"What's *Pokémon*?" I knew, but I wanted him to talk to me. I brushed his blond hair away from his forehead, partly to see if he was running a fever today. He launched into the description of the game and how it's now a television show and how he plays it on his iPad at school sometimes and at home when his mom allows him. He was animated and excited, and I knew this kid was going to be a gamer. "Don't forget to eat. We only have a few minutes left before we have to leave."

"I like this stuff on the toast," he said and held up the piece for me to inspect it.

"It's cinnamon and sugar." I tapped the side of his leg. "Finish up. I have to clean up the mess I made. I want shoes on your feet and a belt around your waist in five minutes."

The dishwasher was loaded and ready to go by the time Noah returned with his backpack in hand.

"Seven minutes." I folded my arms across my chest and leaned up against the counter.

"I couldn't find my belt."

"Tuck your shirt in. Let's go."

He slung his backpack over his shoulder and walked with me. I melted as he slid his tiny fingers in my hand and didn't let go until I had to set the alarm. "Get yourself buckled into the car."

We made it to school with five minutes to spare. Al let me park out front and high-fived us as we dashed up the stairs and into the building.

I signed us in and grabbed a visitor's pass, much to Noah's surprise, and walked him to class.

"Cassie. So nice to see you again." Trina's smile was infectious. I smiled back at her. She looked adorable in her wool skirt and cream-colored sweater, and I loved her knee-high boots.

"Thanks for thinking of me for the festival."

She gently squeezed my forearm. "I'm going to put you to work, so you've been warned."

"Do you have time to talk about it now, or should I come back? We're running late because Noah wasn't feeling well last night, so I kept him home for as long as possible."

"I have lunch from eleven thirty until noon. It's only a half an hour, but if you have time, we can have lunch here. I can introduce you to cafeteria food," Trina said. She fidgeted with her watch and avoided eye contact when she suggested lunch.

I made her nervous, which gave me confidence. I couldn't remember the last time I made another woman nervous. Even though I had class today, I knew I could skip out early. This was far more important to my social well-being. "Not a problem at all. I'll check in with Mary and meet you here?"

She finally looked up at me. "That sounds good."

I lifted my eyebrow at her and smiled. "I'll see you later." I waved to Noah on my way out and returned my visitor's pass to Mary, who pretended she didn't know who I was. Then I headed back to the estate to switch out cars. Ecology lecture lasted from ten to noon and had a two-hour lab afterward, but I could skip out for an hour or so. I was riding a low A in that class, and even if I got docked for missing an hour, it'd be worth it.

❖

"The food is actually good here. It's not like public-school food." Trina led me down the line, pointing out all the good things and steering me away from the bad.

"It's very healthy. Which is good," I quickly added for fear that Trina was super healthy or vegan. I ended up with a veggie burger, sweet-potato fries, cole slaw, and a small piece of carrot cake. "This is a lot of food."

Trina swiped her card for both of our trays, and I followed her back to her classroom. Being there felt clandestine, or maybe I was being too hopeful.

"Thanks for lunch."

She closed the door to her classroom, and my stomach jumped a little. She slid a chair to the other side of her desk. "You're welcome."

"So, tell me all about this fall festival. Is it to raise money for anything?"

"It's just a fun thing for the students and their families. The money goes back into the school for maintenance or a new facility, if needed."

"A new facility? Like what? This place is nicer than my school."

"You're a student?" Her voice registered surprise.

"Working on my master's." My chest puffed out a little bit. "I dropped out of medical school after a year and decided to get my master's in environmental sciences."

"Wow. That's impressive."

"Which part? Because if you ask my parents, they'd tell you nothing about my decision was impressive." My bitterness was hard to hide. I needed to find some way to get over it. I briefly explained my parents' decision to help me leave the nest.

"That just makes you brave. I take it that's the reason you're working for the Wellingtons?"

Touchy subject ahead. "Yeah. It's a really good job that helped me out of a financial bind. I like Noah. He's a fantastic kid."

"He really is. Quiet, but very nice and empathetic."

I watched Trina as she chewed her food. She was delicate the way she covered her mouth when she answered my questions and asked several of her own.

"We have five minutes left, and we haven't even talked about the fall festival. I know it's to raise money for the school to design a sculpture out of gold. What will my part be?"

Trina laughed until she almost choked.

"Good news. I know CPR and have had one year of medical school. I'll save you," I said after it was apparent she was okay.

"I love your dry sense of humor." She took a drink of water, her eyes never leaving mine.

Lunch just got a hundred times more interesting. I leaned back. "It's obvious we aren't going to accomplish a lot in the next five minutes. Are you interested in meeting me for coffee or a drink tonight? I work until seven."

"Sure. How about a drink at the bar at the Pearl?"

"It's my favorite place." It really was. I wondered if Lacy worked tonight. Even though I was making money now, it was hard not to still want to cut corners by getting a free meal or two. I squelched the need to text her for a handout. I stood up when the bell signaling lunch was over blared over the intercom. Trina had to head down to the cafeteria to retrieve her students. "Okay. I'll see you tonight, and we can get down to business."

"I'm looking forward to it," Trina said.

I winked at her on my way out, stupidly putting it out there that I was interested. If nothing else, I knew women and how to read all the signs that they were into me.

Chapter Seven

My skirt was a little tighter than I remembered. I attributed the few extra pounds to the three meals I was eating a day versus grabbing something here and there whenever I had time and money. I wore a simple white blouse and switched out my boots. I spent a few extra minutes on my hair, styling it casually, and reapplied my makeup. I was treating this as if it were a date, but I honestly had no proof that Trina was a lesbian. I got the vibe from her, and I was rarely wrong, but I didn't want to assume, especially since she was Noah's teacher.

The restaurant was packed, but I found Trina sitting at the bar sipping on a glass of white wine. She had on the same clothes she wore to school, and for a split second, I thought I'd read her all wrong. When our eyes met and her gaze traveled up and down my body, I had my answer. She was interested.

"How are you?" After she moved her jacket, I slid onto the stool next to her.

"I'm good. This seat is good real estate. What would you like to drink?" She signaled the bartender to get my drink order.

"Hey, Cassie. I have a new single malt. Want to try a glass?" Rick was Lacy's favorite bartender. She bragged about how he always filled her orders first. Lacy and I had spent many hours up at the bar drinking whatever Rick wanted us to try. I gave him the single nod, but I threw in a smile.

"Well, you weren't kidding when you said this place was one of your favorites." Trina leaned closer to me as the crowd of people around the bar thickened.

"My friend works here. She's great. You'll like her." I turned to Rick. "Hey, is Lacy working tonight?"

"Yeah. She's got the private dining room. She already has the drink order, but I'm sure she'll be back up here in a few." Rick slid a tumbler of amber-colored scotch in front of me, added a few drops of water, and waited for me to taste it. "It's eighteen years old. Legal."

I sniffed, took a tiny sip, and let it rest on my tongue. "It's good. Really good. What is it?"

Rick handed me a bottle of Highland Park. Scotch was a drink I was just getting a taste for, though my go-to was always a martini or a gin and tonic.

"I like it. I approve."

I turned to Trina. "Would you like a sip or your own glass?"

She reached for mine, and I watched her lips cup the crystal rim and her tongue flit across them after she took a sip. Trina had full lips, the kind I wanted to press mine against. She grimaced and handed back the glass.

"I'll stick with my wine. That's a bit strong for me."

Rick left us to wait on customers at the other end of the bar. I finally had Trina all to myself.

"Okay. Fall festival. My job. And go."

She smiled at my playfulness. "We need volunteers to run the booths. I'm doing the caramel-apple booth and would love your help."

"I'm allergic to apples."

Her eyes widened. "Shut up. Really?"

I shook my head. "No. I'm just playing. I'll gladly help you with the apples."

She laughed and touched my knee. "I like that you're playful. The booths will be set up, but I'll need help making the caramel and slicing the apples to order."

"Caramel's delicious. This is the best volunteering job I've ever had."

"It's hard work. The festival is from ten until six, which means I need you there by eight. Is that too early?" She cringed.

"No. I'm up early on the weekends." Not true, but she didn't need to know that.

"This is the best news I've had all week." She finished her glass of wine and signaled Rick for another. "I should probably eat something like an appetizer. Have you had anything yet?"

"I ate with Noah about an hour ago, but I could go for an appetizer or two. What sounds good to you?" I leaned forward as she looked over the menu. She smelled clean, like lavender and baby powder.

Her breath was warm against my cheek when she turned to face me. "I could go for the lobster dip and maybe the crab cakes?"

I didn't lean back. We were in each other's personal space, but neither of us moved. Tonight had just taken a turn. I went from wondering if she was a lesbian to how I could sneak her into my apartment without anybody finding out. "That sounds delicious." A guy who was too drunk to be standing around bumped me from behind, and the moment was gone.

"Sorry, babe," he said.

I rolled my eyes and turned to Trina. "Let me see if I can score us a table." I headed to the hostess stand and asked Linda if anything was available. It was Monday night, and even though the bar was hopping, the dining room wasn't. I worked my way back to Trina, who was politely avoiding the drunk guy. Then I slipped my hand into hers and pulled her gently from the stool.

"Thank you." She didn't pull her hand away from mine, and I didn't shake her loose. We walked into the restaurant hand in hand.

"I have a table in the back. It's near the kitchen, but not as loud as the bar," Linda said. We followed her, weaving in and out of tables, until I saw the empty two-guest tables tucked in a corner.

I wasn't paying attention to anything other than Trina holding my hand, until a flash of long white-blond hair caught my eye to our right. I made eye contact with Brook, and it took a solid five seconds to register it was her. Her eyes went from mine, down to our entwined hands, and back up to my eyes, showing no emotion at all. I was sure I looked guilty as fuck. I felt cold as my confidence slithered away. Just as I was about to stop for no other reason than to explain myself, us, to her, she gave me her dismissive nod and returned to her company, who was a very tall, very striking woman who gave Brook her total attention. That was definitely a date.

Trina slightly tugged me back. "There's Brook," she whispered.

I nodded. "I don't think she wants to be disturbed, though."

We sat, and I stupidly took the chair that faced her table. I couldn't stop staring at her. How did she beat me here? Who was watching Noah? Who was the woman with her? Was this a date? A twinge of jealousy ribboned through my veins. I tried to concentrate on Trina, but I couldn't focus on anything but Brook. Her back was to me, and the dress she wore revealed a lot of skin. Definitely a date. Sophistication. That was the perfect word to describe everything about her right at this moment. The regal way she sat in her chair with her sexy legs crossed, the graceful way she held her wineglass, and the lilt in her voice that I heard from here. Definitely sophistication.

"Cassie?" Trina waved her hand in front of my face because clearly calling my name wasn't cutting it.

"I'm sorry. I'm just so surprised to see Brook here."

"Really? She's a beautiful woman. Let her have fun. I can't imagine she has a lot of downtime."

"Agreed. I only see her dressed in conservative suits. I don't see this side of her."

"The sexy, confident woman who obviously gets what she wants?"

We both sighed. I wasn't the only one who had a crush on Brook. I didn't blame Trina, but whatever was happening here wasn't really going to happen. Not that I didn't trust Trina, but I didn't need an unnecessary entanglement that resulted in my termination. It was one thing thinking I could sneak around with Trina, and another going in with Brook knowing I was out with her. My job was more important than getting laid.

"Maybe we should think about dinner instead of appetizers?"

Trina was still on a date. I couldn't imagine eating food right now. "I can only eat a few bites. If you're hungry, go ahead and eat. I'll just order a small plate of something. I really just wanted to get away from the bar. That was crazy." I was trying to deflect and not bring up Brook, but I was ten feet from her. Somehow, over all the smells in the restaurant from sautéed garlic to freshly baked bread, I could detect her perfume. Trina, who was sitting right across from me, smelled fresh and sweet, but Brook's spicy perfume a table away kept my attention. It wasn't strong. It was just her.

"I'll have the special. Cassie, what do you want?"

I stared at the waitress and wondered how she got there. The control that Brook had over my thoughts tonight amazed me. "Just the crab cakes. The appetizer portion. And an iced tea." I handed the menu back to the waitress. As much as I wanted to drink my confusion away, I needed to have a clear head. At least until I got out of there.

"You're having the same reaction my kids have when they see me outside of school. It's kind of funny. For some reason, it's hard to see teachers or, in your case, bosses, out in the real world."

"Nah. I'm all right. Let's talk about something else." I played with the empty glass I'd carried from the bar. "Tell me more about you. You like to volunteer for things like the fall festival. And what else?"

She smiled at me and slipped right into an autobiographical account of her adult life. Trina loved cats, reading history books, hiking, and wine. She preferred white, dry wines. She volunteered for everything because she had the time. "What about relationships?"

That question jerked me back into the conversation. "What about them?" I cocked my head and smiled when she mimicked me.

"Are you for them or against them?" She thanked the waitress, who carefully and quickly slipped a glass of water in front of her and handed me the iced tea.

"Right now, I'm not in a place to commit to anything, but I do like them and all the benefits they offer." I couldn't keep my eyes from drifting to Brook. Her arm rested along the back of the empty chair next to her, her fingers running smoothly back and forth across the textured fabric. At that moment she turned her head slightly and flashed a look my way. Our eyes met for the briefest of seconds, and my heart slipped into a higher gear. I sat up a little straighter to keep her attention, but she turned away.

"What do you mean, you aren't in a place to commit?" Trina asked.

Trina was the girl you took home to your parents. She was the girl who remembered your birthday and made a big deal out of it every year, even though you played it off like it wasn't important. She would drive by your house when you didn't feel well just to see if you needed anything. She was perfect for somebody, but it just wasn't me. Hooking up with her would be detrimental to her and to my working relationship with Brook. Now how the fuck was I going to explain holding her hand to Brook? Did I even need to? "My job is tricky. I work a lot, go to school, and study on the weekends."

"Come on. I'm a big girl. I can stay out past seven o'clock. A dinner or movie here and there could work."

She was making it hard to say no. If my boss wasn't Brook and Trina wasn't Noah's teacher, then definitely. "That's true. And it's nice to have new friends." I barely had time for Lacy, but I needed to branch out. I just wondered if we could keep it at the friendship level.

"Then let's toast to new friends." She held her glass up, and we clinked to our new friendship. I wondered how long it would last.

❖

I held my hand against my stomach as I walked into the kitchen for fear that it would lurch when I saw Brook. I'd barely slept, and my dreams were punctuated by visions of her disappointment in me.

"Hi, Cassie."

Noah was already at the table eating a bowl of cereal, the good kind with sugar. Two percent milk was on the table next to him. Not almond or soy, but straight-from-the-cow goodness.

"Hey, buddy. How was your night?" I placed my messenger bag on the counter and sat next to him.

"It was okay. I went over to Mom's and played with the twins." He took another big bite of cereal.

"Twins, huh? I guess I didn't know that. Cool. I wish I had a twin." I wanted a bowl of cereal, but my stomach was too unsettled. I also wanted to know the history of the twins and what that meant. Did Noah have half siblings? Were they older or younger? "How is it just now seven and you're ready for the day? Usually I have to beg and plead for you to get dressed," I said.

"I stayed the night at Mom's, and she gets up really early." His voice held a note of sadness.

"Oh, that makes sense. So you're telling me that you've been up forever. Is Miss Trina going to call me today and tell me you fell asleep in class?"

"No. I went to bed early last night. It's kind of a rule with the twins."

That probably meant they were younger. "Did you get enough sleep, though?" We didn't have a schedule for naps, and I didn't know if they were encouraged.

He nodded and tipped the bowl to drink the milk. A little dribbled down the side of his cheek that I quickly wiped away with the napkin on the table. "We don't want you to have to change. I know how you are about clothes." I pointedly rolled my eyes until he giggled. It was such a sweet sound.

Brook's clicking heels on the hardwood floors announced her arrival with just enough time for me to sit up straight before she entered the kitchen. She was wearing her dark-gray power suit, my favorite, and black heels, also my favorite. She looked fierce and formidable. I stifled a shiver.

"Good morning, Cassie."

"Good morning, Brook."

I watched as she poured herself a cup of coffee, her hands steady and sure. What had happened after I left the restaurant? Did she go home with her date, or did her date go home with her? Oh, my God. Was her date still here? Did I have to get Noah out early?

"I'd like to have a word with you in my study before you start your day," she said.

Shit. "Right now?"

She looked at me. "If you can, yes."

"Don't forget to put your bowl in the sink," I said to Noah. I followed Brook and her clicking down the hall. She shut the door behind me.

"Let's talk about last night," she said.

I sat in the chair opposite her. "Last night was interesting."

"Not that I want to tell you who you can date, but is it really a good idea to date Noah's teacher? What happens if he sees both of you leaving your apartment? Or what happens if it doesn't work out?" When I started to defend myself, she held up her hand. "I'm just telling you to be careful. Situations like this tend to be sticky."

"Speaking from experience?" I could have kicked myself for asking that. For the first time since I'd known Brook, I saw anger pinch her features. Her brows furrowed briefly, and her eyes narrowed. I swallowed hard but kept my cool.

"I don't think that's any of your concern. I just don't want to put Noah in a bad spot. If he sees you together and something happens, he'll be right back where he was with me and Lauren. I know you can't understand that, but I have to protect him. Our breakup was really difficult for him. He's just now at a place where he trusts her again."

I knew that dating Trina probably wasn't a great idea, but Brook's explanation made me feel like complete shit. "For the record, we aren't dating. We were out only because she recruited me for Hessick's fall festival. I was holding her hand to pull her away from the drunk dudes at the bar. We took separate cars there, and I was home before ten."

Brook leaned back, crossed her arms, and stared at me. At least the anger was gone. I relaxed for the first time since I sat down.

"I don't feel good about this. Your private life should be your private life. I know living on the estate puts you in a bind, but I also need to do what's best for Noah."

I held my hands up in surrender. "I get it. I really do. Lacy was only here one time, and Noah saw her. I'm sure seeing his teacher and his nanny together would be confusing. Dating Trina isn't going to happen. I don't have time to date anyway." I clamped my mouth shut and told myself to stop talking.

"Okay, so we're done here. Thank you for understanding."

She stood, indicating we really were done talking. I followed her back to the kitchen, where Noah was playing on his iPad.

"Noah, have a good day. You, too, Cassie."

I got the single head nod as she grabbed her coffee and left the room and watched her the entire way until she closed the door to the garage. Then I sighed and turned my attention back to Noah, whose attention was on me, not on his iPad.

"What did you and my mom talk about?"

Oh, the fate of my vagina and the sex life I'll never have as long as I'm your nanny. "Just boring business stuff. I did tell her what a terrific kid you are." I ruffled his hair as he tried to dodge me. I wasn't wrong. He really was a great kid.

Chapter Eight

"What do I need to do to get a caramel apple around here?" The gruff voice added to my panic as I stood up from trying to salvage what was left of the sliced apples and my dignity. "Were you hiding?" An older man with perfectly coiffed gray hair and kind eyes smiled at me. Blue shirt, dark blue sweater, wool pants. Everything about him screamed money. Before I had a chance to explain myself, a small voice I recognized well interrupted us.

"Hi, Cassie." Noah ran up to the counter and stood up on his tippy toes just to see over it.

"Noah. You made it." I knew he was going to be there. I was just expecting him to be with Brook.

"Cassie. I've heard your name a lot lately. Nice to finally meet you. I'm David Wellington, Noah's grandfather," the older man said.

"Nice to meet you, too. I'm going to have to excuse myself because I have a mess that I need to clean up before anybody else sees the utter chaos down here."

David peeked over the counter to the piles of apple slices that had tumbled out of the barrel and landed on the wooden lid.

"I won't say a word as long as my order comes from the apples still inside the barrel. And I don't want to know what's happening to the caramel." He pointed to the pot on the burner behind me.

"Shi—" I stopped just short of dropping the *t*. Burnt sugar wasn't a good smell. "I'm going to need some help over here." I stirred the hot caramel, careful to avoid touching the bottom of the pan.

"You had one job." Trina slid into the booth with me, smiling at my panic. "What happened?"

"A squirrel ran through. Or what I thought was a squirrel. Anyway, I've burnt the caramel, and the apple slices were trying to make a quick getaway. Suggestions?"

Trina turned off the burner, grabbed a ladle, and scooped the caramel into a smaller pot. "This will have to work for now. You'll have to be stingy with the portions until we can cook up more. Rinse off all the apple slices, but throw away the ones that hit the ground. Don't cut any more. They'll just have to be made to order." She was so in control, and I just stood there in the way. "Why don't you fix Mr. Wellington's order, and then we'll clean up."

I smacked my palm to my forehead. "Of course. Sorry, Mr. Wellington." I put on fresh gloves, grabbed a bowl, dug out the best apple slices under his scrutiny, and gave him more caramel than I should have, especially since I had to make a whole new batch.

"Hello, Father."

I stiffened at the voice, knowing full well Brook had arrived. The tingle that traveled up my spine and raised the hairs on my arms was unmistakable. Powerful and sexy. I licked my lips out of nervousness.

"Hi, Cassie. Hi, Trina." Brook slid into her father's one-armed embrace and put her hand on Noah's shoulder.

"Cassie spilled the apples, and Miss Trina had to come over and help," Noah said.

I gave Brook a quick wave and quickly avoided eye contact when I handed her father his order. I also avoided Trina when she brushed up against me while getting the ingredients together for another batch of caramel.

"I see. Are you sure they're safe to eat then?" she asked. I couldn't tell if she was joking or not.

"A little dirt never hurt anyone." David slipped a hundred-dollar bill in the tip jar on his way to the next booth. All tips and donations would go back into the school, but the booth with the highest tips got a gift card to one of the Wellington grocery stores. Even I felt competitive with the kettle-corn booth next door. They were getting a lot of business, but autumn in the northeast meant apple everything. Cider, doughnuts, caramel covered, pies, vinegars, sauces, and anything else people could do with apples. Kettle corn was universal. And boring. That didn't stop me from asking for samples. I gave them samples, too. Like Mr. Wellington said, a little dirt never hurt anyone.

"I think we might have a shot at winning. I never win. Although, to be fair, this is only my third year doing it," Trina said.

I eyed our tip jar and the kettle corn's tip jar and figured we were really close to being even. "Are you friends with them?"

"Patricia and Ellie?" she asked. I nodded. "They're nice, but really obnoxious when they win."

"Well then, let's not let them win." I flagged over some people who were meandering in the little courtyard set up for the festival. "It's dessert time. Come on over and get some apples before we run out." It was a hard sell, but I got rid of two bowls, then another two, until we had a line. The kettle-corn girls did, too, but by the end of the afternoon, I swore we were ahead.

"Cassie. Do you have any apples left?" Noah was back at the booth with Brook right behind him.

I took my finger out of my mouth and slowly put the pot of semi-burnt caramel down. This was awkward and embarrassing. "Sorry, buddy. We're all out." I looked at Brook and shrugged. "You probably shouldn't have seen that, but I haven't eaten a lot today."

"Are you done here? Or do you have to stay to help clean up? We can take you to dinner if you want," Brook said. Did she just ask me out? I mean, I knew it was just probably a quick dinner somewhere fast, but it was Saturday, and I had no obligation to them, nor they to me.

"I think I have to stick around and clean up. I helped set up, so I'm sure I'll have to break it down, too, but thanks for the offer." I wiped my hands on my apron, trying to figure out how I could do both, but knew I had to stay.

"Go on." Trina took the caramel pot from my hand. "There's nothing left to do. Everything here will get carted up to the kitchen. Our job here is basically done."

"No. I told you I'd help. Plus, I want to know if we beat the librarians," I whispered so Brook couldn't hear the conviction in my voice.

"Get out of here. I'll text you later."

I turned back to the Wellingtons. "I'm available if the offer still stands." I took off my apron and handed it to Trina. "Definitely text me later."

Noah slipped some money into the tip jar while I gathered my things. It was another hundred, and I pretended not to see it.

"Where do you want to go? How about that place that serves burgers and all the fries you can eat?" Noah looked at me like it was my choice.

"It all depends on your mom and where she wants to go."

He slipped his hand into mine. I couldn't look at Brook. "Can we go to Happy's? That's a fun place." Noah looked back at Brook, who was a step behind us.

"It's going to be packed. How about we grab a burger at Ruby's?" Brook took his other hand and moved up to walk with us.

"But that's Uncle Anthony's restaurant. We always go there," Noah said.

I squeezed his fingers gently. "I've never been. Is it good?"

"Yeah. It's just more for adults."

"But today was all about kids, right? Maybe tonight should be about the adults," I said.

He looked at me and nodded. "Okay. Let's go to Uncle Anthony's."

"Do you want to follow us?" Brook stopped at her SUV.

I'd completely forgotten that I drove to the academy. I stopped short of sliding into the passenger seat and quickly opened up the back door for Noah instead. "Sure. I'll meet you there. The one on Elm Street, right?"

Brook gave me the single nod and slipped into the driver's seat. As much as I loved her in her power suits, she looked even better in fashionable form-fitting pants and an oversized sweater. With her hair up in a messy bun, she was a mix between sexy and flirty. I couldn't have felt frumpier in my jeans and flannel shirt if I tried.

At the first stop light, I dug around in my console for any makeup or a hairbrush, knowing full well I kept my new car clean. I pulled out a pack of gum, a wheel lock, an air freshener the dealership had thrown in it, and a hair tie. Damn it. I flipped down the visor to check out what ten hours on my feet looked like. How long had the speck of caramel been on my cheek? Was that a piece of apple in my hair? At least my cheeks had some color. I smoothed down my hair and threw it back in the hair tie. Then let it down again. I didn't want to look like a teenager. I took a deep breath and waited for the light to change. Noah turned around and waved. I smiled and waved back.

Chapter Nine

"How was the festival? Did you hook up with the teacher?" Lacy's voice was loud through the speakers. I quickly turned down the volume.

"No, but guess what I'm doing right now?"

"Noah's teacher?" She laughed.

"Shut up. I'm going out to dinner with Brook and Noah." I leaned back in the seat as if she was in front of me and I'd just dropped the mic.

"Are they in the car with you?" Her whisper was low, but the concern was unmistakable.

"No. I'm following them to the restaurant. Brook's brother owns Ruby's."

"You're taking a kid to that place? It's kind of not really kid friendly. I think I applied there when they first opened."

"Get this. I'm wearing flannel. And jeans. And muddy hiking boots. I'm basically a hot mess who can't tell her boss no."

"Well, what's she wearing? Flannel, too? No. She's too classy."

"Oh, thanks a lot. But you're right. She's wearing tight pants and a big sweater, and she looks so relaxed and adorable with her Daenerys hair and big blue eyes."

"Oh my God. You work for the mother of dragons. By the way, I'm so far behind on that show. Don't tell me what happens. But do tell me what happens tonight after your date."

"It's not a date, but I'll text you later and let you know all about it. And the kid will be with us." I shook my head. "Okay. I'm parking now. I'll talk to you later. Bye." I dragged out *bye* in an annoying way.

"I really hate that." She hung up during my laugh.

Noah greeted me at my car door.

I rolled down the window. "Can I help you, sir?"

He giggled. "Come on. I'm hungry."

"Are you placing your order, sir? Is that for a cheeseburger and fries?"

"Come on, Cassie." He opened my door and reached for my hand.

"Wait, wait. I need to roll the window back up." I locked the car and looked at Brook for the first time. She gave me a tight smile. Everything inside me fluttered. I gave her a half smile back. "So, this is your brother's place?"

"He got tired of the family business, so he got to do what he wanted." She held the door open for the both of us.

"Thank you," I said. Brook was completely in my personal space, closer than she'd ever been before, and I felt self-conscious. She was so close I heard her smile when a man approached us and hugged Noah.

"Hey, big guy. I just got your message. I'm glad you made it."

I assumed this man who leaned very close to me to reach Brook was her brother. Brook's arm brushed my shoulder, and I moved to the side to give her more room. I wasn't prepared to feel her hand lightly touch my waist as she leaned past me to kiss his cheek. "Hello, Anthony."

She was formal with him, though not as casual as she was with her father. I definitely detected love, but it was more restrained.

"Hey, big sis."

"Big sister by what? A year?" I said.

"Sixteen months. Wow, our mother couldn't wait," he said.

"Um, hello? We have guests here." Brook held her hands over Noah's ears and gave her brother the best older-sister look, which even made me shrink back.

"Hi. I'm Anthony." He stretched out his hand to shake mine. It was a firm yet friendly handshake.

"I'm Cassie. I'm with Noah."

"I've heard about you. All good things."

"I was going to say don't believe everything you hear, but in this case, do."

"I know you're appreciated. My sister's pushed to her limits.

Come on. Let's get you a table in the kitchen so I can show you how awesome I am."

I liked Anthony. He treated Noah like a kid and knew how to talk to him. I wondered how often he saw his nephew. Today was the first day I'd met anyone from Brook's family. Both her father and her brother seemed good-natured and relaxed.

I sat opposite Brook with my back to the wall so I could see everything. I watched as she reviewed the menu with Noah, allowing him time to read it first before explaining things. Lacy was right. This was not a kid-friendly place. Quail? Quince? Quiche? I checked to see if there were any foods that started with the letter *z*.

"Are you looking for anything in particular? I'm sure my brother can whip up whatever you want," Brook said.

Her eyes were so piercing. And her lips. I couldn't tell if she was wearing lipstick. They were full and not too red but had just enough of a tint that made me question whether she toned it down with a neutral color or if that was just her natural look. Her makeup was light, with a tiny bit of eyeliner, a touch of mascara, and a hint of blush. Were her eyelashes as light as her hair? Her eyebrows were darker, but that was normal for blondes.

"Cassie? Hello?"

I gave her my best impression of a deer in headlights. Holy shit, she'd caught me staring. "I'm sorry, what?"

"Is there anything you want?"

Yes, your body next to mine. Your lips on mine, kissing me everywhere, your hands with your painted nails on my back. "Everything looks delicious." I shrugged and found something very interesting to look at on the wine list.

"I'm having a cheeseburger and fries," Noah said.

"Hi, Noah. Hi, Brook. Nice to see you again."

A waitress swooped in and took our drink orders and placed a basket of bread and butter on the table. Noah reached for a piece immediately.

"Only one piece. I don't want it to spoil your dinner."

"Mom, can I have your phone?"

She unlocked her phone and hit the app he wanted. And then it was just the two of us. I took a sip of water for lack of conversation while she rummaged through her purse.

"Tell me about school." Brook focused her attention back on me, interlocked her fingers, and placed her hands on the table. At least she was making the effort.

"It's definitely keeping me busy."

"More than you expected?"

"Not more, just different. See, before I had to worry only about school. Now I have school and a job. I didn't have to be concerned about money before." I took another sip of water. It wasn't that I didn't want to talk about it. I just wasn't over my anger at my parents, and I didn't want to come across as bitchy or ungrateful. I was both, but I didn't want Brook to know.

She nodded more than once. "I get it. Anthony was kind of in the same situation. Our father wanted one thing, and he wanted another. He got this restaurant all on his own, much to my father's amazement and chagrin."

I cocked my head and pursed my lips as though I didn't believe her. The man I'd met today was kind and nice. He didn't seem the type to cut off his own family. Plus, after hearing Lacy's horror stories for years, I knew how hard it was to run a restaurant.

"You don't believe me. Yes, he has the Wellington name, and not too many people are going to tell him no, but the money is all his own. I'm proud of him for that." She took a bite of warm bread and licked the crumbs from her lips. In response to watching her, I licked my lips, then quickly took another sip of water.

"It's not that I don't believe you. I mean, all families have their histories. Your dad seemed like a cool guy, and your brother is obviously chill. I just thought everything was perfect in your world. You seem like a really close family."

"Oh, we are. It just took a lot of time to get there. So, even though you're dealing with issues of your own, there's hope." A smile. A genuine smile popped up on her face, and I melted. I'd believe anything she said right now.

"It'll take a bit. With Thanksgiving right around the corner, I'm still trying to figure out if I'm going with Nana to my parents' or if I'll hang out with Lacy. Her family always has a good turnout. I'll blend in there." My heart stopped when Brook placed her fingers gently on mine. It was completely out of character for her, at least the Brook I knew.

"You are more than welcome to come to Thanksgiving dinner with my family. You've met my father and my brother. That's half the battle right there. My mother's easy to get to know, and my sister, well, she's very protective."

She pulled her hand back, and I was so tense I swore I heard my heartbeat. I casually put my hands on my armrests and squeezed out the excess energy her touch suddenly gave me. It was the first time she'd treated me like a friend, not an employee. Looking at her under the dim lights, relaxed and comfortable, it was hard to think of her as my millionaire boss. Come to think of it, I didn't know what Brook actually did.

"Tell me about your job. What do you do for Wellington Enterprises?"

"Ah, deflection. I know it well." She winked at me. Winked!

I smiled sheepishly. "I honestly don't know. I mean, I know Wellington does import and export things, and you have grocery stores, but what's your actual job? You run it all, don't you?"

She took a sip of wine. "We have a board that technically runs it. I'm the COO. My father is still CEO. I report to him when I need to, but he leaves a lot of the decisions up to me. He'd rather travel and vacation with Mom than deal with company issues."

"Do you travel?"

She shook her head. "With Noah in school, I won't even try. I can't do that to him."

"With an import and export business, wouldn't you have to travel? Or do you have a team that does that?"

"My father and his number one usually close all overseas business deals. I just maintain them. This can't possibly be exciting to you."

I was leaning forward so much, I had to reach back for my wine. I slowly sat back. "You'd be surprised what fascinates me." Well, that was laced with more sexual innuendo than I wanted.

She lifted her eyebrow at me and saved us from several awkward moments of silence by continuing to question me. "Tell me why you're studying environmental sciences. And why did you leave med school?"

Her voice held only interest, no judgment. It was a relief to talk to somebody who wanted to know why. Most of my friends and colleagues thought I was stupid for dropping out of med school, especially after completing the first year.

"Both my parents are doctors. They pushed me down that path, and I let them. When it got down to it, I didn't want to. I dreaded school, yet I love learning. So, I broke the news to them, they cut me off, and here I am." I was proud that I kept my voice even and emotionless.

The food arrived just as I was getting ready to launch into my new educational path. I desperately wanted a cheeseburger and fries like Noah, but settled on chicken and asparagus. That was an adult enough meal. Brook went with a filet mignon and new potatoes.

"Look at that. You're not going to be able to eat it all." I pointed to the stacked burger that was half the size of Noah's face.

"Whoa. Look at this, Mom," he said.

"I see that. Are you hungry enough?"

Brook and I both knew he would eat maybe a third of it.

"I'm going to help you with your fries, okay?" I said.

He carefully picked out one and handed it to me. I wouldn't have cared if his hands were covered in mud. I was going to eat it.

"Yum. Thank you." I looked at Brook, who smiled at me. A cheesy grin slid onto my face, and I couldn't stop it. I glanced at my plate. "This looks really good, too."

"My brother's a pretty good cook. Even better than Patrick. Just don't tell him that because I don't want him to get a bigger head than he already has," she said.

There was a moment of companionable silence as the three of us dug into our food. The chicken was juicy and tender, with just enough char on it. I had to slow down to stop myself from eating it like a caveman.

"This chicken is probably the best I've ever had. I almost want to cry at how good it is."

"Can you say that again, please? And speak into my phone. I'm going to share this with Patrick," Brook said.

I stared at her for a solid three seconds before I realized she was joking. Then I choked on the bite already in my mouth. My eyes watered, and I discreetly tried to swallow before I made a complete ass of myself.

"Are you okay?" Brook's beautiful eyes were huge as she leaned forward to check on me.

I nodded, even though my eyes watered, and I was trying to breathe through my nose while I coughed to dislodge the chicken.

"Cassie, are you choking?" Noah looked just as concerned as his mother.

I held my finger up to them and drank some water. That helped. I sighed when I finally swallowed the piece. "I'm okay, I'm okay."

"Was it my joke?"

I nodded. "Completely unexpected and hilarious. I'm sorry I worried everyone."

Even the couple in the booth across from us kept glancing my way. I smiled at them, and they returned to their conversation.

"That was embarrassing."

She waved me off. "Don't joke with Cassie. Check." She drew an imaginary check mark with her forefinger.

"Are you kidding? This is great. Thank you for inviting me."

"Thanks for volunteering at Noah's school. You didn't have to, but we both appreciated it."

"Full confession. I like my job. Noah's really sweet. The school is gorgeous, and I know he's getting a top-notch education. He's smarter than other kids his age. He makes it easy," I said.

Another genuine smile from Brook Wellington. Happy pings twitched inside me as I tried to play it cool while we finished dinner. This was nice. Anthony came over a few times to chat with us until his employees pulled him back.

"You never answered me about why you're getting your degree in environmental sciences. What drew you to that field?" Brook asked.

"I've always loved botany. Plants are incredible. I learned how delicate our ecosystem is and how that affects everything in life. Very few people care. I mean, we have a ton of organizations that educate, but a lot of people ignore the facts. I want to do something about it." I refrained from shrugging. I realized I polished my vocabulary and sat straighter in front of Brook. Even though we were in a relaxed environment, I was tense.

"Ah, youth. It's refreshing."

I bristled. Visibly.

She leaned forward. "No offense. I mean your ideals and beliefs are nice to hear. I deal with dejected people and ballbusters daily. Your enthusiasm is appreciated. Truly." She placed her hand on her heart to emphasize her message.

I stared into those stark-blue eyes and saw nothing but sincerity, so I smiled. "I can say *ballbusters* and that's okay?" I mock-whispered and looked at Noah.

She covered her mouth. "Oops. Usually it's just me and Noah at mealtime. I'm not used to adult dialogue."

We looked at Noah, who was engrossed in his game again.

"I'm so glad I never got involved in video games," she said.

"Well, don't visit me. I have all the systems. Not that I have the time anymore, but if you need guidance, suggestions, or tutoring, I'm your girl." I pointed my thumbs at my chest and realized that I was too comfortable, so I dropped my hands even though I saw a tiny smile in the corner of her mouth. "I'm pretty sure you were too busy studying and learning the business in prep school to learn *Mario* and *Sonic* and whatever games were out." I stopped. Did I just say that? I got the single eyebrow lift. Fuck. I did. "Well, you know what I mean. Games have improved so much just the last few years."

"Want to stop while you're ahead?" Her voice was slightly menacing, but the smirk on her face told me she was teasing.

"Definitely. Thank you."

"Ladies, and sir, how was everything?" Anthony showed up a final time, putting his hand on Brook's shoulder. She relaxed and leaned into him.

"Fantastic. Best chicken I've ever had. Next time I'm getting the cheeseburger, because that looked amazing, too."

"Thank you. The chicken is our most popular dish. Except for the seafood specials."

Noah asked me a question, and I had to break away from their conversation to answer him, even though I was trying hard to listen to what they were saying. Thanksgiving was going to be at the restaurant, and all the Wellingtons were invited and expected to bring whatever they wanted or nothing at all. Anthony's wife and her sister would cook the bulk of the meal. Brook volunteered something, but Noah's explanation of the quest he was on drowned out the rest of her words.

"I've invited Cassie, too."

"That's great. You don't have to bring anything. It's a very casual, fun day," Anthony said.

Noah rolled his eyes. "I'm like the only kid."

"That's not true. You have two cousins who'll be here," Brook said.

"They're too young to play with."

"Come early, and you can help me in the kitchen. I heard you like to watch Patrick cook. Maybe you could cook the turkey," Anthony said.

"No way. I can't cook. I'm six," Noah said.

"You can still help. Then you won't be so bored."

Brook stood and helped Noah slip his jacket on. I guess we were done. I shook Anthony's hand and complimented him again on the food.

"See you next week," he said.

I now had a plan for Thanksgiving. Nana was either going to be disappointed I wasn't going to my parents' house or scold me for getting too involved with the Wellingtons. At least I felt welcome.

"Thanks for the invite and for the meal. I had a good time." I helped Noah into his booster seat and shut the door before turning my attention to Brook. Our eyes met over the top of the sedan. Something passed between us. I didn't know if it was a spark or a flash of desire, but I knew our relationship had taken a slight turn tonight. I wasn't just the nanny anymore.

Single nod. "I'll see you Monday, Cassie."

I smiled and gave her a single nod back before I slipped into my car and followed her home.

Chapter Ten

I spent more time getting ready for Thanksgiving dinner than I should have. It took forty-five minutes to fix my hair, fifteen minutes to perfect the very-little-makeup look, and ten minutes to contort into clothes that I should have slipped on before I even started with hair and makeup. Damn, I looked good. My boots gave me the height that also boosted my confidence. I grabbed my keys and headed to the garage. Brook texted that she was going there early with Noah so he could help. Dinner was at three. It was only a ten-minute drive, but I wanted to be early and sit in a corner watching the family, instead of walk in late and be the center of attention.

There were so many cars in the parking lot already. I took three deep breaths before I opened my car door and walked into the restaurant.

David Wellington spotted me immediately. "Cassie. Come on in. Let's show you around." He introduced me to his wife, Camila, whose resemblance to Brook was unmistakable. Same light-blond hair and piercing blue eyes, except her hair was cut in a stylish bob.

"I understand you've been such a help to Brook. Noah talks about you nonstop. It's so nice to finally meet you." She shook my hand and squeezed it before letting go.

"Thank you for allowing me to share Thanksgiving with your family," I said.

"Let's go meet some people."

I met Brook's uncles, aunts, and cousins and remembered none of their names. The crowd was overwhelming. I looked down when I felt tiny fingers tug my hand.

"Cassie. You're here," Noah said.

I excused myself from the conversation and bent down so that my face was even with his.

"Hello, gorgeous." I brushed his hair away from his forehead. "How was cooking? Did you make all of it yourself?" I exaggerated my voice, and he smiled at me.

"I pasted the turkey."

"You pasted the turkey? Do you mean basted it? Like with a giant eye-dropper thingy?" I knew how to speak six-year-old.

He nodded.

"I'm sorry I wasn't out here when you arrived," Brook said.

I looked up and felt light-headed. Brook was wearing slacks and a V-neck sweater that showed off her beautiful skin. Her hair was down and wavy. She looked incredible. As beautiful as Brook was every day, this casual, chic look left me breathless.

"I forgot your hair is wavy." *That's the thing I say to my boss? Not thanks for inviting me or I'm so happy to be here, but your hair is wavy?*

She smirked and lifted her eyebrow.

I shook my head. "What I meant to say was hi. Thank you for inviting me."

"I hear you've met my family. Well, except for my sister."

"Cassie, sit by me, okay?" Noah asked.

"Let's just wait and see, okay, buddy?" Noah nodded and left to go play with his smaller cousin, per Brook's request.

"Where's your sister?"

"She's chronically late, but on her way." Brook handed me a glass of wine. "It's the house, but it's very tasty."

It was a little dry for my taste, but I wasn't going to complain. I was sharing space with a woman I admired and admittedly crushed on. I drank it.

"You look nice."

"So do you. It's good to see you relaxed." I blocked out the night she was on her date. Every time my mind conjured up Brook in her sexy, open-back dress from the Pearl, I tamped it down. I couldn't afford for her to take up more of my time, even if my thoughts were pure fantasy.

"It's nice to be relaxed. We aren't allowed to talk about business during the holiday get-togethers or family dinners. My mother won't let us." She leaned a little closer and whispered, "She's the hard-ass of the family."

I looked for Camila and pointed my glass to the other side of the restaurant. "I think you're safe. And I seriously doubt that she's a hard-ass."

She shrugged. "You just met my mother. Just you wait."

"Uh-huh. Sure." I nodded. I didn't believe her for one second.

"Hi, Aunt Brookie."

A tiny girl about three or four grabbed Brook around the waist and knocked her off balance. She reached out and grabbed my arm, her fingers grazing my breast in the process. I turned bright red and coughed. Brook muttered a quick apology and squatted down to give her niece a hug.

"Frances, you made it."

I took Brook's glass so she could remove her niece's coat and mittens. "I'm Cassie."

"Is she your girlfriend?" Frances asked.

I gulped the rest of my drink and was tempted to finish off Brook's. I stood there and smiled.

"No, sweetie. She's my friend. Where's your mom?"

"Talking to Grandpa. Where's Noah?"

"In the kitchen with Griffin. Why don't you go find them? It's almost time to eat."

A tarnished version of Brook with darker hair and darker eyes approached us. She was striking. "Brookie, how is it we only see each other on holidays, even though we live so close? Now that you have a live-in babysitter, I can drop off Frances, and we can go out for a night on the town." She was also bitchy. I was taken aback by her rudeness.

"Gwen, meet Cassie. She's Noah's nanny and our friend, not my live-in babysitter." Brook turned to me with her hand on her hip. "I apologize for my sister. She always leaves her filter at home. Cassie, this is Gwen."

"Oh, I'm sorry. I just assumed she was your date. I didn't mean anything by that. It's nice to meet you." She waved her hand in front of us as if shooing off a gnat, like trivializing me wasn't a big deal.

"Same."

Brook looked at me and gave me the single nod.

"Wellingtons and guests. We are ready for dinner," Anthony announced while carrying a giant turkey to the table. Several sides were already on the row of square tables pushed together to make one huge table.

I had no idea where to sit, so I stood around until David started pointing to chairs. I got seated next to Brook's cousin, George, and Anthony's wife, Erica. Brook and Noah sat directly across from me, which made Noah happy and me extremely nervous. I gladly accepted another glass of wine as bottles were being passed around.

David clinked his knife against a crystal glass to get everyone's attention.

"Family and friends. Thank you for being here for the Wellington tradition. Anthony has cooked a beautiful meal for all of us to enjoy. I'm proud of him and all of my children. Brook is doing a fantastic job with the businesses, and Gwen has done more work with our charities than ever before. Our family is strong and supportive, and I couldn't be happier."

I tried to pay attention, but my mind wandered to my own family and our struggles. What was going on at the house? Did Nana make the sweet potatoes this year, or did she only make the rolls? My mother had the meal catered because she couldn't take the time to cook, but my Nana always made something because she felt it was necessary and helped the experience feel more like a family affair. The clinking of glasses interrupted my thoughts as everyone toasted one another. I reached out and tapped Noah's water glass. It was a good thing I had a long reach, or else my enthusiasm would have been embarrassing.

"Happy Thanksgiving, Cassie." Brook's tone was low and sultry, and even though I'm sure it was innocent, a wave of hunger rippled through me.

I tilted my glass back at her. "Thank you again for inviting me."

Once dinner started, it was hard to have a conversation with anyone other than the person sitting next to you. Hearty laughter and storytelling by the person who spoke the loudest punctuated the low murmur of voices. It was hard to keep up with conversations, but I always perked up when I heard Brook's name.

"So how long have you been working with Brook?" Erica asked. She filled our glasses.

I liked her. She seemed genuine and was clearly supportive of

Anthony and his dreams. And she didn't treat me like the help, unlike Gwen, who barely registered I was there. I was thankful she was sitting at the other end of the table.

"Since school started about three months ago. Noah's such a good kid."

"He really is. And he's so good with Griffin. I know he wishes Griffin were older, but in a couple of years, they'll have more in common and Noah won't feel like he's babysitting all the time. So, tell me more about yourself. Brook said you're a student?"

Her eyes were only on me, so I knew she was actually interested. I poured another glass of wine and told her everything. It only took a few questions for me to open up. I'd like to think I was fair to my story, but the wine clouded my memory of the moment.

"I'm sure your parents were doing what they thought was best, but good for you for getting out and proving them wrong." Erica toasted me and we both giggled.

"Okay, okay. I think you both have had too much wine." Anthony replaced our wineglasses with coffee. "It's pie time anyway. The coffee will taste better than the wine, trust me." He leaned down and kissed Erica's cheek.

Anthony was right. Most people were up and about, spread out and talking in groups. The desserts were on a separate table, buffet style.

"How's it going over here, you two?" Brook asked. She slid into the chair next to me.

"I really like her, Brookie," I said. I looked at Brook's lips, her gorgeous full red lips, and leaned forward. The need to be close to her was overwhelming. I was tired of always being on guard around her. Today was nice.

"Yeah, I bet you do. Why don't you stay here, and I'll get you a piece of pie to go with that hot coffee."

"No, no. I've got this." I stood up, felt the room spin once, then sat back down. "Okay, maybe not."

"Both of you. Stay here. I'll be back," Brook said.

I watched her walk away, admiring her form and the sway of her hips. "She's really attractive."

"Agreed. I hope that when I'm almost forty, I'll look that good," Erica said.

"You look good, too." I meant that. Erica was cute and perky and had a nice body. She just wasn't as curvy as Brook.

"It's hard to stay in shape being a mom, working full-time, and being married to a chef."

"A phenom chef."

"Exactly. And then I have to eat pie." She took the plate from Brook and fake-cried while she took the first bite.

"Thank you," I said to Brook. Much to my surprise, she sat next to me again. "Where's Noah?"

"He's with Anthony and Griffin in the kitchen. You don't have to worry about him. Tonight you're our guest."

I leaned closer to her. "You have a really nice family."

Erica put her hands on my leg as she bent forward to hear what I was saying to Brook, but she slipped, and her face landed in my lap. I burst out laughing, as did she. Within seconds we were laughing so hard we couldn't catch our breath. Brook helped Erica back upright in her chair because I was too busy wiping away tears to help.

"All right. Okay. Erica, stay here," Brook said. She turned to me and pointed. "And you stay here, too. I'll be right back."

"Are we in trouble?" I asked.

"No. Brook wasn't mad. I've seen her mad before, and this isn't it."

"Let's drink our coffee. Maybe that'll make her happy," I said. We were two tipsy women trying to play it cool. Thank goodness nobody was paying attention to us. "It's hot, so be careful," I warned her after burning my tongue on the bitter brew. I knew Brook liked her coffee black, but I was a cream-and-sugar kind of girl. "And really strong."

"Cassie, put on your coat."

"Wait. Are we leaving already?" I stood and wobbled. Both women reached out to steady me.

"It's probably a good idea. Come on. Let's say good-bye."

"Crap. How much did I drink?"

"Probably a glass too much."

"I wholeheartedly agree." I waited until I was balanced, hugged Erica, who wobbled with me, and followed Brook to her parents.

"It was so nice to meet you, Mrs. Wellington. Thank you for inviting me. I had a wonderful time." I heard myself stress the word *wonderful* even though I was trying hard not to seem drunk.

"Cassie, you're such a delight. Take care, and I hope to see you soon." Camila hugged me.

"You should come by and visit," Brook said. "Noah and I would love to see you."

"I'll do that," Camila said.

I believed her. I waved a little too enthusiastically to Brook's cousins on my way out the door. "Hey, we can't forget Noah."

"He's fine. Anthony's going to drop him off tonight. Let's get you home."

I managed to get into the car and close the door, but couldn't latch the seat belt. Brook reached over to help.

"Quit wiggling and stop looking down. Move your hands. You're not helping."

I raised my arms high and stared straight ahead until we heard the click. Then when she moved her hands from my thigh, I sagged in my seat.

"Thank you. Hey, I really like your sister-in-law."

"She liked you, too. My whole family did."

"Do you think they knew I'd been drinking?" I held my hands out on the dashboard to steady myself as Brook twisted and turned through the streets to drive home. I didn't want to further embarrass myself by puking in her car. Being drunk on wine was a horrible feeling, and my stomach often revolted when I imbibed too much.

"Probably. My family's pretty smart."

"It's nice to see you chill for a change. And you're so pretty. You should wear your hair like that more. And I really want to call you Brookie." My confessions didn't sound real. I heard them but felt like I was in a dream and none of this was happening.

"Brookie might be pushing it," she said.

I knew she wasn't driving fast, but it felt like it. I held the handle. "Are we almost home? We should stop and pick up some ice cream."

"We should really get you home and into bed."

I grinned at her, the sexy grin I reserved for women I was trying to charm. "Oh yeah? Just like that?"

"Not like that. You. Alone."

I frowned. "Fun sucker."

"Fun sucker? Really?"

She didn't sound upset. I looked over and stared at her profile. She was perfect. Smooth skin from her forehead down to her neck and full lips she licked out of habit when she was deep in thought. Even in the dark, I could see her light-blue eyes. They fascinated me.

"Not really fun sucker. I know you're capable of fun. I just wish you were fun with me. I'm fun."

"Without a doubt you're fun. You are really good with Noah, and he already loves you."

I sighed with relief when we pulled up to the gate and hummed the *Jeopardy* song while we waited for it to open. Brook giggled.

"Did you just giggle? Is my voice that bad?"

"If nothing else, at least you're a fun drunk." She parked the car and looked over at me. "Are you ready?"

I pointed to the seat belt. "This fucker isn't working again."

Another laugh and a loud click. "There. You're free."

I opened the door and stumbled out, catching myself on the Range Rover. "Hello, beautiful. I'll see you Monday."

"Are you talking to the car?"

I turned around, swayed, and denied everything that she might have just heard.

"Come on. I'll help you up the stairs." She was so close I could feel her body heat even though we were both wearing coats. I licked my lips and leaned forward. "Your eyes are so blue. The bluest I've ever seen. I thought maybe they were tinted contacts, but then I met your equally gorgeous mom, and she has the same eyes."

"Nope. All mine. All real."

She helped me up the stairs, both of us wobbling and holding on to one another for different reasons.

She guided me to the door and asked me to punch in the code. After three times of missing the buttons, she asked me for the code and gently pushed my hands away from the pad.

"You told me not to give it to you. Will I have to change it again?"

"I'm not going to break in. I'll forget the number as soon as I use it. Then you won't have to change it. Fair?"

That sounded logical. "Okay. Five, five, five, five, five."

"That's your code? Do you realize how easy that is?" She shook her head at me and steered me inside after I refused to budge when the door opened. "Sit on the couch."

I gasped when she knelt in front of me and put her hands on my knees. I reached out and gently touched a strand of her hair. She didn't stop me. I felt her fingers on my calf searching for the zipper. I didn't tell her they were pull-on boots. I liked her hands on me. "Do you watch *Game of Thrones*?"

She stopped and leaned back on her heels. "Not you, too."

"Wait. You get that a lot?"

"Let's just say I'm known as the mother of dragons at work, and even though people tell me it's because I look like a character, I know it's because I'm a hard-ass." She figured out I didn't have a zipper on the boots and tugged on them instead.

I fell back against the couch and sighed. "You're not a hard-ass. When I first met you, I knew you weren't the ice queen everybody thinks you are. I saw you with Noah. You're so sweet with him. But your ex? I don't like her. One day we'll have to sit down, and you'll have to tell me what went down there."

"I barely know myself." She found a blanket in the closet and instructed me to lie down.

"Can you stay and talk to me? I promise to keep my hands to myself."

"I know you will, but Noah will be here soon. Don't worry about your car. It'll be safe at the restaurant. We'll pick it up tomorrow. Sleep well." She closed the door softly, not giving me a chance to respond.

I closed my eyes and replayed the night to the best of my knowledge. Bits and pieces floated in my mind, and I couldn't distinguish between reality and fantasy. Did I tell Brook I thought she was attractive? Shit, I think I touched her hair. Or did I just want to do that? I fell asleep not really knowing what happened and hoped that in the morning, I would wake up and not remember any of it.

Chapter Eleven

"Go away." I rolled over on the couch. The loud, incessant knocking pissed me off in record time.

"Cassie, I thought maybe you'd like to get your car. Noah and I are leaving this afternoon, and now is the only time I can drop you off."

I sat up when I heard Brook's low voice on the other side of the door. My head started pounding. Wine hangovers were the worst. "Uh, can you give me a few minutes? I need to put some clothes on." I looked down at yesterday's outfit wrapped and wrinkled around me and wondered how I was able to sleep.

"Okay. I'll just meet you in the garage in five minutes."

As soon as I heard Brook descend the steps, I headed for the bathroom. I winced when I turned on the light. Hello, raccoon face. I scrubbed my face, brushed my teeth, and threw a hat on to cover my unkempt hair. I wanted to wear sweats but threw on jeans and a sweater instead and ran down to the garage.

Brook, refreshed and polished, greeted me with a head nod. I could barely look her in the eye, not after the scattered pieces I remembered from the last time we were together.

"Thanks for doing this."

"No problem. I'm just glad you didn't drive last night."

Guilt trip served. "No way. I would've used Lyft. I should have done that today to get my car instead of inconveniencing you."

Brook put her hand on my arm. "It's not a big deal. It's ten minutes away." She backed out, and we headed to the restaurant in silence.

I turned to her "I'm very sorry I lost control last night. I hope I didn't embarrass you in front of your family. And I hope that, whatever came out of my drunk mouth, you took with a grain of salt."

"You don't remember? Hmm." The way she said that made me concentrate all the harder to distinguish fact from fiction. "It's okay. You and Erica weren't the only ones drinking. There's nothing to apologize for. I'm glad you had a good time."

"I'm sorry I didn't spend more time with Noah." I really missed the kid when he wasn't around.

"You spend plenty of time with him. I'm sure being around adults was a welcome change."

She parked next to my car and waited for me to get my keys out of my purse. "I'll wait here to make sure your car starts. Just so you know, Noah and I will be away for the rest of the weekend. He's with my mother right now."

I opened the door and thanked her again for giving me a lift. Just before I shut the door, she stopped me.

"If something comes up, call or text me."

"Yes, ma'am. And I promise no more wine for a long time." Brook lowered the window on the passenger side to say one last thing, and I leaned over to hear her better.

"Cassie? I know last night was fun, but so we're clear, don't ever call me Brookie again."

Just when I was about to drop to my knees to apologize profusely for being so forward, she winked and drove away.

❖

"You look like total crap," Nana said.

"Thanks. I love you, too." I sat at the kitchen table and reached for the Uno cards. I really wanted to be at my place, but guilt had driven me here. I shuffled the cards and dealt us the first hand.

"Did you catch a cold? Are you running a fever?" Nana felt my forehead. I dodged her attempt to squeeze my cheeks. For some reason, she thought that was a viable way to check my temperature if my forehead felt fine.

"I'm fine. Just had a little too much wine last night."

"Did you go out with Lacy after all?"

"No. I was at the Wellingtons' party. We were all drinking. And before you get all grandma-judgy on me, everybody had a good time. Erica, Brook's sister-in-law, and I easily put away two bottles."

Nana sat down and tapped my hands. "Was that the smartest thing to do? I know you think people didn't care, but let me tell you something. Brook cared. People like that don't like people like us."

I pulled away and scowled. "What does that mean? There's nothing wrong with us. We come from decent money. Hell, Mom and Dad probably go to the same country club as the Wellingtons."

"I just mean you should watch yourself. She's still your boss whether you're on the clock or not."

I wanted to stop talking about last night's faux pas. "How was dinner?"

Nana paused and studied me before going along with the change of subject. "We missed you and talked about you a lot."

I rolled my eyes. "Somehow I'm sure it was all about the mistakes I'm making or the bad decisions I've already made." I stood and headed for the refrigerator. I needed something in my stomach to settle the churning. I grabbed the almond milk and found a bagel and cream cheese.

"Are you done whining?"

I leaned against the counter and crossed my arms in front of me while I waited for the toaster. "For today, yes. For the rest of my life? Not by a long shot. It's part of your job. Taking care of me and listening to me whine." I topped off her coffee and offered her half of my bagel, which she promptly waved off.

"I think the roles are starting to reverse, and it's my turn."

"I think you're dreaming, old lady."

Nana winked at me and reached out for a hug. I welcomed it. I loved this woman and all her spunk. "I'm sorry. You've always been my champion. Tell me good things that happened yesterday. Even if it involved my parents."

"As you know, I can't show up empty-handed."

Nana launched into the whole dinner from the time my father picked her up until she got home. I detected a sadness to her voice, but she kept the story light for my sake. "Your mom did a great job of decorating the house. And the Elliots from next door brought over a cherry cobbler that was really good. They're fun people."

"Yeah. I remember them growing up. They used to get mad at me for kicking my soccer ball over the fence and into their yard. Mr. Elliot was always nicer than Mrs. Elliot."

"That's still the case. I just think she's really guarded around your mom. You know how your mom can be around other women."

As successful as my mother was, she had very little self-confidence. As unsuccessful as I was, my self-confidence was off the charts. People saw my mother as bitchy, but I considered her cautious. "I don't even know why. I mean, Mom is attractive, successful, and has everything she could want."

"I don't think your mother has been happy for a long time, and I don't know why. She does have it all."

"She doesn't have me," I said.

"Well, because of her stubbornness, it's going to be up to you to extend the olive branch." She grabbed my hands and squeezed my fingers gently. It was her way of making sure I was listening "Honey, I miss my small family. I love all of you, and Thanksgiving made me realize how much I need everybody together. Can you find it in your heart to at least try? Christmas is coming up."

Nana had kind eyes that hypnotized me if I stared at them too long. She was right. I needed to grow up, even more than I already had, and be proud of what I had accomplished, given the rocky start to my independence. I sighed and leaned back.

"You're right. Let me really think about it, and maybe we all can do Christmas early. I'm still intending to leave for the ski trip on the twenty-sixth and get back before New Year's Eve."

"This is wonderful news. I'll talk to your parents and see what works best for them."

I rolled my eyes. "Less talking, more playing." I pointed to the Uno game we'd barely started.

"You're so pushy for being so young," Nana said.

"You're so pushy for being so old."

❖

I spent the rest of the Thanksgiving-holiday break studying. Finals were in a few weeks, and with Noah's school schedule, Hessick Academy's holiday play practice, and violin lessons, I knew study time during the week would be scarce. I was expecting all As, maybe one B+, and I was good with that. I had a relatively light load this semester because I'd been aware I would have to work, but now that I had perfected my nanny gig, I had better control of my schedule. I knew how far I could stretch myself and not sacrifice.

My phone rang. I didn't recognize the number, but it looked familiar. For a split second, I thought it was my mother. I wasn't mentally prepared for that battle. "Hello?"

To my surprise, it was Natalie, Noah's music teacher. "How are you, Cassie?"

I couldn't help but smile because I was surprised. I wasn't expecting her call. Ever. "Natalie, hi. I'm good. Just studying. What's up?"

"I have a keyboard on a stand that a student surrendered to me, and I wanted to know if you were interested in lessons. I remember you said you wished you would have stayed with music."

"That's super sweet to think of me, but I really don't have the time right now. You know, finals, the holidays, and I just signed up for classes for next semester and am taking an extra class to catch up."

"I understand. If you change your mind, just let me know."

She kept the conversation going for about ten minutes. I really liked her. She was always so patient with Noah. Sometimes during his practices, I wanted to storm into the library, grab the bow from his tiny hand, and break it over my knee. I was patient, but she was chill on a Zen level. She invited me to coffee, but I had to decline and study. Five minutes after we hung up, my phone dinged again.

Noah wants to know what you're doing.

Brook sent a photo of Noah baking. Ingredients were scattered all over the counter, his shirt, and the floor. I zoomed in and saw flour handprints on the refrigerator.

Is any adult supervision happening?

He wanted to surprise you. Can you come over or are you busy?

I sat up. This was unusual for Brook. This was personal. And fun.

Give me about ten. Are you making cookies, and should I bring milk?

I raced to my closet and pulled out a chunky sweater, leggings, and a pair of Uggs. I needed to look comfortable and not too dressy since Brook knew I was studying. She didn't need to know I'd been wearing oversized sweats and a long-sleeved T-shirt with a stain I didn't know the origin of. I put on some light makeup and pulled my hair up. Twelve minutes later, I let myself into the kitchen.

"Hello?" I called out softly, because this didn't feel real. Did I misread her texts and was breaking into their house?

"We're in here." Brook laughed at something, then I heard, "No, no, no."

A loud boom exploded in the kitchen right when I walked in. Noah had dropped the bag of flour and was absolutely covered. I burst out laughing. Noah seemed in total shock. His face and sweatshirt had received the brunt of the drop. Brook stood there with a look of disbelief on her face. Then she stared at me.

"That did not just happen," she said. She rounded the counter and stood there shaking her head at the mess.

"I'm sorry, Mom," Noah said.

"It's okay, honey. It was actually kind of funny."

I took the long way around them to the pantry to find the broom and dustpan. Then I dragged the garbage can out and started sweeping around Noah.

"Cassie, give that to me. I didn't call you down here to clean up the mess."

I kept sweeping. "You brush the flour off his shirt until you can take it off. We don't want it all over the house." I handed Brook a dish towel so she could dust off his face and shirt. After most of it had settled on the floor, Brook took off his shirt and picked him up. I took off his shoes, and she put him down away from the pile.

"If the timer goes off, please take the cookies out of the oven. We'll be back in a few minutes."

"No worries. I'll just clean up the best I can."

She gave me the single nod before disappearing down the hall. "Thank you, Cassie."

I swept up most of the flour, wiped down the counter, and mopped the floor before they returned. Noah was fresh from the shower with wet hair and pajamas.

"The cookies are out of the oven, but I waited for you both before I ate them all."

"Cassie, did you eat one?"

His sweet little face looked so concerned. I squeezed his cheeks but stopped when I realized I was doing exactly what Nana did. Plus, Brook was watching, and for whatever reason, I was nervous when she observed our interactions.

"Not a single one. Not even a crumb. Not even the dough that I want to eat," I said and made a big production of smelling it.

"You can't eat that. It has raw eggs," Noah said.

I looked at Brook. She shrugged. I rolled my eyes at her.

"You're right. We shouldn't eat that. Come on. Let's finish baking. That's why you called me down here."

Noah crawled onto a chair by the counter and awkwardly stirred the batter. I pulled out a fresh cookie sheet, greased it for him, and put it within reach. Since he was standing on the chair, Brook supervised from behind him, in case he slipped. We were a great team.

"How was your trip?" My question was directed toward Brook, but Noah answered.

"It was fun. And warm. I wore shorts."

"What? Look outside. There's snow here. Shorts?" I saw Brook smile, which ramped up my confidence.

"We went to Texas," Noah said.

"Texas. What's in Texas?"

"Mom's friend, Aubrey. We saw giraffes and goats and so many animals."

"It sounds like you had an awesome time. And Texas is warm. Did you have fun flying?"

"We took Grandpa's plane."

I looked at Brook and rolled my eyes again.

"My best friend from college lives in San Antonio. We haven't seen her in a few years. Her son is ten, but the boys still had fun," she said.

"Did you go to a zoo? Or does your friend have giraffes living in her backyard?"

Noah laughed. "Nobody has giraffes as pets. We drove through a park and saw the giraffes in it."

"Did you feed them?"

"No. They wouldn't let us. We had the top off the Jeep so they leaned into the car, and one tried to eat my hair."

"Well, your hair does look like marshmallow fluff."

"What's that?" he asked.

I looked at Brook and slowly shook my head. "How have you not introduced your son to this deliciousness?"

"I don't even know what you're talking about," she said.

"Stop everything right now. Neither of you have had fluffernutters?"

"Fluffer what?" Noah asked.

"Let's put the cookies in the oven, and then I'm going upstairs and coming back with magic."

"We already ate dinner," Brook said.

"It's barely real food. Do you have regular bread here?"

"Regular bread?" Brook raised her eyebrow.

"Yes, regular bread. Like white bread. Not wheat, or whole grain, or gluten-free. Just bread, bread."

Brook asked Noah to sit on the chair, opened the pantry, and held up half a loaf of sourdough. "Will this work?"

"Absolutely not. Hang on. I'll be right back."

To look as cool as possible, I walked out of the kitchen casually, but once I was out of sight, I raced to my apartment. I found fresh bread, grabbed the jars of peanut butter and marshmallow fluff, and headed back to the house. They were pouring three glasses of milk and had a plate of freshly baked, warm cookies on the counter.

"Can I help you, too?" Noah asked.

"No, buddy. This is way messier than baking cookies."

I washed my hands and quickly made one sandwich that I cut in quarters. Something told me Brook wasn't going to like fluffernutters, but this was more about Noah and introducing him to something I thought every child should experience tasting. "It's a good thing you have milk poured, because you'll need it after this."

Noah took a square, investigated it, smelled it, and finally took a bite. Brook followed suit, and much to my surprise, both Wellingtons smiled and made happy noises. I proudly took a square off the plate and joined in.

"How have I missed out on this my entire life?" Brook asked.

She looked so adorable with a tiny bit of fluff smeared on the corner of her mouth. I pointed to my own mouth and stared at hers until she got the hint. She smiled and grabbed a napkin, and in that moment, she wasn't my boss. She was just a very attractive woman in yoga pants, thick wool socks, and a large Harvard sweatshirt. She'd changed her clothes when Noah cleaned up. Her hair was pulled back in a loose ponytail, and she was breathtaking.

"What do you think, buddy?" I turned my attention to Noah, who took the last square off the plate. "Well, I guess that means you like it. Can I have a cookie now?"

We spent the next twenty minutes eating cookies and drinking milk. Noah animatedly recapped their vacation—roaring, barking, and making various other animal noises to emphasize his excitement. Brook jumped in to clear things up or add to the story. It was nice to see her relaxed and playful with Noah. I didn't have the opportunity to see them interact a lot.

"It's almost time for bed. Why don't you say good night to Cassie and go upstairs and get ready? I'll be up in a minute to tuck you in." Brook kissed the top of his head and squeezed his shoulder. Noah slid off the chair and surprised us both by wrapping his hands around my waist and hugging me.

"Bye, Cassie. I'll see you tomorrow."

I reached down and held him against me for a fraction of a second before letting him go. It was the first time he'd hugged me. I tried to hide the surprise, but Brook saw it. We watched him disappear down the hall.

"He really does like you," she said.

"You've done a great job with him. He's adorable." The silence dragged on. I turned the plate of cookies just to have something to do with my hands. "I should go. Thank you for inviting me over."

"Stay for a bit. I want to talk about your holiday plans. Will you excuse me while I tuck Noah in?"

The look she sent me wasn't sexual or smoldering, but it had a hint of something I couldn't identify. Longing? Hope? Whatever it was, I was definitely sticking around.

Chapter Twelve

I pretended that it wasn't a big deal to be alone with her after hitting on her the other night, but my heart was thumping. I sat at the counter and pulled my phone out to check messages, but my hands were shaking so I gave up. My mind raced at all the possibilities of our conversation. I hadn't asked for anything special over Christmas break. I wanted to go skiing with Lacy, but I didn't want to ask for vacation time. My job was more important than a ski trip, but I was almost certain I had that week off.

"I'm sorry it took so long. Noah was amped from all the sugar. He's allowed to read for fifteen minutes, then lights out."

"No worries. I just checked my email and stuff."

She slid past me and reached into the cabinet. "Would you like a glass of pinot?"

"Sure."

I wished it were something stronger, but I managed to not make a face when I took the first sip. I'd sworn off wine just three days ago, and here I was drinking it again to impress a girl. The same girl.

"Let's go into the living room and get comfortable. My back hurts from sitting on these stools all night."

I followed her and tried everything to keep my gaze from drifting over her, but I failed miserably. Brook Wellington was perfect. Even dressed down, she had an aura of confidence I admired. She sat on the couch and motioned for me to sit next to her. I chose a spot far enough away to keep me out of trouble, but close enough to be personable.

"Tell me your plans for Christmas." She curled her legs underneath her and spread a blanket over her lap.

"I'm not sure what time I have off. I wanted to talk to you about it. I don't know that we ever discussed time off."

"A bad oversight on my part," she said.

I smiled. "I needed a job, so I didn't really review the contract well."

"I needed a nanny, so I didn't really review the contract well either."

We both laughed.

"Do you have plans? I mean while you're on break?"

Something made me shake my head and tell her I had no plans. Maybe it was wishful thinking. Maybe it was lust. Either way, I was going to listen to what she wanted to say.

"The family is going to Vermont for four days between Christmas and New Year's Eve. If you're not busy, we'd love some help with the kids. It would be Noah, Griffin, and Frances. And only when we need you. Not seven to seven, but whenever we go skiing during the day. You'll still have plenty of time if you want to ski or go out during the day. Your nights will be free. And you'll be compensated. You'll have your own room and transportation if you want it."

My heart sank. I knew she wasn't going to ask me as a date because I was just the nanny, but sometimes I wished my fantasy life would come true. If I accepted her offer, I could still ski, but Lacy wouldn't be there. But Brook would be, and it would score me brownie points. I knew I should have said no, because I wanted to go for all the wrong reasons.

"That sounds like fun. The kids and I can go sledding and build snowpeople," I said. I wasn't super excited, but it would be a relaxed environment, and Brook was always different when she wasn't facing a day of business deals and contracts.

"Thank you. I wasn't sure what your plans were. Did you talk to your parents over the weekend?"

"No. I hung out with Nana Friday, but she highly recommends I try to work things out with my parents for Christmas. Thanksgiving was boring without me."

"I honestly believe that. Hopefully you had a good time with us."

She took another sip of wine and looked at me over the rim of her glass. It wasn't the look so much as it was the gracefulness of it. Brook was suave. She didn't glance away or try to avoid eye contact. That confidence was sexy as hell.

"I did. I'm just sorry I got a little carried away." I covered my face with my hand out of revisited embarrassment. Then I felt her hand on my knee and barely stopped myself from jumping under her touch.

"You were fine. Erica really had fun with you. She'll be excited to know you're coming on the trip." She moved her hand from my knee, and I relaxed.

"She's really cool. Laid-back and a lot of fun."

Brook poured herself another glass of wine, but I waved off the offer to top mine off. I couldn't go through another night like Thursday, especially at Brook's.

"We're taking the family plane, so we'll have some fun on the ride. We'll leave for the airport about noon on the twenty-sixth. I have to wait until Noah gets home from Christmas with Lauren." An expression of sadness washed over her, and she took another sip to cover it up.

"Why does Lauren get him over the holidays? If you don't mind me asking." I didn't want to pry, but she looked so sad I thought maybe she wanted to talk about it.

"We switch every year. When I get Noah over Thanksgiving, she gets him over Christmas. Next year it'll be opposite."

"When does she get him over his break?" I didn't even think about days I might have off when Noah was with Lauren.

"Break starts on the nineteenth. She'll get him the twentieth until the twenty-sixth. Then I'll have him."

"Do you think she'll keep him the whole time? I'm just curious because we both know her track record." In the three months I'd been watching Noah, Lauren had showed up only three out of the nine Wednesdays.

"Who knows? She'll probably only want him Christmas Eve and part of Christmas Day. Her twins are almost two, and Noah's great with them, but she doesn't like to take Noah to her husband's family events. Like Noah is an embarrassment. He hates it, and I try to make him understand that his other mother loves him, but it's hard when she doesn't follow through with anything."

I heard bitterness in her voice and could feel my own blood starting to boil. "Why does she do this to him?"

Brook finished off her second glass of wine and poured a third. "You really want to know?"

I nodded, both scared and intrigued.

"Money. It's all about money. She knows that if she doesn't at least try, I'll take her back to court. She gets a lot of child support with very little responsibility. It pisses me off no end, but Noah loves her, and we made the decision to have him together."

"I don't like her. I hope that's okay to say. I would never say anything disparaging in Noah's presence. Nor would I be rude to her, even though she was rude to me."

Brook leaned forward. "I'm sorry. She used to be nice a long time ago."

"How did you meet her?" This was new territory for us—a casual night drinking wine and getting to know one another.

"At a fund-raiser. Well, because of a fund-raiser for Hasbro Children's Hospital. Lauren was responsible for reaching out to companies who had previously donated, and I took her call. We met several times before the event. She was charming and confident, and I fell for her. That was twelve years ago. We were married two years after that and divorced a year and a half ago." I tried working the math in my head without being obvious but failed. "Doesn't add up, does it? One day she came home, informed me she'd met somebody else, was pregnant, and wanted a divorce."

"Holy fuck." I didn't even try to hide my disgust. "Well, now I hate her."

She waved me off like it was no big deal. My blood was boiling over something that had happened years ago to somebody I didn't know that well. It was a shitty thing to do to anybody.

"I take a lot of the blame. My father gave me a lot more responsibilities when I returned to work after having Noah. I hit the ground running. I wasn't home a lot. Lauren was home with him, and I didn't give her enough time."

Brook raised the empty wine bottle and held it up to the light. "Did I really drink all this?"

"No. I had a glass."

"You're still working on it."

I laughed. "After Thursday, I hesitate to drink wine."

Brook stood and apologized. "You should have told me. I could have poured you anything. The bar's stocked." She was wobbly on her feet, so she plopped back down.

"The wine's fine. I have a hard day tomorrow at school, so I need to be sharp."

"Ugh. Tomorrow's a tough day for me, too. It's always hard to get into the swing of things when I've been out of the office for a few days." She leaned back against the couch and closed her eyes. She was quiet for so long, I thought she'd fallen asleep and quietly put my glass on a coaster.

"Are you leaving already?"

I looked at the time. "It's almost ten. I have this Kraken of a boss who wants me in the office at seven in the morning." I did air quotes around the word *office* and stood to make my exit.

In a surprising move, she grabbed my hand and pulled me down onto the couch. She didn't let go of my hand, and I sat frozen with her fingers interlocked with mine.

"Am I that bad a boss? I never thought I was. I always considered myself professional." She held up our hands and stared at them. "Well, maybe not completely professional. You have such nice hands, Cassandra. Strong yet feminine. I've always admired them."

"I was teasing. You're not a bad boss at all." I hated that my nails weren't painted or nicely filed. I chewed the skin around my thumbnails to help harness my stress levels while studying.

"I wish everybody was like you. Sweet, adorable, willing to give me a chance." This was a side of Brook I wasn't prepared for. I'd fantasized about thawing her ice walls, but for them to come down without any work on my part derailed me.

"You're fine. I was scared of you at first, but only because being Noah's nanny is a huge responsibility and you're a Wellington. I have to be careful. I'm just thankful Noah hasn't broken any bones."

"He's a very cautious kid, never does anything to rock the boat. I kind of wish he would do kid things, but I think he's shy and worried he's going to upset me or Lauren."

"Oh, give him time. One day he'll be a teenager, and then you'll wish he was six again."

"Wait a minute. Back up. You were scared of me? I hate that." She frowned and gazed at me. A jolt of lust blasted in my veins when she looked down at my lips and then back up to my eyes.

I sat up straighter and moved slightly away. "But I think you're a nice person with a good heart."

She groaned. "You're just saying that."

"Seriously, if you and Noah were flying a kite at a park and I was there reading a book, I would totally approach you. I would try to say something charming or funny." We were still holding hands, and I could feel my palm growing sweaty with my confession. I needed to turn it down because I couldn't afford to lose my job over a crush.

"I'm so much older than you. You'd probably ask to play with Noah."

I couldn't help but laugh. Totally something I would do, but only to get to her. "Not true. I'm almost twenty-five. And you look like you're twenty-eight, so it would have worked out. I would have asked if Noah was your kid brother."

She tweaked my side and made me laugh. "And I would have called bullshit. Ah, it's too bad life is the way it is."

My heart bobbed, riding each wave up and down with every word she said. I was more confused now than when I first met her. Was she interested? This entire exchange was all over the place. Alcohol. As much as it loosened us up, it really fucked with my head.

"Okay, it's getting late. I need to go finish studying." Why was I jeopardizing any shot with Brook?

"I can't feel my face," Brook said.

I watched as she rubbed her hands over her face. That's right. Because she was drunk. I was doing the right thing like she did with me. "Come on. I'll escort you upstairs, and I'll set the alarm when I leave. Deal?"

She was so close to me. And that smile. And those eyes. It took all my strength to not kiss her.

"You know where my bedroom is? Have you been in my room without me?" She poked me again, teasingly, as if I'd just gotten caught doing something naughty.

"You gave me a tour when I first started. I know where your bedroom is, but I've never been inside it. I promise."

Grabbing my hand again, she walked me to the stairs. I put her free hand on the railing. Getting her upstairs was more of a chore than I realized. It took a few minutes to steer her to her bedroom.

"We're here." I opened the door for her.

She leaned against the frame and put her palm on my chest, her fingers stroking my neck. "Thank you, Cassie. I'll see you tomorrow." She turned and started taking off her sweatshirt.

I quickly closed the door and rested my forehead against it. "I'll lock up. Get some sleep. Good night, Brookie."

She whipped open the door, causing me to stumble. She was wearing only a thin camisole and her yoga pants. Everything about her was firm and toned. "I told you not to call me Brookie."

"You weren't supposed to hear that. Now go to bed," I said. She took a step toward me, and I took a step back. "Brook Wellington—Wait. What's your middle name?"

"Addison. It's my mom's surname. My full name is Brooklyn Addison Wellington." She put her hand back on my chest, and I softly removed it. She frowned.

"Brooklyn Addison Wellington, go to bed." My voice held an authoritative note I didn't feel.

"Brooklyn Addison Wellington. Never Brookie." Thankfully, she turned and crawled into bed. I closed the door quietly once I saw she was under the covers.

Jesus, that was a close one.

Chapter Thirteen

"Good morning, Cassie."

Brook walked into the kitchen as if last night didn't happen. She looked refreshed and beautiful. After I left last night, it took forever to fall asleep. I kept thinking about the crazy holiday weekend. Thursday, Brook took care of me, and Sunday I took care of her. That crossed all professional boundaries, yet here she was—guarded, professional, and sexy as fuck in her business suit and kitten heels.

"Good morning, Brook. How did you sleep?"

She poured coffee into her travel mug before she turned to me.

"I slept well. Thanks for asking. I should be home early tonight. I have a million meetings today, but I think they will wrap up quickly."

Whenever Brook had a long day of meetings, she wore one of her wool pantsuits. Today it was the charcoal one with a light-blue blouse that made her eyes pop. She had a silk scarf loosely draped around her neck that added flair and fall colors. The entire ensemble was conservative, but it didn't deter from her beauty. Her hair was up and her makeup light. I guessed she had all in-house meetings with the board. When Brook met with clients, she wore more makeup, and her lipstick was bright. Today's lipstick was more natural and subdued.

"That works for me."

She kissed Noah good-bye, grabbed her coffee, gave me a nod, and disappeared into the garage. I barely had time to process what had just happened. I wasn't expecting her to be all cute with me like she was last night, but I expected something warmer than her single head nod.

"Are we going in early today, or are we sticking around here?" I asked Noah.

"I want to go in early because Matt has a Nintendo Switch, and he said I could play it. We can only play before or after school."

Both Wellingtons had better things to do today than hang out and talk to me.

"That's cool. We still have a few minutes. I'm going to study in the kitchen." I set the alarm on my phone. My finals were scheduled for late next week, and I felt confident in my toxicology and plant physiology classes, but I was a little worried about my ecology lab. I couldn't study for it though. The written test would be a breeze, but labs always scared me. Hands-on experience was tough—another reason I quit medical school.

"Is it time?" Noah yelled from the sitting room.

I checked the alarm. We still had a few minutes, but by the time Noah rounded up everything he needed, we'd get to school right when it opened. "It's close enough. Go ahead and put on your boots and your sweater." I packed my things and waited for him. He came around the corner with a big smile on his face. He deserved friends, and I knew how shy he was with other kids.

"Is your mom okay with you playing Nintendo? What game is it?"

The last thing I needed was Brook to find out I'd been taking Noah to school early just so he could play shoot-'em-up games.

"He has *Minecraft* and *Super Mario*."

Those were kid-friendly, but I would have to talk to Brook about this, because she wanted to hold off as long as possible before Noah gamed. Taking him to school early to play them was enabling him, but it was also encouraging him to socialize with his classmates.

I waited until the last possible moment to pick up Noah. He had violin with Natalie in less than twenty minutes, but I wanted to give him time with Matt. He greeted me with a huge smile. I tousled his hair and smiled back.

"Good day today?"

He nodded. "I'm going to ask Santa for a Switch. We played it before and after school."

"Sounds like you had a ton of fun today. How was school? Did you learn anything interesting?"

Noah rushed to tell me all about his day while I signed us out. He grabbed my hand when we reached the stairs leaving the school and didn't let go until we reached the car. That was always the highlight of my day.

"So where is Matt from? Ms. Trina says he's new to the school."

Noah shrugged. "His dad works for the airport."

"Is he a pilot?"

"I don't know. I wasn't really paying attention."

I wasn't that invested anyway. I was sure, with impending play dates, I would find out soon enough. "Miss Natalie is going to be at the house about five minutes after we get there. I need you to get changed and race to the library to start practicing."

I pulled into the garage and helped him out of his booster. "Okay, go."

He ran through the house on a mission. I grabbed his backpack and rifled through it until I found the permission slip for Brook to sign. Noah's class was invited to go on a field trip to Winter Wonder Days at the zoo. It sounded like a ton of fun, and they wanted volunteers, but it was next week, and I had to study. Break couldn't come fast enough. A month off with nothing to do but watch Noah, and for only part of the time. I was going to binge-watch all the shows I'd missed because of school and work.

The intercom buzzed right when Noah returned to the kitchen with his violin. We stared at each other, wide-eyed as if we'd done something wrong.

"Go." I pointed to the library and he scampered off.

After I buzzed Natalie in, I straightened my sweater and smoothed down my hair. Even if I knew nothing was going to happen with her, it was still nice to be noticed. It was amazing how a crooked smile or the simple touch of a woman could put me in a good mood. I held the front door and waited for her. She was bundled from head to toe, and I wondered how she could drive like that.

"I can't believe how cold it is." She squeezed my arm when she walked by me.

I took her coat and hung it in the hall closet, a chill following her in. "It's supposed to snow later. I always say I'm going to move somewhere warm, but I'll never leave here," I said.

"I don't mind the four seasons. I traveled around a lot as a child."

The sounds of Noah practicing reached us. "Guess I'd better get in there."

"Okay, good luck," I said.

I pulled out my laptop and started reviewing my notes. In what felt like no time at all, Natalie was back in front of me, and I looked at her in surprise. Had it already been forty-five minutes?

"That was quick," I said.

She leaned over me, her hair falling over her shoulder and tickling my neck. "Toxicology. Interesting. I thought you were studying environmental sciences."

"It's a part of it. One of the electives for the degree."

"You're studying poisons. Should we be worried?"

"I do know a hundred and one ways to use hemlock effectively." I smiled.

"Remind me never to come over for dinner." There it was. The smile. The tuck of hair behind her ear. A quick dart of her tongue as she captured her bottom lip between her teeth before she smiled. She was definitely flirting.

"I promise that I will never cook for you. You'll just have to cook for me." Now why did I say that? I'd opened a door I was trying to close with all Noah's teachers.

"Hello, everyone." Brook breezed in and put her bag on the counter. I leaned away from Natalie out of guilt. I knew it looked bad and sounded worse than what was actually happening.

"Hi, Ms. Wellington. I was just leaving. Noah is improving, so the additional practice is paying off," Natalie said.

"We've been working a few extra minutes every night. I've noticed an improvement, too."

I sat there awkwardly trying to figure out what to do. Leaving wasn't an option because I was still on the clock. Brook was home early, and Noah was nowhere to be found.

"Have a good night. Walk me out, Cassie?" Natalie asked.

"Sure. Let me get your coat." I avoided eye contact with Brook and followed Natalie into the foyer.

"Be careful and stay warm." I helped her put on her coat and closed the door behind her. Brook was pouring herself a glass of wine when I walked back into the kitchen.

"Are we going to have the talk again? So soon?"

"What do you mean?" I knew, but I wanted her to say it.

"I don't think it's a good idea for you to date Noah's teachers. It will confuse him, and if things go south, then it'll be uncomfortable for him."

I hated that she looked so good, so confident standing there with her hip against the chair, her hand gracefully holding the wineglass. Her hair was completely down, and her suit jacket was carefully placed over the back of one of the kitchen chairs. The first two buttons of her blouse, once tight under her chin, now were undone. I couldn't see any cleavage, but I did admire the swell under her blouse and her smooth skin.

"First of all, we aren't dating. I was being friendly. She's a nice lady."

"I know flirting when I see it. I don't want this to complicate things."

"What's the matter, Mom?" Noah walked into the kitchen, concern etched on his face. My heart sank.

"Nothing, sweetie. Why don't you go upstairs and read until dinner. Patrick's due any minute," she said. Her voice was so soothing that for a brief moment, I even believed her.

The look she shot me after he left the room made my blood go cold. This was the angry boss I never wanted to see. I braced myself for the onslaught.

"I think that sums it up." She took another sip of wine and slowly circled the table. I could tell she was holding back.

"Look, I'm not seeing Natalie, and I'm not seeing Trina. We are friends," I said. She snorted. I took a deep breath. "I respect you as my boss, but you don't have the right to tell me who I can be friends with. You can't claim every person I meet through this job is off-limits. That's not realistic or fair."

Brook didn't move but stared at me for a very uncomfortable ten seconds before saying anything. It made me nervous, but I was standing my ground. Everything was at stake right now.

"Cassie, you're right. You are more than welcome to be friends with anyone, but between seven and seven, minus school hours, you have a job to do. And that job is Noah. On my time, he is your only priority. That's what you're getting paid for. The only thing I ask is that you don't have a relationship in front of my son."

I almost saluted her. My anger was bubbling up and I needed to walk away. "I get it. Seven to seven." I collected my things. "Since you're home early, am I excused, Boss?"

She nodded once. I stormed off, pissed at her, pissed at myself. I seriously couldn't figure her out. She was all business, then sweet and kind, then bossy, then complimentary. No wonder she was single. No wonder Lauren left her. No, that was mean. I didn't know, but damn it, she infuriated me. I walked into my apartment and threw my bag onto the couch. Ugh. I hated that I needed this job. No. I didn't hate it. It was a good job and Noah was wonderful. I hated that she was right.

I paced my apartment, feeling trapped. I wanted to go outside, but it was starting to snow. I took a deep breath and looked out. The grounds were beautiful here, even with the trees barren and the grass a dark straw color. The backyard was well lit. Every tree, every bush, every statue had lighting of some sort. The pool had ample lighting even though it was covered. Wait. What was Noah doing out by the pool inside the gate? I banged on the window.

"Hey! Noah. Get away from the pool!"

I knew he couldn't hear me, and by the time I opened the window, the unthinkable happened. One minute he was walking by the pool, and the next, he disappeared. I had looked away for one second while I was unlocking the window. He must've fallen in. I sprinted down the stairs and burst through the kitchen door.

"Brook! Brook, call 9-1-1."

Patrick dropped bags of groceries on the floor and reached for the phone. Brook came running in from the living room.

"What's happening?"

"Noah fell into the pool!" I ran past her.

"Noah's up in his room," she said.

I pushed through the side doors. The far corner of the pool's cover wasn't tethered down, leaving a five-foot area of exposed water. I jumped in, fully clothed, and swam under the cover. The lights inside the pool were off, so I had to feel my way around. Even though the pool was heated enough to keep it from freezing when not in use, it was still a shock to my system. But nothing mattered other than finding Noah.

My lungs felt like they were about to explode, but I pushed myself and kept swimming. I heard screaming and felt the water shift. Brook and Patrick were taking the cover off. I came up for a single gulp of air and then swam down to the next corner of the pool. Every part of me told me to go back to the surface. Just when I let out the last bit of air left in my lungs, my fingers brushed against his coat. I grabbed the fabric and hauled him toward the opening that Patrick and Brook had made. When I breached the surface with Noah in my arms, Patrick lifted him out of the water.

"He's not breathing," Brook said. She fell to her knees in front of Noah and gently shook his shoulders. "Come on, baby. Breathe. Breathe."

I climbed out and crawled over to him. "I know CPR. I can help." Brook didn't move. I yelled, "Patrick, move her now." I put my ear against Noah's mouth and placed my hand on his chest to see if he was breathing. He wasn't. I tilted his head, lifted his chin, pinched his nose, and blew two breaths inside his mouth. "Come on, Noah. Breathe."

"Noah, breathe, baby. I need you to breathe." Brook was leaning over us, crowding me as I repeated the breaths.

I counted to thirty and gave him two more breaths. My arm kept bumping Brook. I looked directly at Patrick. "Patrick, please give me space."

He nodded and pulled Brook back. She fought him for a bit but took a step back.

I gave Noah two more breaths and listened. Still nothing. I repeated the breaths. Water dribbled out of his mouth, and he started coughing. I rolled him to his side so he wouldn't choke.

"That's it, buddy. Cough it up." I rubbed his back in tiny circles until his coughs turned into cries and he reached for Brook, who had dropped to her knees and was over us again. She scooped him up. I advised her not to because we weren't sure if he'd hit his head or injured his neck, but he held on to her tightly, so I doubted anything was broken.

"Let's get him inside," Patrick said.

Brook carried Noah while Patrick put his arm around me and walked me in. Every muscle and joint hurt. It was hard to catch my breath. I was shaking and weak, but he prevented me from collapsing. Noah was half crying and half trying to talk.

"The cover...were fighting." His sentences weren't coherent, but the message was clear.

"It's okay, baby. Don't worry about anything. You're okay. Cassie's okay," Brook said.

"You—You need to get him out of his wet clothes," I stammered.

She stripped Noah down, wrapped him in a warm blanket, and rubbed down his tiny body with her hands. Patrick handed me a blanket. I clutched it but didn't wrap it around myself. I heard sirens fast approaching, and even though the tense moment was over, it was a welcoming sound.

"He's still too cold," Brook said.

"I can't get her to put on a blanket either," Patrick said.

I couldn't stop my teeth from chattering. "I'm too wet."

"Switch with me, Brook. I can hold him to warm him up, and she needs to take off her wet clothes," Patrick said.

"Okay." Brook handed Noah to Patrick, who wrapped Noah in his arms. Brook headed over to me. "Cassie, we need to get you out of these clothes."

"I'm okay."

"No, you're not." It was ridiculous that I was fighting her, so I nodded. She pulled my sweater over my head and dropped it on the floor. It felt like five pounds left my body, but I was shivering more. Without hesitation, she unbuttoned my shirt and tugged it down my arms. She wrapped a blanket around my shoulders and unfastened my pants. My wet cell phone clanged to the floor, and the screen cracked all over.

"Fuck," I said.

Brook didn't correct me or stop to check on it. She untied my shoes and had me kick them off, along with my pants. The blanket she cocooned me in was already warm, and I sighed at its comfort.

The doorbell rang, followed by rapid, loud knocks and the fire department announcing their arrival. Patrick carried a very bundled-up Noah to the front door.

"How'd they get through the gates?" I asked.

"The alarm company allows police and fire up to the house. It's going to be okay. Here, sit on the couch." She found another blanket and wrapped my legs in it after peeling off my wool socks.

Patrick returned and handed Noah back to Brook. He was followed by paramedics.

"What happened here?" one of the firefighters asked. His gruff voice boomed through the room, startling Noah, who started crying again.

Patrick spoke up. "Noah fell into the pool, and Cassie went after him. He wasn't breathing, but she resuscitated him."

The captain looked at me. "How long was he under?"

"Probably two minutes." I gave him my background just so he and everyone else could relax a little. I was adult- and child-CPR certified, and had a year of medical school. It was mostly classroom education, but we did a lot of lab work and simulations.

While we discussed the events with the captain, the paramedics checked Noah thoroughly. Brook hovered over them, peeking over shoulders, encouraging him to cooperate. He was whiny and confused, and Brook insisted they take him to the hospital for a full workup. She directed one of the paramedics to check me out even though I was only cold. I didn't breathe in any water, and my body temperature was fine. I was uncomfortable, but not in danger. Patrick started a fire, and soon I was almost too warm.

"I'm fine. Really. Just worry about him," I said.

They brought in the stretcher and strapped Noah in. Brook disappeared for about thirty seconds and returned with some warm clothing for me and a pair of pajamas for Noah. Before leaving with the ambulance, she gave Patrick instructions to look out for me. Once the flurry of activity left the house, Patrick sat down beside me and took my hand.

"You saved that sweet little boy," he said.

"It's my job." I shrugged like it was no big deal, but I was still shaking with adrenaline. What if I hadn't gotten to him in time? What if he'd been under too long and had brain damage?

"How about a hot cup of tea while I make soup? Or is there anything else you'd like?"

"That sounds perfect. I'll go put on these dry clothes."

He stood and helped me up. "You got this?"

I nodded. "I got this." I walked slowly to the bathroom. When I finally took off my wet bra and panties and dried off, I felt better. Even though what Brook gave me to wear wasn't sexy at all, it still felt intimate. I was wearing her clothes. The sweats were too short, but the thick socks reached halfway up my calves. I found a hair dryer in the closet and used my fingers as a brush. By the time I returned to the kitchen, Patrick had a cup of hot tea waiting for me and soup on the stove.

"That smells wonderful. What is it?"

"It's a creamy mushroom soup. I've diced some chicken that I'll add if you want."

I nodded. "I can't believe how hungry I am."

He pulled out a plate of cheeses and small breads from the refrigerator.

"This looks delicious." I grabbed a piece of raisin bread and spread cream cheese on it. Thankfully, Patrick had seen me eat like a starved wolf before, so I didn't have to be on good behavior. I shoved the entire piece in my mouth and moaned at the taste.

"I'm so glad you were here tonight. We couldn't have saved him without you," I said.

"I'm glad you saw him out there. I can't think about what would have happened if—" He was getting choked up.

I grabbed his hand. "It's all right now. Everything's okay. Let's eat, and then you can go home and spend time with your family."

"I called them. They're fine without me for one night."

"I'm completely okay. After we eat, I'm kicking you out for the night."

He laughed. "We'll see."

We sat at the counter and ate soup and laughed. It was nice. He told me about his culinary-school experience, his first marriage, and the time he and his friends got kicked out of Vegas. The entire city.

"No. They can't do that. Can they?" I asked.

"Have you ever been to Vegas?"

I shook my head. "I never really had the desire. I mean, I probably should have when I had the money, but now I need every penny I make."

After dinner Patrick made me sit in front of the fire and brought me another hot tea. "Brook just texted that Noah's lungs are clear."

"That's a relief." I finally was able to relax.

"I'm going to clean up. Do you need anything else?"

"You've spoiled me already. Thank you, I'm good."

Fifteen minutes later, ten of them reassuring him I was fine and healthy, Patrick put on his coat. "If you need anything at all, here's my number. You did an amazing thing today, Cassie. We'll always remember this. Now, go get some rest. I'll set the house alarm when I leave. Brook texted that they should be discharging Noah soon."

I was tired, but this wasn't my place. I needed to go up to my apartment, put on my clothes, and go to sleep, but a fire was still burning. I couldn't just leave. I missed fireplaces. I snuggled down on the couch, and before I convinced myself to get up and go home, I fell asleep warm, safe, and alive.

Chapter Fourteen

Somebody was stroking my hair, softy, sweetly. For a moment I thought I was at Nana's house. When I was growing up, she used to play with my hair until I fell asleep. When the fingertips traced my cheek and down to my neck, I knew it wasn't Nana. I struggled to open my eyes, but I was so tired, and my body felt heavy. I heard footsteps walk away from me and return. Another blanket was tucked around me. Warm lips touched my cheek. The haziness was starting to clear. The memories of the evening flooded my thoughts, and I forced my eyes open.

"Hi. I didn't mean to wake you. I just wanted to make sure you were warm."

Brook was on her knees in front of me. The soft glow of the dying fire illuminated the room just enough for me to see her face. Her eyes were pink and puffy. Her hair was loose around her shoulders. She looked vulnerable.

I quickly sat up. "Is Noah okay?"

Brook put her hands on my knees and nodded. "We just got home. He's completely fine. Already upstairs asleep."

I rubbed my face and tried to wake up. "I should have gone with you. What time is it?"

"Just after midnight. Go back to sleep. We all have the day off tomorrow." She smiled.

"I'm sorry I'm still here." I stood and almost stumbled over.

"Sit down, Cassie. You don't have to go anywhere."

I not so gracefully plopped back down on the couch. "Thanks for giving me dry clothes."

She touched my cheeks, her palms cupping my face. "Thank you for saving my son. I don't know what would have happened if you hadn't seen him fall in." Tears welled in her eyes, threatening to spill at any moment.

"That's why I'm here. That's why you hired me." I didn't mean for it to come out as shitty as it sounded, but I was answering her question. And shit, I just woke up.

"Stop. Please stop. I'm sorry about earlier. I was just jealous and bitchy, and I wasn't being fair to you."

Maybe it was because we both had almost lost the one person who had brought us together, or maybe it was because we realized how lucky we were that he was still alive, but for once we weren't guarded. She put her arms around my neck and let me hold her. She shook as the tears fell. I clutched her to me, hating myself for noticing how she was pressed against me instead of only comforting her. I waited until her tears and sniffles subsided.

"Wait. You were jealous? Of what?" I leaned back and brushed the tears from her cheeks.

She looked down, not able to meet my eyes. "Of how casual and comfortable you are with other women. It's stupid, I know, but it just reminds me of how far removed I am from everyone. Remember when you saw me at the Pearl? That was my first date in forever."

"That was a night of misunderstandings," I said. Sort of.

"My date told me I was distracted. The night didn't go as planned for either of us, because of us," she said.

I looked at our fingers entwined and couldn't remember who reached for who first. "Today was an emotional day. You have to be exhausted. Go upstairs and get some sleep. I'm going to my place and do the same." I tucked a few tendrils of hair behind her ear. "Call me when Noah wants some company. Maybe I can bring over a gaming system, and we can play for a bit. I'm warning you now. He has a new friend, and his friend loves to play Nintendo Switch."

Brook laughed through her tears. "Shit."

I stood and carefully pulled her so she was almost flush against me. I put my forehead against hers. "I'm so happy Noah is okay." Without even thinking, or maybe because it was always on my mind, I lightly pressed my lips against hers. They were softer than I imagined.

She kissed me back tenderly. When I felt her tongue touch my bottom lip, I knew this kiss had forever changed us. Ever so gently, afraid she would back away, I pulled her closer to me and deepened the kiss. Brook was in control of every aspect of her life, from the boardroom to the home, but right here, in my arms, she gave me control. She molded herself against me. I moaned when she opened her mouth to me. I ran my hands down her back and pulled her hips closer to mine and was rewarded with a gasp and a moan. This was the perfect first kiss. Before it got out of control, I pulled back.

"Okay. That wasn't supposed to happen."

Brook stood there and stared at me, silently.

"Not that I minded, because obviously I didn't, but today was an exhausting day for all of us. Go to bed, Brook. Let's see how we are in the morning."

She nodded and stepped away from me. I wanted to reach out to her, hold her, protect her, but we needed separation. Too much was at stake in the moment, and I wanted Brook to want me for me. Not because I saved her son, but because she desired me. She said she was jealous of Trina and Natalie, but was it for the right reasons? Was it because of me, or because she liked winning? I was definitely overthinking it. I needed sleep.

"You're right. If you come over in the morning, I'll make us breakfast," she said.

"You can cook? All this time and I never knew it?" She laughed and walked with me to the garage. "Pancakes. Let's see if you can make us pancakes."

She playfully pushed me through the doorway. "Go to bed, Cassie."

"Pancakes, Brook. Pancakes."

She shut the door, but not before I saw her signature single nod.

❖

I got out of the shower at nine and wanted to text Brook but remembered my phone was damaged. After our kiss, it was hard to fall asleep. I kept replaying it. The one thing I wanted, she gave to me so willingly, but was it out of relief or out of need?

I pulled on jeans and a school sweatshirt. It wasn't sexy, but after looking like a drowned waif yesterday, I was sure I could get away with being comfortable. I pulled my hair back in a ponytail and dabbed makeup on. I looked tired, but at least I had some color in my face.

I knocked on the door only because it felt weird and too comfortable for me to barge right in, even though I did it every morning and Brook was expecting me. But that was my job.

"Come on in," Brook yelled.

I marched in with my Wii. I was sure after almost drowning, Brook didn't want Noah jumping around, so I only brought controller-based games. "Hey, buddy, how're you feeling?"

"Good. Is that your Wii?"

"Good morning," Brook said. She handed me a cup of coffee with cream and sugar. How did she know how I took my coffee?

I thanked her and tried not to stare. Her hair was down and still damp from her shower. She had on very little makeup and looked at least fifteen years younger than she did in business suits and heels. She was wearing yoga pants. Her toenails were painted a pale pink. I'd never seen her look so relaxed or vulnerable. I turned my attention back to Noah.

"Yes. It is, and I brought several games we can play." Even though I had a class, I wasn't going to miss quality time with them. We were probably going to review things for the final, but I'd call my study partner for notes. I emailed my instructor and told her there was an emergency and I wouldn't be in. Because of privacy issues, I couldn't divulge any information, but I doubted she gave a shit.

"Do you have *Mario Kart*?"

"I have all the *Mario* games, and I have an oldie but a goodie, *Sonic*. He's a hedgehog, and you'll have fun with him."

"You get one hour of games. Make it count," Brook said.

I hooked up the system in the living room and sat on the couch next to Noah, Brook sitting on the floor in front of him. I played a quick level of *Sonic*, much to Noah's delight and Brook's chagrin.

"Okay. You'll have to tell me what's going on here. I'm so out of touch," Brook said.

"You have to collect emeralds as fast as you can. I just want to show Noah this one, but we can play *Mario Kart*. You can play together."

TEMPTATION

"I'm going to make breakfast now. Would you like another coffee, Cass?"

That was the first time she'd called me that.

"Yes. A tad more cream, please." I barely registered her presence when she returned with a cup because I was busy instructing Noah about how to play the game. When Brook returned with two plates of pancakes, I sat up straighter and paused the game. "You really made pancakes."

She smiled and handed me a plate with a tall stack dripping butter and syrup. Her plate had only one pancake. Noah started the game back up.

"Where's Noah's?" I asked.

"He's six. He ate at seven because he was starving and didn't want to wait until you woke up."

"So, you made me breakfast?"

She shrugged. "Well, you did save my son, so it's the very least I could do. Oh, and here. I almost forgot." She handed me a present wrapped in pale-pink paper with a white bow.

"What's this?"

"Open it."

I put my plate on the table and unwrapped the latest iPhone, along with a new case.

"Since yours got destroyed in the pool," she said.

"You didn't have to do this, Brook, but thank you very much." Was this version even out yet? And how the fuck did she get me a phone already? "It's beautiful." I didn't know whether I wanted to play games, eat, or call my cell-phone company and start my own plan.

"I didn't know what color you had, so I went with silver. It's the most neutral."

"It's perfect, thank you again, but you didn't have to."

My cracked iPhone was sitting in a bowl of uncooked rice. I knew full well it was destroyed, but I was optimistic. I picked up my plate. I knew I was going to eat every last bite, even if Brook only ate half her pancake.

Game time lasted over two hours, and Noah had a smile on his face the entire time. When somebody buzzed the gate, I assumed it was a delivery or the cleaning staff. I wasn't expecting Lauren to show up.

I was unhooking the game when she blew into the living room. I didn't care if the cords were properly banded together. I grabbed the unit and controllers and tried to get the hell out of there quickly.

"I find out about this the next day?" Her voice was loud and so shrill that I winced.

"If you'd have taken my calls last night, you would have known about it then." Brook was cool and calm and showed no emotion.

Lauren was livid and pacing back in forth in front of Noah. "You could have left a message or texted me 9-1-1."

The look on Noah's face broke my heart. I took his hand. "Hey, buddy. How about we go get a snack in the kitchen?"

"Don't you dare touch my son. Leave him right where he is," Lauren said.

I could take disrespect up to a certain point, but I wouldn't let Noah get hurt. "You're obviously mad, and it's upsetting Noah. I'm just going to take him out of this environment while you two hash this out. He doesn't need to hear this."

The anger in Brook's eyes changed to calm as she turned her attention from Lauren to Noah. "It's okay, sweetie. Go with Cassie. You can see Mama in a bit."

I didn't hesitate. I grabbed his tiny hand and hustled him to the other room. We could still hear their elevated voices.

"You have no right to be rude to any of my guests in my house. And perhaps you should talk to your husband, since he and I spoke last night, and he knew exactly what happened."

I realized the kitchen wasn't far enough away, so I made a decision. "How about we go up to my apartment and play some *Mario*? Then we don't have to listen to adults." I rolled my eyes for effect. If I didn't act concerned, he'd know it was going to be okay. "Oh, and that's not even the best part. I think I have all the stuff to make fluffernutters. Remember them?"

His face finally lit up. "Yum. Let's go."

I wished I'd grabbed my new phone, but no fucking way was I going back into the living room. I scribbled a quick note to Brook and left it on the kitchen counter. Since Noah only had socks on, I lifted him, piggyback style, and walked him up to my apartment from the garage. He laughed the entire time.

"Your place is awesome."

"Really? Is this your first time up here?"

He nodded.

"Awesome, huh? If you need to go to the bathroom, it's that door over there. If you don't, have a seat on the couch. I have to hook everything up."

"Your television's small." He said it matter-of-factly, not condescendingly.

"It is, but it works. If I had a big TV, I wouldn't study for school. I'd miss so much," I said. It didn't hurt to try to instill a quick lesson about how all-consuming gaming and television could be. "Okay, you ready?" I handed him a controller and sat next to him.

By the second game, Noah almost beat me. "You're a pro at this!" I groaned and fell back on the couch.

"It's easy." He pressed start on game three, and I barely grabbed the controller in time.

The banging on the door startled us both. I opened the door to find Brook standing there, arms crossed over her chest as if we were guilty of something bad.

"Your game is loud. I've been standing here a while."

"I'm sorry. Video gaming isn't a quiet sport." I stood back and invited her in. "And I'm sorry I took him, but I figured it was a good idea until things simmered down. He's on the couch trying to beat me at a game he just learned." I leaned forward and whispered so Noah couldn't hear. "It's very kid-friendly." Brook surprised me by coming in and sitting next to him.

"I hear you're a champ at this stuff." She ruffled his hair as he tried to dodge her hand.

"Mom, this game is awesome. Maybe I'll get a system for Christmas."

"We'll see."

I tried not to roll my eyes because that usually meant no. "I'm going to fix Noah a fluffernutter, if that's okay."

Single nod. We were back to that. I made Noah a half sandwich and threw grapes and pretzels on the plate.

"Hit pause and eat up while I show your mom how to play this game."

Brook had to tap him on the arm before he looked up at me and obliged. "This is what I was afraid of."

"Trust me. He'd be this way even if he was watching a movie. This is the attention span of a six-year-old." I wasn't one hundred percent sure about that, but it sounded good.

"So, how do you play it?" Brook held the controller limply and pointed it at me.

I sat next to her and held the other one. "You just have to learn what all the buttons do."

"Mom, it's really easy. Just move the controller to turn. The buttons on the very top make you jump," Noah said, his mouth full of peanut butter and fluff. Or that's what it sounded like.

"Don't talk with your mouth full," Brook and I said at the exact same time. We smiled at one another.

"Okay, let's give this a try," she said.

I started a new game and was shocked by how horrible Brook was at it. Even Noah groaned at her lack of dexterity and how she couldn't seem to grasp the concept. After ten minutes, I took the controller from Brook and handed it back to Noah.

"And yet you close multi-million-dollar deals weekly."

"My skills are elsewhere." Her eyebrow hitched ever so slightly, and heat blossomed all over me. I looked away. We hadn't talked about the kiss. Not that we'd had time, but I was obsessing.

"Five more minutes, bud. Then we have to go."

"Aw, Mom. Really?"

"Yes. We have a few things to do, and I'm sure Cassie could use some downtime."

I hoped my disappointment didn't show. It was nice to have them over, especially since yesterday had been such an emotional day. I didn't want to sound needy, so I played it cool.

"Life gets back to normal tomorrow. I'll see you in the morning. I think I'll head out and do a little holiday shopping alone, since you've told me a million times how you don't like it," I said.

"Are you going to buy me something for Christmas?" Noah asked.

"Noah," Brook said.

"What?" He looked so cute. "I'm going to get her something."

"Cassie does enough for you. And she let you play her games. She doesn't have to get you anything."

I waved it off like it was no big deal, but I was touched that he was so thoughtful. "I'm sure I'll find a little something for you."

"Okay, finish your game. We have to go," Brook said. She took his empty plate back to the sink.

I followed her. "So, do you think you'll get him a gaming system? I could get him a few games I think he'd like."

"You really don't have to get him anything."

"I want to. We spend a lot of time together, and I'm more than happy to give you suggestions," I said.

"Let me give it some serious thought, and I'll let you know what I decide."

I leaned a little closer. "It's inevitable. Every child in America has a system."

"Including you," she said.

"Ouch."

Chapter Fifteen

"Are you done?"

"Child, don't push me," Nana said.

As much as I loved to shop, the stores Nana wanted to go to and the stores I wanted to go to were completely different. She liked yarn and material, and I liked clothes. I dragged my feet while we walked down the rows and rows of yarn. How many types and thicknesses does anyone need?

"Eight pairs of knitting needles? This is like a lifetime supply for the old folks' home." I held them up, a rainbow of colors and different sizes, and dramatically rolled my eyes.

"Please keep whining. That just makes me walk a little bit slower," she said.

"Turnabout's fair play. You know how I normally just buy clothes? This time I'm planning to try on every little thing in the store. And make you wait."

She scoffed at my threat, knowing it would drive me crazy, too. I followed her with the cart, scrolling through my phone, checking text messages, hoping I'd hear from Brook. I should have been home studying, but I had too much energy to stay caged up in my apartment. She'd kissed me last night. Kissed me.

"What do you think of this?"

"Nana, they're virtually the same color. Blue. We're in a sea of blue."

"No. This is a deep blue, and this other one is a royal blue."

I rolled my eyes at her and kept pushing the cart forward. I heard her scuffle behind me as she made her choice and tossed three rolls of yarn into the cart.

"Are you working tomorrow?"

"Of course. Do you need me to take you somewhere?"

"So saving a child's life is worth only one day off?" she asked. I could tell she disapproved.

"We're both fine. He's going to school tomorrow, and so am I. Today was a perfectly acceptable day to play hooky."

"Well, I think you should get the week off. That water was freezing, and you're probably working on catching a cold." She mumbled something else, but I couldn't hear what it was.

"The pool was heated. It wasn't a big deal."

"I'm glad you saw the little boy fall in. Brook's very lucky to have you," she said.

I didn't tell Nana everything. I left out the argument and the kiss. She didn't need to know, and I didn't need the third degree from her. "I'm happy I got to him in time."

"Look, honey, I know you don't want to talk about this, but we need a plan for Christmas. You stood me up over Thanksgiving, and I really want the family together during the holidays."

I didn't go straight to anger this time. My heart felt sad. Nana was right. This feud was futile. Secretly, I missed my parents—not because they were good, but because they were mine. "Let's have Christmas dinner at your house. Neutral ground. I can agree to one meal for starters."

She stopped and cupped my face with her hands. "That makes me so happy. I promise it'll be so much fun. Your mother will be on her best behavior. And stop rolling your eyes at me."

I broke free. "I can't promise the same from me."

"You be you and things will be fine. Now let's pay for this and get out of here before I spend all my money here."

"Admit it. You can't wait to go clothes shopping with me."

I managed to dodge a swat from her right before I ran into a pole.

"Karma. She's a bitch and my best friend," Nana said.

Nana and I stayed out for five hours, then ended the evening with a nice Italian dinner. I ordered an extra set of breadsticks and sent the leftovers home with her.

While we shopped, I found an antique pocket watch for my father, a bottle of perfume for my mother, and a very nice silk scarf that I told Nana was for Lacy, but was really for Brook. I thought she'd appreciate the colors. Nana was busy looking at other things and didn't see how much I paid for it. I wasn't even sure if I'd give it to her, given everything that had happened.

I pulled up in her driveway and hopped out of the car to carry the bag of a zillion knitting needles and yarn to her door. She kissed my cheek. "Okay. Dinner will be on Christmas Day at five. Don't be late. And don't worry about bringing anything. I'm going to cook it all. Good luck on your finals. I know you'll slay them."

"I'll come over after I'm done with the semester, and we'll decorate your living room." I felt guilty that my only contribution this year was getting the Christmas tree down from the attic. Between nannying and studying, my free time was sparse. I still had to think about what I was going to get Lacy. There was a cool whiskey-of-the-month club I thought she might like, but that seemed overly adult. I signed up Nana to join the fruit-of-the-month club. Food and drink clubs were easy. Overpriced, but less for me to do.

With Lacy on my mind, I decided to call her. We had to play catch-up for the last few weeks, and I knew she was off on Mondays. "Hey, what are you doing?"

"I need you to come here and give me a foot massage. I'm dead. I can't wait till the holidays are over. If I make it to the new year, it'll be amazing."

"I just dropped off Nana. I can be there in fifteen. Need anything?"

"Why was Nana with you? Didn't you work today?"

Lacy didn't know about what happened. "Oh, there's a story."

"Holy shit. Did you get fired?"

"Uh, no. Thanks for thinking of the worst. We'll talk about it face-to-face. I'll see you in a bit." I ended the call and wondered how much I should tell Lacy. By the time I pulled up to the condo, I'd decided to tell her everything except for the kiss. She would be totally judgy, and I didn't need that. I knew such behavior wasn't professional and that Brook and I had crossed a line, but I needed to know from Brook what it all meant. I didn't want to share my crush with Lacy, have her scold me for something I already knew was wrong, and then end up purely professional with Brook. That was probably the most logical result, but

I liked my fantasy. I knocked on the door and held up a six-pack so she could see it through the peephole.

"Get in here right now," she said. She grabbed the beer, tucked it under one arm, and hugged me with the other. "Tell me all the good things. And why did you spend the afternoon with Nana?"

I shrugged off my coat and sat on the couch. "Where's your roommate?"

"Who knows? She's never here. She has a boyfriend I hate, so they always stay at his place. Come on. Tell me what's up."

"I got in this massive fight with Brook."

"Shut up. You really did get fired." Her eyes were so big I couldn't help but laugh.

"No. We argued about, get this, me dating Noah's teachers."

"Wait, wait, wait. You're dating Noah's teachers? Plural? How many gay teachers are there at his school?"

I held up my hand to stop the barrage of questions. "I only know of one. His homeroom teacher, but his violin instructor is also a lesbian. Both are cute, but I'm not dating either of them."

She opened two bottles and handed me a beer. "So how did the conversation come about? Like I saw you staring at his teacher. Stop it?"

"Well, I did meet his homeroom teacher for drinks that night at the Pearl when I barely saw you, but nothing happened. That was a get-together to talk about the fall festival. Brook said it wasn't a good idea for Noah to see me with his teacher in case things didn't go well. One breakup was hard enough on him."

"Hold up. She has no right to tell you who you can date."

I held my hands up in frustration. "Exactly my point. That's what the whole stupid argument was about. I told her she had no right, but it didn't matter because nothing would happen with his teacher. And then there was his violin teacher."

"She's gay, too, right?"

I nodded. "Anyway, Noah overheard us arguing and Brook sent him upstairs, but instead he went outside. I stormed off and saw him by the pool from my window. One minute he was there, and the next he was gone."

"She doesn't have a cover on it?"

I nodded. "She does, but the corner was loose. Noah said he was trying to fix it and fell in. He can swim, but he panicked because of the cover. Plus, he was wearing a heavy coat. He couldn't get out. So I jumped in and pulled him out. I had to resuscitate him."

"Oh, my God! You saved him." She squeezed my arms. "Is he okay?"

"He's perfectly fine. Like nothing happened. But it scared the shit out of me."

"Yet you didn't panic. Come on, Cass. Your parents have to hear this story. And I'm pretty sure you'll never get fired. I'm so proud of you. You saved somebody's kid. That's amazing. When did this happen?"

"Last night, so we all got the day off today. Brook made breakfast and invited me down. Noah and I played video games until Noah's other mother showed up yelling at everyone. Brook tried to call her last night to tell her what happened, but she didn't answer her phone." I helped myself to a bag of cheese curls from Lacy's pantry. Even though Nana and I had just eaten, I needed something to nibble on. A lot had happened over the last twenty-four hours, and I had nervous energy to expend. My favorite activity was eating.

"She sounds like a total bitch."

"Totally," I said. I shoved more into my mouth before I continued. "It was so awful I had to leave. I took Noah upstairs, and we played games."

"All of this is so crazy," Lacy said.

"I know. Oh, and also I'm having Christmas with my parents."

"You're fucking amazing."

I gave her a toothy smile full of cheese curls and orange teeth. "Don't forget irresistible."

The rest of the week proved to be just as normal as the other weeks. Brook never mentioned the kiss. If anything, she was even more standoffish than usual around me. I got the normal head-nods daily and a "good luck on your finals" Friday night. One of my finals was Saturday, and the rest were during the following week. I spent the weekend studying everything from the textbooks, my notes, and even reading journals from the library's database to clarify things I wasn't a hundred percent on. I was overprepared. Saturday's test was easy, so I doubted everything and overthought each question. I barely finished on time.

The rest of my finals were more straightforward. My last one was on Friday, but Noah's school let out early, so Brook arranged for her mother to pick him up. Brook texted right before my test that I had the rest of the time off until the twenty-sixth at noon, but I felt deflated. I was hoping for a quick Christmas celebration with them. Brook had never said whether she was getting Noah a gaming system, so I ended up buying him a three-wheel scooter. Their driveway was huge, so he could learn to use it there before I took him out to the park.

I called Nana before I headed to her place to help decorate. "What do we need?" The tree was done, but I wanted to hang lights and have fun things around. When Papa died five years ago, Nana stopped over-decorating. I couldn't handle going from one extreme to the other so I always made time to help her set up the nativity scene and the Christmas village, hang a garland across the fireplace, and dig out the stockings. This was the first year I wasn't excited to hang them. It was sad Papa wasn't around, and I wasn't on speaking terms with my parents.

"Maybe more cotton for the village? I can't seem to find it."

"No worries. Snow. Got it. What else?"

"Those Italian cookies for Santa." Nana said it so quickly that I laughed.

"Okay. Cookies for..." I paused for effect. "Santa. What else? Do you need milk?"

"I have everything else. Just get over here. Bring your pajamas in case you get snowed in," she said. We were expecting four to six inches of snow. As much as I wanted to be at my own place, I knew Nana missed me, and it wasn't fair that I didn't spend a lot of time with her.

"Will do. See you within the hour."

I hung up and shoved some clothes and toiletries into a backpack. I only planned to stay one night but packed for two, because I knew how convincing Nana could be. She could lay a guilt trip on me faster and better than anyone else in my life. I headed to the local Walgreens and bought three bags of artificial snow and three cans of spray snow. It was a bitch to clean up, but I liked to frost Nana's windows. It made it seem more grandmotherly. I stopped at the grocery store for the cookies and texted Lacy to have a safe trip with her family.

Nana opened the door and took the grocery bag from my outstretched hand. "How did your finals go?"

"I'm pretty sure I aced them all. I'll check later. I got an A-minus in Toxicology 431, and that was the class I was worried the most about."

"Straight As this semester?"

"I think so. It'll be nice to share that fact with the parental units."

"Just so you know, they're very excited that we're all doing Christmas together." She wasted no time in opening the cookie packages.

"Hey. I thought those were for Santa."

"You're looking at Santa, kiddo."

"What? All this time?"

She pulled me into her arms for a hug. "I really do miss you."

Chapter Sixteen

Uncomfortable wasn't really the right word to describe Christmas. My parents were their typical stoic selves. My father avoided eye contact for the first ten minutes, and my mother sighed a lot and tried to make small talk. It was funny how suddenly they didn't have power over me anymore. I poured a glass of wine and offered it to my mother. My father declined a glass. Still no eye contact.

"Thank you, Cassandra. I trust you are doing well." My mother was talking to me, but she was concentrating on the wine. It wasn't what they were used to, but it was something I liked and cost less than twenty bucks.

"I'm doing really well. I have a good job, my own car, and school is everything I'd hoped it would be."

I didn't need to throw that zinger in about school, but it gave me a few moments of victorious pleasure. I hid my smile as I took a sip.

"How's babysitting?" Mom asked.

I'd forgotten how callous she could be when she wanted. "Well, nannying is a little bit more complex than babysitting, but the Wellingtons are a wonderful family, and I really love the kid."

"Don't you just pick him up from school and play with him until his mother gets home?"

"Ruth." My father finally spoke up.

"What? It's a legitimate question. I just thought 'nanny' was a formal way to say babysitter." She shrugged and poured more wine into her glass.

"I do more than that, but it works with my school schedule, and I get paid well. Now I can get the degree I've always wanted, pay off my loans, and have a decent car to drive." I looked at Nana and smiled. "No offense." I'd fixed the heater in her car, but the dripping oil was there to stay. I couldn't afford a new transmission yet, but I carted her around on weekends whenever she asked.

"None taken. The food is ready, but I need help carving the turkey," Nana said.

I never saw my dad move so fast in his life. "Here, I'll help." He disappeared quickly, leaving me alone with my mom. It was quiet for a moment. Then we both started talking at the same time to fill the void.

"I wanted you to know—"

"I think Nana did a good job—"

We smiled at one another. She held her palm up for me to continue.

I cleared my throat. "I wanted you to know that as much as I hated what you and Dad did, I understand why you did it."

Mom took a step toward me. "I'm sorry it seemed like such a harsh thing, but we felt it was time." She could have done a better job explaining herself, but that was just how she handled things. Direct and to the point. I got my emotional side from my dad.

"It was shitty, but at least now I'm on my own. Oh, and you can take me off your phone plan. I have my own now."

She nodded. "Yes. I noticed that."

"The phone fell into a pool and died."

My mother raised her eyebrows but let it go. "I hope we can put all this behind us and be a family again. This has really upset Nana." Typical Mom behavior. Deflect any and all emotions onto somebody else.

I took a deep breath. "Baby steps, Mom. Let's just get through Christmas."

We weren't a close family. Nana was our glue. My parents were too involved in their own lives, and I grew up self-absorbed. Dad and Nana interrupted the moment with food. I followed Nana back into the kitchen and grabbed the basket of rolls and the gravy boat.

"And? What happened? I saw you and your mother talking." She thought she was whispering, but her voice definitely carried. I looked over my shoulder. My parents pretended they couldn't hear us.

"It was okay. I'll tell you later," I said.

The meal was relatively quiet. My parents talked about their jobs, Nana raved about me and school, and I stayed pretty quiet. Our gift exchange was amicable. My dad liked his watch, and my mom actually smiled when she opened her perfume. It wasn't a bad night. It just wasn't a Hallmark fluffy Christmas. I wanted them to go so Nana and I could drink eggnog laced with too much bourbon and talk about the night and the early Christmases she'd shared with Papa.

"Well, I have an early shift tomorrow." My father stood, indicating he was ready to leave. My mom grabbed their coats and hugged both of us.

"Have fun on your ski trip. Be safe," she said.

I'd mentioned to them I was out of town until December thirty-first, and before they even asked my plans, I told them I was going to Lacy's New Year's Eve party. In the past, we had dinner at the country club on the last day of the year. It was a big event that they dragged me to every year up until I started college.

"Thanks. And thanks for agreeing to dinner." I sounded mature, but to be fair, I was tired of fighting my anger. It just wasn't there anymore.

Nana gave a little victory fist pump after she shut the door. "That was wonderful. Thank you, sweetie, for doing this for me. For the family."

"Let's skip the egg part and drink the bourbon straight," I said.

"You completely deserve it. Now tell me everything your mother said."

We sat down and relived the night, the bottle of bourbon tucked between us on the couch.

"You aren't going home tonight, are you?"

"Why? Are you getting me drunk?"

"I want to make sure you don't drive."

I knew better. We'd lost Papa to a drunk driver one summer night when he went to the store to surprise Nana with her favorite mint chocolate-chip ice cream. It was a head-on collision, and the driver was still in prison. It was his second driving-while-intoxicated offense, so he wasn't getting out for at least another five years.

"I don't have to be anywhere until eleven tomorrow, so I'm yours for the night. Let's drink to a marginally successful night." I clinked my glass with hers, and we stared into the crackling fireplace.

"You are the best granddaughter in the world."

"You're just saying that because I'm fun, smart, sexy, hilarious, and only a phone call away." I leaned over and kissed her weathered cheek. "And also your only granddaughter."

"That's true, but you have a kind heart, and I know tonight wasn't easy, but it's a great start, and I haven't seen your mother this happy in a long time."

I snorted. "Happy? Mom? She looked out of place the entire night."

"To you she did, but I saw what you chose not to."

"Mr. Miyagi, you are so wise."

"Who's that?" she asked.

"Never mind. Want to watch a movie? I'm sure Hallmark's got all the good ones on tonight." I picked up the remote and turned on the television.

"Let's watch something dangerous."

I laughed. "What do you mean dangerous? Like a thriller or a slasher movie? Is that really how you want to celebrate this Christmas? I thought for sure you wanted something like *It's a Wonderful Life* or *A Christmas Carol*."

"Nah. Let's watch *Die Hard*. That's a Christmas movie."

I gaped at Nana. "How do you even know about *Die Hard*?"

"It was out before you were born. It's a classic. They talk about it all the time on television."

I must have missed that episode of *Murder, She Wrote*. "What shows do you watch?"

"*Brooklyn Nine-Nine*."

I laughed and said "Cool" repeatedly like Jake Peralta. "Okay, but don't crawl into my bed tonight when you get scared."

She put a throw over our laps, and I started the movie. Halfway through I couldn't keep my eyes open and rested my head on her shoulder. It was the last thing I remember. I woke up when Nana turned off the television and lights and felt her kiss my cheek when she covered me with the blanket.

"Merry Christmas, sweet girl."

I mumbled something back and rolled over, snuggling the blanket to my chest. I almost fell right back to sleep but then remembered I couldn't be late tomorrow. Nana was always up early, but I needed to be out of there by nine. "Can you make sure I'm up by eight?"

"Yippee-ki-yay," she said.

I smiled at her *Die Hard* reference. "You're so weird, and that's probably why I love you so much."

❖

The panic didn't set in until after my shower. I had an hour and a half to pack, but no idea what to wear. I would be gone for five days and had a giant pile of clothes on my bed that I felt like I needed. In reality, I would only wear half, maybe a third. I rolled up three sweaters, two pairs of jeans, two snow pants, wool socks, and absolutely nothing sexy. My evenings were free, so I packed something nice for at least one night. I had to sit on my suitcase just to close it. And then I had Brook's and Noah's presents. The scooter was in a big box, so it would be awkward carrying it around and making sure there was room on the plane.

I have Noah's present, but it's in a big box. Do you want me to save it until we get back, or should I bring it?

Bring it. He'll be excited. He has something for you, too. We have plenty of room in the cargo hold.

I was surprised she texted me right back. *You say that now, but you haven't seen my bag or my backpack. Five days. One would think we're going overseas.*

LOL I know what you mean. Try packing for a kid. The dilemma of if I don't pack it, he will surely need it. And then he'll wear only two things.

I wanted to see her. We'd never talked about the kiss. When she'd texted me to tell me about the surprise time off, she asked about finals. I answered, she congratulated me, and that was it. Phone silence until now.

I'll see you in a bit.

I grabbed my bags and dragged everything down to the garage and waited. It wasn't my place to barge into the house. I scrolled through social media and liked the photos and said all the right things on my friends' celebrations about life. Cool sweater, cute puppy, miss you, let's get together soon.

Where are you? Brook's text snapped me back to reality.

In the garage.

Get in here, silly girl. We're snacking before we head to the airport.

I stood, straightened my sweater and jeans, and walked into the kitchen.

"Cassie. You're here." Noah jumped up and threw his arms around my waist. I stumbled back a few steps with the force of his happiness.

I put my hand on his small back and gave him a quick squeeze. "Hey, buddy. I missed you. How was Christmas?" I squatted so we were at eye level.

"It was great. I got a PlayStation!"

Brook walked into the room, and my attention moved from him to her without hesitation. I loved it when she wore her hair down. Her teal sweater was flattering, and I couldn't stop my ear-to-ear smile when our eyes met.

"PlayStation. Good choice."

"I'm glad you approve. See? I do listen to you."

It was as if nobody else was in the room. "It's a shame I'll have to learn new games."

She winked at me. I melted.

"Hi, Cassie."

I stood. Erica was on the other side of the counter from me. I hadn't even noticed her there. "Oh, hi."

"Are you ready for some debauchery?" She wagged her eyebrows at me.

"What's debotch?" Noah asked.

"It's nothing, honey. An adult word you'll learn when you're in college. Now go find Griffin and tell him lunch is ready," Brook said. She shot a look at Erica that made her innocently raise her arms.

"I didn't think he'd repeat me," she whispered.

"They hear and see all. Trust me." Brook rolled her eyes.

I wanted to go back to the debauchery comment. What did that mean? Did Brook tell Erica? Or was that just her way of saying there will definitely be fun times ahead?

"I can vouch for that. Noah's retention level is astounding," I said.

Erica squeezed my hand. "I'm so excited you're coming. Not just because you'll be there for the kids, but because I have a wine buddy who's not afraid to let go." She gave Brook a playful scowl and was rewarded with an eye roll.

I didn't want to burst her bubble and tell her wine wasn't my favorite drink, but I was so happy to be a part of her plans that I decided I'd drink wine if it killed me. It was nice to belong to something, to have plans that didn't involve school or kids.

"The good thing about Anthony is that he knows the evenings are mine. Or at least that's what I'm going to tell him," Erica said.

"Yeah, good luck there. You know how much Anthony likes his cigars and whiskey around the fire," Brook said. She walked around Erica, and her arm barely brushed against mine. Instant chill. "Cassie, grab something to eat. The flight isn't long, but by the time we get up there and unloaded, it'll be dinnertime."

"And wine time. Don't forget wine time," Erica said.

I nodded and nibbled on cheese and crackers. It took everyone thirty minutes to eat and clean up. By then, the SUV to take us to the airport had arrived. Their family dynamic was entertaining. Brook was fun with her sister-in-law, but more formal with her brother. The boys were running around playing a game of tag, but Noah was laughing and happy, and I knew it was going to be a good few days.

"Are we ready?" Brook's voice boomed out, getting everyone's attention.

Shouts of joy and instant pandemonium erupted. The driver loaded our bags while Erica buckled Griffin into his car seat. Noah happily buckled himself into his booster, and before long we were on our way.

David and Camila were already waiting for us at the airport. This time, Anthony busied himself installing the kids' seats. Erica, Brook, and I boarded the plane, Gwen, the evil sister, already in the back. Frances was a row ahead of her, asleep. Camila was sitting across the aisle from Frances. That meant that Brook and I had a shot at sitting together. I tingled in anticipation. Accidental touches, laughing, every romantic subtle gesture popped into my head.

"I'm sitting with Cassie. I need to get to know her better," Erica said.

And just like that, my mood fouled. Hours next to Brook would have been heavenly. Instead, I was subjected to Erica's idea of getting to know me better. I answered so many questions I felt I had no mystery left after an hour.

"Are you single?" she asked.

I dreaded the question. I didn't want to explain my dating situation, but I also didn't have anything to hide. I knew the second I answered her that Gwen, who was busy with her phone and laptop, would jump into the conversation.

"I am single. School is my number-one priority."

"I thought Noah was," Gwen said.

"Nobody asked you, Gwen. Go back to your laptop," Brook said.

"Yes, he is, but as far as my personal life goes, school is first, and women are second."

And just like that, I outed myself in front of Brook's family without even thinking of the consequences. If they thought I was straight, then we would have moved on from the conversation eventually, but now every single person was focused on me. Fuck.

"You're gay?" Erica asked. Her voice wasn't accusatory. As a matter of fact, she seemed excited.

"I don't like labels really." I shrugged like my relationships were fleeting, boring, nonexistent, but suddenly my gender preference was the rage of the cabin.

Gwen piped up again. "Have you dated men?"

"Hey, everyone, let's quit subjecting Cassie to an inquisition," Brook said. "Surely we have better things to talk about."

I looked across the aisle at her. She winked, and I couldn't stop a smile from sliding onto my face.

"Yes, Gwen, leave Cassie alone. By the way, Gwen, how long do you want Frances to sleep?" Camila asked. "She'll be wired all night if we don't wake her up soon." Camila had been quiet during most of the flight, but kudos to her for changing the subject.

"Mom, nudge her awake. That's probably a good idea," Gwen

said. "I have *Peppa Pig* on the DVD player, if you can turn that on for her."

While Brook was helping Camila figure out the movie, Erica leaned over, her voice low so only I could hear her. "Oh, we're not done here, but we can continue this talk over wine tonight."

I rolled my eyes at her. "I'm not that exciting. Really," I whispered back.

"Are you kidding me? The electricity in this plane alone is combustible."

Chapter Seventeen

Mountain Ridge Resort was spectacular. I was expecting something like a hotel with individual rooms, but we had a massive cabin with snowy mountain views visible out the floor-to-ceiling windows. I was in awe. Of course, I was traveling with millionaires, so I should've expected nothing but the best.

"Cassie, you can pick any of the bedrooms upstairs." Camila pointed at the cute loft area that overlooked the living room.

"Thank you, Camila." I was glad somebody had said something because I felt awkward standing there with my bags and nowhere to put them.

I was the only one staying up in the loft. Noah fought for one of the smaller rooms up there, but Brook was adamant that he room with her. Two huge suites and two other large bedrooms flanked the giant stone fireplace downstairs, and even though I felt a little bit like the help being separated from the family, I appreciated having my own space.

When I opened the door to the first bedroom in the loft, I gasped. It was gorgeous. I didn't even have to look at the others to know I wanted to sleep here. Plus, it was the only bedroom that wasn't over one of the suites or bedrooms on the ground floor. The bathroom was spacious and had a jacuzzi tub. I missed those. I dropped my bags, freshened up, and headed back downstairs. Even though there was a full kitchen, I doubted anyone wanted to cook.

Brook met me at the bottom of the stairs. "We're having dinner at the main cabin."

"Oh, do you want me to watch the kids?"

"Absolutely not. You're joining us. I told you that your only responsibility is during the day. At night you're more than welcome to hang out with us, or you can do your own thing. And you have access to the car service. They usually send a driver in about ten minutes."

"Thank you."

"Come on. Let's head to the main cabin so we can find a table or two to accommodate us all."

Noah's little mittened hand grabbed mine. "I have to tell you all the things I got for Christmas."

His shining face was so adorable I almost leaned down and kissed his red cheeks. I missed him so much. "I can't wait to see what games you got for your PlayStation."

"I only got two, but Mom says we can go out later and pick more out."

"I still have to give you your present." I made a big deal out of it, but really, what was he going to do with a scooter up here in all this snow? I should have insisted that we wait.

"We have yours, too. Mom, can we open gifts after dinner?"

Brook, holding his other mittened hand, nodded. The walk up to the main cabin wasn't bad. By the time we reached the kitchen, we were swinging him between us. He giggled and asked if we could do it on the way back.

"I don't think I have the strength for that," Brook said.

We asked for a table to accommodate ten of us. Brook, Noah, and I sat at one end and waited for the others to show. They slowly trickled in, giving us enough time to get caught up. It was hard to look at Brook. We were in such a different, more intimate setting, and Brook was so beautiful. It was hard to remember this wasn't a date and I was an employee who was just on a little bit more personal level than most.

"It'll be a nice break for you. When do classes start back up?" Brook stared at me, gave me her full attention as I told her about my upcoming schedule. It was unnerving and made me tingle everywhere. Her eyes went from mine down to my lips, then back up to meet my stare. I had to remind myself I wasn't on a date, but damn, I wanted to kiss her. Again. I wanted to feel her against me. I wanted to knock her walls down and pull her into my arms and melt the ice around her heart. I wanted to make her happy. And smile.

"How's work? Are you going to be able to relax this week?" I asked. She gave me a small shrug, and I laughed. "I thought so. I'm sure with the whole family here, most of your conversations will be work-related."

"Want to bet?"

"Oh. Oh, this could get good." Flirting was harmless, right?

She laughed and took a sip of wine. "My mother has a no-work policy at meals. We can talk about anything else. Don't you remember when we were at Anthony's restaurant?"

I groaned and dropped my head into my hands. "I can't believe I drank so much," I whispered to her over Noah's head.

"You were fine. I think we're even now."

"I promise to be on my best behavior."

"Don't make promises you can't keep." Brook dropped that bomb right when her parents sat down.

"Cassie, what do you think of the place?" Camila picked up the menu and perused it even though she probably knew most of what was on it. This was a foodie family, especially since Anthony had his own restaurant.

"This, all of this, is just gorgeous. For some reason, I thought the lodge would be like a hotel. Separate rooms, not separate huge cabins. Thank you again for inviting me."

"We're glad to have you." She squeezed my hand. I was appreciative of how sincere Camila was, not like Gwen. I kept my poker face on when she and Frances arrived. She was going to be the one to treat me like an employee.

True to what Brook said, the conversation steered clear of all work-related topics. I kept quiet unless someone asked me a question. I was soaking up this large-family atmosphere. Erica sat on the other end of the table so I knew she wasn't going to ask me any embarrassing questions. That would be for later. By the time dinner was over, the kids were practically asleep and had to be carried back to the cabin. It was after eight, and I was beat, too.

After all the kids were tucked in, the men went outside under the heat lamps and smoked cigars. I was invited to drink wine with Erica, Gwen, and Brook. Camila excused herself early, but the rest of us settled around the fireplace. Erica was the talkative one, bouncing from one subject to the next. It was obvious Brook and Erica were close. But I couldn't put my finger on Gwen. She was standoffish but funny. She wanted attention but never wanted to be the topic of conversation without her consent. Brook was charming and funny, and I tried desperately not to stare at her. Erica caught me several times and smiled knowingly. After the fifth time, I feigned exhaustion and excused myself, telling them I'd be ready for the kids at ten.

"Sleep well," Brook said.

"Sweet, sweet dreams." Erica winked at me. I thought I saw Brook reach out and smack her arm when I slipped into my room, but I wasn't sure.

❖

Playing in the snow lasted a measly eight minutes, twenty if you counted how long it took us all to bundle up and locate missing gloves and get boots on the right feet. Noah wanted to snowboard, so I told him I'd take him out later when it was just us. The other two kids were just too small and didn't want to be out. I didn't blame them. The powder was light and great for skiing, but not great for building snowpeople. So I marched them to the main cabin for an hour-long arts-and-crafts class. We drank hot chocolate, ate hot dogs, and colored. It was fun, but I could tell they needed a nap. I leaned down to Noah. "When your cousins go down for a nap, we can play a game. I packed my Switch." I held my fingers to my lips when I noticed he was about a second away from whooping and drawing too much attention to us. He nodded emphatically instead. "Let's keep this between us. Less sharing time."

"Hey, you want to go back to the cabin and nap?" Noah asked.

"Noah, that's the worst thing to ask a kid," I said. "How about we head back to the cabin and watch a movie?"

That suggestion obviously sounded more appealing. We gathered up our snowpeople made of construction paper and cotton balls and headed back to our cabin. I put the little ones on a sled and dragged them down the hill as Noah raced ahead, twirling and laughing at the snow that had started to fall again. Away from home and school, he really embraced his freedom. It was adorable to watch him.

"*Peppa Pig*," Frances chanted while I unzipped her coat and pulled off her boots.

Griffin waited for me to do the same for him. Noah was already turning on the television and pulling up Netflix.

I had them line up on the couch by height, so Frances had the best seat. She was the smallest and needed the most advantage. I scrolled through the movies until they all decided on *The Incredible Journey*, about two dogs and a cat traveling cross-country to find their owners. I was hoping for *Peppa Pig* but was outvoted. I found blankets for the kids and settled on the floor in front of them, my back against the couch. Frances played with my hair until she fell asleep twenty minutes in, Griffin close behind her. When they were both out, I ruffled Noah's hair to get his attention.

"Want to play a game, or do you want to keep watching the movie?"

"Can we finish the movie and then play?"

There was still forty minutes left of the movie. I nodded and quickly ran upstairs to get the Switch. I didn't want it to be a big production of bringing a gaming system downstairs. I didn't know if the kids were allowed to play, so the Switch was a nice small alternative.

"Come sit with me." Noah patted the recliner beside him. I made sure Frances and Griffin were covered and moved over to Noah.

"Scoot, scoot."

I waited until he gave me more than six inches to sit down. "Ready?" I asked him.

"For what?" he asked.

I hit the button on the side of the chair, and he giggled as it lowered and reclined us. He snuggled in the crook of my arm, and we sat like that until the movie was over and the gaming started. I didn't hear Brook come in, which not only made me the worst babysitter ever, but probably the first to die in a home invasion.

"How long have they been asleep?"

Her voice startled me, but her hand firmly on my shoulder kept me from jumping up and dumping Noah in the process. Noah looked up from the Switch.

"Hi, Mom. Look. I'm playing Cassie's game."

I leaned back to look up at her. "I hope that's okay." She licked her lips and looked down at my mouth. I wondered if she always did that, or if I'd just started noticing since our kiss. "And those two have been asleep for a little over an hour."

Brook nodded and took a step back, while the rest of the family breezed through the front door.

"The last thing I want to do is break my leg out on the slopes," Gwen said.

Her eyes traveled from me to Brook and back down to me. Erica's eyes did the same, but she had a giant smile on her face, while Gwen's was pinched in a scowl.

"What have the children been up to?" Erica sat down and rubbed Griffin's legs until he stirred awake.

"We gave up on playing in the snow, so we went up to the main cabin for arts and crafts, ate lunch, and came back here for a movie. You're back early," I said. I set us upright in the chair and untangled myself from Noah.

"We wanted enough time to get ready for dinner," Gwen said. She woke up Frances by tickling her neck and whispering in her ear until she giggled. It was nice to see her interact and lose her bitchiness, even if only for a few seconds.

"Tomorrow we're going tubing. I signed us up before lunch. I think that'll be a big hit."

Camila put a teakettle on the stove. "Cassie, will you be joining us for dinner?"

I didn't want to get too attached to this family, and I definitely didn't want to overstay my welcome.

"No, thanks. I think I'll head up to one of the bars at the main cabin and watch some hockey. I'll just grab something there." I didn't care about the game, but I needed an excuse to do my own thing. I was starting to care about these people, and even though Brook insisted I was a guest, I was also her employee. Gwen was always so kind to point out that fact.

"Are you sure?" Brook asked.

"Yeah, I'm sure. But thank you."

"I'm sure you need a break after six hours with these three," Erica said.

"It was fine. They were good. Not fans of the snow, but to be fair, this kind of snow isn't great for kids unless they like skiing. That's why we're tubing tomorrow." I stopped myself from going into too much detail.

"We might see you later," Erica said.

"Okay. Have a good night if I don't."

Brook asked Noah for the Switch back, and after only one round of "please let me keep playing," he handed it to her without any fight. She gave it to me. "See you later."

I smiled and went upstairs to change. Nanny clothes and a night out were completely different. I stayed upstairs until they left, knowing full well the kids would need to eat early. I styled my hair, squeezed into skinny jeans and a gray oversized sweater, and put on makeup. I even accessorized with a necklace, a scarf, and a few rings. When the crowd left, I slipped on my boots and headed out. It felt good to look less like a nanny and more like a twenty-four-year-old out to have fun with new people. I told myself I wanted to look good for new people, but I was really hoping I'd run into the Wellingtons, Brook specifically. She rarely saw me dressed up, and I rarely saw her dressed down.

When I walked into the bar, a cute bartender pointed for me to have a seat. "What can I get you?" She had long reddish-brown hair and dreamy eyes.

I wasn't going to mind staring at her for a few hours this evening. I bet she got a lot of tips and a lot of phone numbers. "How about an IPA?"

She rattled off a few until I told her to surprise me because I couldn't make a decision. "What brings you up to Mountain Ridge? Ski trip?"

"Sort of, but not for me. I'm a nanny."

"We get a lot of nannies up here. Rich families need a break, too."

I ordered a cheeseburger and fries and hung out and talked to her until the bar filled up and the other bartender showed up to help out.

I was on my second IPA when Brook walked into the bar. It was as if something told me to turn around at that exact moment. She walked straight over to me, turning several heads in the process.

"Mind some company?" she asked.

"Of course not." I pointed to the empty chair beside me. "Who's watching Noah?"

"Mom is. My mom, I mean."

"Nice. So, you have the evening to do whatever?"

The bartender popped over to get Brook's Jack and Coke, winked at me after she delivered it.

"Here's to…" Brook paused and looked up as she thought about what she should toast. "Here's to fun vacations away from the real world."

We clinked glasses, and I finished what was left of my beer. I felt relaxed yet full of energy at the same time. Brook smiled at me like she had a secret.

"What?" I asked.

She shrugged. "Nothing."

I put my hand on her knee. "No, seriously. What?" I didn't move my hand. Neither did she.

"Want to get out of here? Get some fresh air? There's a cute little park not too far away."

I hated being cold. I wasn't dressed for a walk on a snowy path in below-freezing temperatures. But was I going to say no?

"Sure. Let me just settle up."

I threw some cash onto the bar and made sure to leave the bartender a big tip. I gave her a small wave when we left. She looked at Brook, then smiled knowingly at me. I smiled back. Apparently my crush on Brook was noticeable to everyone, but did Brook know?

Chapter Eighteen

"I don't mind the cold much, as long as it's not windy," Brook said. She was wearing warm boots, gloves, a nice hat, a scarf, and a coat. I was wearing half that and shivering. I clenched my jaw to keep my teeth from chattering.

"It's not horrible," I said.

She chuckled and linked her arm with mine. My body temperature spiked a few degrees at her nearness. "I'm sorry, but I wanted to talk to you and not around a ton of people."

"Did I do something wrong with the kids today? Oh, crap. I forgot to take Noah snowboarding. I'll squeeze some time in tomorrow."

She walked off the path and into some trees. I held back. "It's safe. Great view past all the trees. I'm not dragging you back here to kill you. I'm almost positive you could take me."

I raised my eyebrow at her. I could definitely take her, in every sense of the phrase. She cleared her throat and motioned for me to follow her. I did. We dodged branches and deep snow until we reached a clearing. The stars were bright and seemed so close to us. The moon was a mere crescent in the night, affording us very little light.

"You're right. This is gorgeous up here."

Brook brushed the snow off one of the benches. "Have a seat."

"Are you going to scold me?"

"Absolutely not. We need to talk about the other night."

"Which one?" I sat down, tucking my hands in my pockets to stay warm.

"The night Noah fell in the pool."

"I know I was wrong to argue with you, but I think—"

She stood in front of me and crossed her arms. "That's not what I'm talking about."

"Oh?" She brought up the one thing I'd been wanting to talk about for weeks, and I acted nonchalant like a teenager.

"The kiss."

"The kiss," I said. I blew out a deep breath. "I shouldn't have done that. It's all my fault."

"Are you upset that we kissed?"

I looked up at her in surprise. "I'm not sure how I'm supposed to answer that."

"I want you to answer with the truth."

"I don't think you do." My brave words belied my nervousness, but I kept eye contact with her.

"Tell me."

Well, fuck. Everything was on the line. My job, my future, my education. I guessed I could pick up a few shifts at the Pearl and maybe a few babysitting gigs. Living with Nana wasn't the end of the world. I could downsize my wardrobe. I stood to lose everything, yet I never wanted to be so truthful in all my life.

"I'm not sorry at all. I've wanted to kiss you before I even knew you."

"That doesn't even make sense."

I stood. She didn't move but looked at me and waited.

"I couldn't keep my eyes off you the first day we met. You were at soccer practice off by yourself, and I noticed everything about you at once. Every part of me was aware of you. Your hair, your clothes, your suit, your confidence. I didn't know who you were. You turned to me when Alex sent the text out to the parents to help me out of the bind, and you looked up at me with your stunning eyes and motioned me to follow you. I didn't hesitate." I was rambling, but I didn't care. This confession was liberating and scary at the same time.

She didn't move. She didn't make a sound. I threw up my hands and sat back on the bench. She was going to fire me. I just gave her this massive confession, and she just stood there with her arms crossed.

"Well," I said, "this has been very enlightening. I think I'll go back to the bar and have another beer."

"No."

"No?"

Her shoulders dropped. "I'm sorry. I'm not very good at this. I've been guarded for a very long time."

I was frustrated. She'd made me puke this confession, and suddenly she didn't want to talk? That wasn't fair. "Not good at what? Talking? You talk for a living."

"That's business. It's different."

Another deep breath. "Okay, did you hate it? Was the kiss horrible?"

"It was a fantastic kiss, and I didn't hate it at all. *At all.* But you're an employee. And everything screams for me to shut up and let things go back to the way they were, but I can't. I can't stop thinking about you or that kiss." She pursed her lips as if preventing herself from saying anything else.

I was too scared to move. This beautiful, smart, courageous woman I'd been dreaming of for months was standing in front of me telling me her thoughts were similar to mine? "So, what do we do now?"

She stared at me, her eyes big and vulnerable, her lips slightly parted. When her shoulders fell a second time, I thought for sure she was going to take a step back. Two steps. Three steps, until she turned around and left me alone on the bench. Instead, she leaned down until her face was only inches from mine.

"Anything we want." Her lips brushed over mine, featherlike and so gently, they felt more like a breath against my mouth.

I pulled back to ensure this wasn't the alcohol talking or a bad decision, but I saw only determination and want. She gained confidence when I put my hands on her waist and pulled her closer. She straddled my lap without hesitation. When I felt her press against me, I groaned and deepened the kiss. Her mouth was warm and commanding. Out of instinct or lust, I spread her legs farther apart so that the most physically intimate part of her was only a few thin layers of material away from mine. I pressed my hips up, and we both moaned.

"We probably shouldn't do this here." I broke the kiss and looked around. We were still very isolated, but civilization was only a few steps away. I'd forgotten about the cold. Fire, passion, and need spread through me, heating me from the inside.

She ran her fingertips over my cheek and across my lips, barely moving her finger away before her lips claimed mine in another intense kiss. I couldn't get enough of her. I refused to let my negative thoughts have the stage. I picked her up and felt her legs wrap around my waist before I dropped us both into the snow. I had to feel all of her against me. I ground my hips against hers.

Brook tugged at my clothes, ripping her gloves off with her mouth. When her warm fingers slipped inside my coat and under my sweater, I gasped. Not because her hands were cold, but because she was finally touching me, and it was everything I'd dreamed it would be.

"Once we get past the trees here, we should be able—Oh. I'm so sorry. We didn't know anyone was up here."

Four people broke the tree line and stared down at us. I pulled back as Brook untangled herself from my clothes.

"No worries," I said. Once I was free, I stood and helped Brook up. I brushed the snow off her back.

They stared at us. We stared back. Three more people showed up. Of all the fucking luck.

"What's going on?" I asked as normally as I could, even though my heart was racing, I was throbbing all over, and the only thing I could feel was Brook's warm hand in mine.

A dude from the second group spoke up. "There's a window of fourteen minutes where we should be able to see the aurora borealis from up here."

"That explains the interruption," I said.

We were both breathing hard. I smiled at her, and she started laughing. Soon both of us were laughing, and our audience smiled at us. It was an awkward situation, but the second somebody saw the lights, we all focused on the night sky. We watched as a small ribbon of green light whipped low across the dark horizon. It wasn't spectacular, but I was already humming with energy, and everything overwhelmed me. I pulled Brook closer and smiled when her hand snaked under my coat to rest against my hip. She didn't say anything, only stood there and held me. Those were the longest fourteen minutes of my life. As incredible as the aurora borealis was to see, the timing was shitty. Not that a pile of snow was the best place to have sex, but had this astronomy bunch not showed up, I would have at least tasted her skin and touched her in places I'd only dreamed of.

"This is beautiful." Brook whispered it as though she didn't want to ruin the moment for the people who'd climbed the hill just to see it.

"Everything about this right here, right now is beautiful." I stared at her until she looked away smiling. Maybe I did have game after all.

When the ribbon faded, we all left. I didn't want to stay there, since our intimate moment was ruined and I was starting to get cold. I had no idea what would happen. Were we going to pick back up somewhere else, like the cabin? Get another place? Or just let this attraction fizzle for a few weeks and try it again?

"Let's go back to the cabin," Brook said.

I sighed. That meant fizzle. No way would she want to have sex at the cabin where her entire family was staying. Granted, it was large enough, but I wasn't exactly quiet, and I doubted Brook was either.

"Okay. I need to warm up anyway."

"I was the one in the snow," she said.

I laughed. "Um, yeah. Sorry about that. I kind of got carried away."

She squeezed my fingers. "I am so not complaining. About anything."

We walked into the quiet cabin, and Brook punched in the code to turn the alarm off after a small ding told us it was activated. She set it again and turned to me.

"I'm going to change and check on Noah. I'll see you later."

I nodded, completely confused. Did that mean later tonight? Tomorrow at breakfast? I didn't want to push, so I went up to my room and slipped into pajama bottoms and a T-shirt. Not sexy, but I didn't want Brook to think I'd packed something sexy for her or that I expected anything. I still looked good. I washed my face, brushed my teeth, and braided my hair back. A very slight two-tap knock came from the other side of my door. I opened it and found Brook in her pajamas. I pulled her into the room and locked the door.

"You're here."

She nodded. "Is that okay?"

I walked her backward until she was pressed flat against the wall. "Definitely." I captured her mouth in a searing kiss. She moaned.

"Shhh. We have to be quiet," I whispered. I ran my fingertips gently down her cheek, down her neck, and traced the vee in her silky top. Her nipples were hard against the soft fabric. As much as I wanted to dive into her, I needed to take it slow. "Nobody can hear us, or we'll never hear the end of it."

"Okay, but you'll just have to remind me. I'm horrible at being quiet."

I moaned at that confession and kissed her hard. She tasted warm and minty. Her hand slipped under my T-shirt, and I shuddered.

"Did I tickle you?" She pulled her hand back.

"No. Your touch just feels good."

We kissed again, finding a rhythm that ramped up our passion. Her breasts felt full against mine, her thighs strong. As much as I wanted to take her to the bed, it seemed so far away, and I was tired of waiting. I slid my hand under the band of her silk pajama bottoms and waited for her to adjust to my touch. This was uncharted territory for us, and as much as I wanted to drop to my knees and taste her, I knew I had to take my time.

She put her hand over mine and moved it to the junction of her thighs, which was smooth and slick. I moaned into her kiss when I felt how swollen and wet she was. I stroked her up and down. When I felt her hand join mine, I lifted her hand out of her pants and laced my fingers with hers. Then I pressed her hand against the wall.

"We have all night," I said.

"But I need you. Now."

I kissed her harder and slipped my hand back inside her pants, but kept her other hand trapped in mine above her head. She tugged her pants down to her knees with her free hand. I smiled at her eagerness and determination. When my fingers slipped inside her, her legs shook, and both of us moaned at the intimacy. She was so tight and smooth and gripped my fingers greedily, wanting more than I could give her at this angle.

"Please, Cassie."

"Please, Cassie, what?" I wasn't trying to control the situation. I didn't know what she wanted me to do.

"Please, Cassie, take me to the bed and fuck me."

I fumbled at her command but slowed my movements. I wanted to stay inside her, to always feel this closeness. Before I slipped completely out, I fucked her hard for about ten seconds. She cried out. I released her hand and clamped my fingers over her mouth.

"We have to be quiet. If we wake everybody up, we can't do this."

She was breathing hard but nodded. With any other woman, I

would have congratulated myself, but with Brook I wanted nothing more than to please her. I was thankful only a tiny light was on in my room, or else she would have seen my desire on my face.

She pulled me to the bed and nestled my hips between her legs. I pushed her silk top off and gently ran my hand over her breasts. She was the most beautiful woman I had ever touched. I leaned over and kissed her softly. I wasn't in a rush. We had at least a few hours just to ourselves, and I planned to take every minute. Who knew what tomorrow would be like or if this was a one-night thing? I hoped it wasn't, but realistically it might have to be. I blocked that possibility from my mind and focused all my attention on Brook.

"You are so beautiful. So soft and so willing."

She stared at me while I touched her. I wasn't shaking, but my hand wasn't as steady as I wanted it to be. I stroked her gently, getting to know her body inch by inch. I held her breast and flicked my tongue over her nipple. She pulled my hair and held my mouth in place.

"Harder."

I sucked her into my mouth while I massaged her other breast. She gasped as quietly as she could. She arched her back. No way could we do this slowly. Our chemistry was almost more than I could handle. I moved up and kissed her, spreading her legs with my own, feeling how wet she was. The need to be naked against her overwhelmed me. I sat up and removed my T-shirt while she helped me out of my pajama bottoms. I pulled the covers back and we slipped between the sheets.

"Are you cold?" she asked.

Embarrassed that I was shaking now that we both were naked, I lied. "Yes, but I'll warm up soon enough."

Brook pulled me into her arms and rubbed her hands on my back. I kissed her shoulder, her collarbone, her neck, and captured her mouth with mine. Her hands were all over me, touching, rubbing, pressing into me whenever I gasped with pleasure. She pushed my hips up so I was on my knees between her legs. I put my hands on her thighs and spread her farther apart. Her mouth opened, and the closer my thumbs inched toward her core, the more rapidly her chest rose.

"Are you just going to tease me?"

I ran my fingers along her slit. "I think you know I'm capable of more." I don't know where my confidence came from, but I wasn't going to stop. I liked the way her eyes roamed appreciatively over me.

"I promise to be quiet," she said.

I could deny her as long as I could deny myself, which was about two seconds. I entered her, and her hands reached out to me. She bit her bottom lip, but true to her word, she kept quiet.

"Yes," she said. I pulled all the way out. "No." I smiled and entered her again. She lifted her hips to meet each thrust and moaned softly. "Faster."

I half expected her to give me a single nod when I leaned over her and answered her needs. For a brief second I thought I'd hurt her as I felt her nails dig into my arms, but when I slowed, she shook her head.

"Don't stop. This feels incredible." She spoke through short breaths. Her legs quivered. She was close.

I leaned down and whispered in her ear, "Come for me, Brook."

Maybe it was because I said her name or the fact that I was in charge at this moment, but she bucked beneath me and came hard and fast. I didn't stop fucking her until her hand stilled mine.

"Oh, my God. I can't. I need a moment."

I kissed her deeply and scooted so I was beside her with our legs entwined. She glistened with a light sheen of sweat, and her chest rose and fell as her breathing evened out. I couldn't stop touching her though. She closed her eyes as my finger fluttered over her pale skin, smiling when I touched places she liked.

"You are so very beautiful. I've wanted to touch you forever."

She reached up and stroked my face. "How am I going to be around you now and not blush or want to reach out to you?"

I grabbed her fingers and brought them to my lips. "You never blush."

She laughed and covered her mouth at her outburst. "I'm pale. I can't get away with anything."

"You have a valid point. And very nice coloring right now." I looked at the flush on her chest and her cheeks. "Too bad it's so dark in here. I'd like to see you better."

She kissed me. It started off sweetly enough, but within seconds, our passion ignited. In a surprising move, she flipped me over and trapped my hands over my head.

"Don't move. At all," she said. When I reached out for her, she stopped me. "Nah, ah, ah. You don't listen very well."

"You're not the boss of me."

I wasn't sure why I said that or how she would take it, but she raised an eyebrow at me and leaned over. Her lips hovered just above mine. "Am I not?"

She never gave me a chance to answer. The second her lips touched mine, I couldn't think of anything but Brook on top of me. She ran her mouth down my neck, nipping and sucking all the way until she landed between my legs. I desperately wanted to wrap my fingers in her hair, but I kept my hands where she told me to. She held my hips as her tongue touched my slit softly. Her warm breath alone was almost enough to put me over the edge. I clenched down and silently begged her to lick me, taste me. It had been a long time, but tonight wasn't just about sex. Tonight was about change.

Chapter Nineteen

I always thought I was in charge when it came to sex. My previous partners pretty much lay back and enjoyed the ride. I had some surprises and a girlfriend who liked to be on top, but I was still the driving force in my sexuality. Brook let me take charge for about ten minutes. The next two hours were life-changing. Not only did Brook know exactly how to build me up almost to my breaking point, but she also showed me how to enjoy the climb. Sex wasn't a race; it was a marathon with her.

I was writhing in need and wanted release. Her wet mouth lavished my clit, while her fingers stroked inside, tapping my G-spot. I wanted to scream in frustration. I wanted her to fuck me hard, but I wanted this euphoric feeling to last. I was hanging on to a ledge, knowing if I fell, this perfect feeling would give me relief, then disappear. I hated and loved it at the same time.

"I need to come." I licked my lips and opened my eyes for the first time in forever.

"So soon?" Brook asked.

My short laugh sounded painful. "But I don't want to. I've never felt this—" I stopped talking when she moved her fingers faster. I barely grabbed the pillow in time to cover my face as I yelled out my orgasm. I dug my heels into the mattress and lifted my hips to grind into Brook's body. I needed to feel her everywhere. I grabbed for her. I felt her smile against my neck as I gulped in air as quietly as I could.

"I'm almost certain everyone heard you," she said.

I turned to her, tilting her back so I could look into her eyes. "Please tell me you're joking."

She leaned forward and kissed me swiftly. "I guess we'll find out in a few hours."

The clock read 1:26. Brook had come to my room a little after ten. Time flew when we were having sex.

"I can't believe it's so late." I dropped my head onto my pillow and pulled her close again. "It's amazing how you make time fly by." I dropped a kiss on her forehead and rested my head on hers. "What do we do now?" I held my breath, afraid of her answer.

"If we plan to function like normal people tomorrow, we should probably sleep."

"You need only four hours of sleep per night, right?" I asked.

"Four or five. It's hard to get more because I'm usually working until about ten, and then I have to work out before Noah wakes up."

"Why do you work so late?"

She slipped her hand under the sheet and rubbed her hand over my breasts and my stomach. "I put Noah to bed, and then I have to check my emails and sometimes make calls. Remember, we work all around the world, so a lot of stuff happens after normal business hours."

"You work too hard. You need to take time for yourself."

She shrugged. "I'm used to it. Besides, closing deals and watching the company grow knowing my hard work is paying off is such a high. I'm certain Noah will always be taken care of. He'll be able to do anything he wants to, whether it's company-related or not. If he wants to be a teacher or an artist, he can."

"I love that you have such a good relationship with him. He's so sweet, and you're so adorable with him. And he's so smart. I can't wait to see how he turns out."

"He really loves you already. Hell, he's probably closer to you than to Gwen."

"Gwen acts like she's allergic to him," I said.

"Gwen acts like she's allergic to everyone."

"Truer words have never been spoken."

"I'm sorry she's not a nicer person. She's always felt separated from us."

"At least you and Erica seem close. I really like her. She's a lot of fun."

Brook laughed. "You can't even imagine the trouble she's gotten me into." She turned on her side to face me. "It's getting late. I should probably go before I fall asleep here."

"You can't leave. It's not even two." I pulled her hand to my lips. "Stay for just a few more minutes."

She pressed her fingertips to my lips. "It's getting late."

I pouted. "But I don't want this night to end."

She placed the gentlest of kisses on my lips, then pulled back but didn't say anything. Maybe this was it. Maybe tonight was all we had. I reached out for her and kissed her the way I've always wanted to—passionately and completely. If this was my one night with Brook, then I was going to do what had been on my mind since I saw her on the soccer field. I touched every inch of her, peppering her pale skin with kisses. She was the most responsive woman I'd ever been with. She wasn't afraid of her body, wasn't embarrassed to tell me what she liked. I ran my tongue up and down her warm slit and moaned at how wonderful she tasted.

"That's perfect." Her voice was low and breathy.

I wanted to take my time with her, but we were against the clock. I held her hips down, giving her the friction she wanted, and continued my seduction. She pressed her fingers against the back of my head and moved her hips until she found a rhythm that brought her to climax within minutes. I wanted to spend the rest of the night between her legs, but she had to leave. I kissed the inside of both quivering thighs and crawled up her body until we were face-to-face again.

"I hate that I have to go," she whispered against my cheek.

"I know." I kissed her softly and untangled myself from her arms.

"Get some sleep. I'll see you in the morning." She slipped out of bed and found her clothes. I loved that she didn't try to hide her nakedness from me. "I need to go. Quit looking so adorable and warm." She slipped her top on and bounced on the bed next to me. "Good night. I'll try to keep the kids quiet in the morning." Brook delivered a quick kiss and tiptoed out of the room.

The warmth disappeared as soon as she closed the door. I fell back with disappointment. The night was a whirlwind, and I was swept away by a blonde who had jumped from my dreams into my arms.

❖

The cabin was empty when I finally woke up at eight thirty. I took a quick shower to get me going, but I still needed to caffeinate. I put on snow pants and a thick wool sweater and headed up to the main lodge. Much to my surprise, Brook and Noah were on their way back down to our cabin.

"Cassie, when are we going snowboarding?"

I squeezed Noah's hand but couldn't take my eyes off Brook. She looked bright and happy, and I took great satisfaction in knowing I had caused that smile.

"Well, we have an hour before we have to find your cousins. Maybe we can talk your mom into going with us?"

"I'd break a leg," she said.

"Are you scared?" I gave her a smug look.

"How about I watch you instead? I like to watch."

A memory of Brook telling me to touch myself to show her what I like flashed through my mind. Watching her watch me turned me on. I almost didn't want to stop, but she was controlling the moment, and I was more than willing to please her.

"Yes, you do. I promise you'll have a good time."

Brook winked at me.

Warmth spread throughout me, and I looked down, because in the light I was sure my face showed all the emotions I couldn't afford to reveal to her.

"Have you eaten anything yet?"

"No. And I haven't had my coffee yet either, so I can't guarantee my greatest performance." I got an eyebrow lift for that.

Brook pulled a granola bar from her pocket. "Here. I picked this up for you. I can't help you with your lack of caffeine, but I can at least feed you."

I took it from her outstretched hand, letting my fingers linger on her palm. "Thank you, Boss."

We walked up to the rental place and picked out three snowboards. A quick text to her family telling them I'd be late afforded us time for a one-hour private lesson.

Noah fell only a few times but jumped right back up every time, full of energy. Both of us had to hold back from reaching out to him when he did fall. A few times I clutched Brook's arm when he fell backward instead of forward. Brook didn't fall at all. After a few close calls, she was right there next to me.

"Don't look so surprised."

I rocked back and forth on my snowboard, eager to show Brook and Noah how good I really was, but afraid to leave them. I felt part of something peaceful and nice. I looked at my watch and sighed. "It's time to collect Griffin and Frances. We're tubing today, so let's go back to the cabin, warm up, and then head back up here."

"But I'm not even cold. And I'm standing up. And I did a few runs," Noah said.

It hurt me to crush his groove. "Buddy, I promise we'll come back. Maybe after dinner we can do some night snowboarding." I knew the bunny slopes were well lit, so I didn't think it would be dangerous.

"This is a lot of fun." Brook unlatched her boots. "But I prefer skiing. More control and less restrictive."

"Why does this not surprise me?"

She playfully gasped. "What are you implying, Cassie?"

I shook my head at her and shrugged, then turned to Noah. "You ready? I promise tubing will be fun."

He grabbed his snowboard, head down, shoulders slumped. I leaned down to him.

"We will definitely do this again, but right now I'm going to need a little help with your cousins. We'll come back tonight."

"Okay." He didn't sound convinced.

"Take the snowboard with you. We'll rent it for the rest of the time here. You can practice up at the cabin," Brook said.

"Woohoo. Thanks, Mom."

"But we still need to go tubing first," I yelled as he took off. I turned to Brook. "That was sweet. I'm glad you did that."

"Small victories."

"Like the PlayStation?"

"Like the PlayStation."

❖

Camila helped me look after the kids, but by four we were ready to hand them back to their parents.

"That was intense." Camila groaned as she fell back on the couch. "I don't know how you do this every day."

"Oh, this wasn't normal for me. Plus, I have only Noah, and he's basically an angel."

"Except for today," she said.

Noah was whiny because tubing wasn't snowboarding, and he complained the whole time. Camila told Brook he wasn't cooperative and now he was grounded for the night. He could practice snowboarding out back but wasn't allowed to leave the yard. I felt bad. I really wanted to take him out on the slopes, but no way was I going against Brook. I hugged him and told him we'd try again tomorrow.

"Would you like to have dinner with us, Cassie?" Camila asked.

"No, thanks. I'm just going to grab something quick and go to sleep. I didn't sleep the greatest."

Erica snorted and choked on her drink. Brook turned and stared at her. "Sorry. It went down the wrong pipe." I saw a small smile on Erica's lips before she opened the almost-empty fridge. I looked at Brook, who raised her eyebrow at me.

I excused myself and headed upstairs to change into jeans and a sweater. Then I waved bye to the family and left. Too much was happening in that space. I wanted a huge dinner, a glass of wine, and my bed.

My bartender was at the bar and slid another IPA in front of me when I sat down. "This one has a hint of citrus."

I saluted her with the glass and took a long swallow. "I was thinking of wine and pasta, but I think I'm going to order a cheeseburger and fries, and sip on this."

"How's your time with us been?"

Ignoring the best night of my life, I answered her honestly. "Watching three kids for six hours a day is a challenge, but my nights are free, and I love the atmosphere."

"I know what you mean. I work four nights a week, but I can ski for free, so the benefits outweigh the work."

I wanted to tell her that applied to me, too, but I refrained. I had a nice salary, health insurance, a free apartment, a space in the garage, and fantastic sex with the boss. I felt a tinge of guilt on the last one, knowing full well that sleeping with the boss in any situation was not a good idea. Plus, I didn't know if it was a one-time deal. I was anxious for the sun to set and the cabin to grow quiet to see if she visited me tonight.

"How long have you worked here?" I asked.

"Eight years. Can you believe that? I started in college and never left."

"What did you go to school for?" I didn't want to assume she graduated.

"Anthropology."

We both laughed. Not that my degree was any better, but I had more options within my field. Yet she looked genuinely happy and was living life to the fullest, according to her.

"Hey, if you stick around, a bunch of us are going skiing around eleven tonight. You're more than welcome to join us."

I groaned. "That sounds like so much fun, but I'm exhausted today. The kids wore me out, and I didn't sleep the greatest." I looked at the time. "Who eats dinner at five thirty and dreams about going to bed at six?"

"Good point." She laughed and gave me another beer.

"This will for sure put me down for the night. Usually I push through the exhaustion, but tonight I give up."

"Sounds like you need a break. Get out of here. I'm taking care of your dinner."

"Oh, no. You don't have to. I can pay for this."

She waved me off. "Go. I'll see you later."

I slid a twenty in the tip jar and thanked her for dinner. I liked her. The cabin was empty when I got there, so I grabbed an apple and a protein bar in case I got hungry later and headed to my bedroom to sequester myself for the rest of the night.

Chapter Twenty

I woke up to a warm body beside me in bed. I'd purposely left my door unlocked, hoping Brook would show up. We'd never talked about last night, even when we had a few moments alone while Noah was far enough away from us snowboarding.

"Mmm." I snuggled into Brook's warmth. She ran her fingertips up and down my arm. I shivered and smiled. "That feels wonderful."

"You're very hard to wake up," she mumbled. "To be fair, I'm pretty sure I fell asleep for a bit trying to wake you up."

I rubbed the sleep from my eyes. "What time is it?"

"Two. I crept in here a few hours ago."

I turned so I was facing her. "Why didn't you wake me?"

"Trust me. I tried. So I gave up and snuggled with you instead."

I kissed her. She was soft and pliant. My heart sped as I processed that she was here with me, that last night wasn't a mistake or a fluke. "I'm so happy you're here."

She responded by flipping me over, straddling my hips, and working her mouth down me. I slipped off my T-shirt as she shimmied my shorts over my hips and down my legs. I hated that she had her clothes on. I'd just slept for five hours and was rejuvenated, the blood pumping through me burning hot.

"Are you cold?" She lifted her mouth off me and stared at the chill bumps that were everywhere.

"I'm burning up."

She smiled and continued her trek. I needed her touch everywhere. We didn't have the luxury of time so I slid her pajama top off. The feel of her bare breasts against my thighs set off another wave of chill bumps. I reached for a pillow to cover my face as a moan escaped. Brook wasted no time spreading my thighs and running her tongue up and down my slit.

"You're so wet already."

She wasn't wrong. I was gushing. She slid two fingers inside me as deep as she could. I moaned into the pillow again, digging my heels into the mattress and raising my hips to greedily greet every thrust. "I think you like this." Her voice was thick and low.

I nodded and lifted the pillow long enough to answer her. "Oh, I definitely like this."

With her fingers still inside me, she moved up me. "Move the pillow, Cass."

I obliged. Her face hovered above mine.

"I want to watch you."

"I want to kiss you." I leaned up to capture her lips in mine, but she moved away.

"Not yet."

She slid a leg between mine and held her knee against her hand, keeping her fingers deep inside me. I moved against her hand.

"Give me more," I said.

She relaxed her leg and worked a third finger inside me. I took a deep breath at the girth.

"You're so tight." She kissed me and slowly moved her fingers in and out. I gasped into her mouth, tugging at her bottom lip with my teeth, careful not to hurt her, but enough to let her know I liked what she was doing to me. We nipped at one another for a few minutes, but once her hand picked up speed, our kiss deepened, and we forgot the playful biting. Her tongue and fingers were deep inside me, and I wasn't sure where to focus or even if I could. I let my instincts take over and moved against her, with her, until she gave me exactly what I needed. Her kiss stifled my moan, and I broke the kiss to gasp air.

"Damn. You should wake me up like that all the time."

She smiled and rested on me. Her head was on my shoulder, her arm draped over my waist. After pulling the covers over us, she snuggled into me. The adrenaline was still coursing through my veins, and I couldn't sleep, so I lay there quietly as not to disturb her. Several minutes later, when her fingers drew little patterns on my skin, I realized she was still awake.

"Only one more night, and then we head back. It's been fun. I'm sorry I haven't spent more time with you," she said.

I turned to look at her. "You're here with your family. Don't worry about me. Are you at least having a good time with them?"

"I love spending time with Erica. My sister's just hard. I never know what version of her I'm hanging out with. Sometimes she's a ton of fun, and others she's a complete killjoy. Of course, my parents are great."

"They are surprisingly down-to-earth."

"For rich people, you mean?"

I nodded. "Not exactly. My parents are well off, but they aren't nearly as fun and relaxed as yours."

"How was Christmas with them?"

"Eh, okay. The dynamics of our relationship have changed, so I wasn't overly stressed. I'm surviving nicely." I gave her a quick squeeze and pulled the blanket up to below our chins. Now that my body temperature was dropping back to normal, I was cold.

"Look at my parents and then look at Gwen. She loves having a staff to boss around and making sure people know she's superior. Anthony and I are very different from her," she said.

I didn't point out that Brook fit the classic definition of an ice queen. But whereas Gwen was mean, Brook had a good heart. She was just all business. And even though we'd had sex several times just in the last two days, we never talked about our emotions or what all of this meant. This relationship was still employee and employer, and at some point, we were going to have to address the situation. Right now, I just wanted to taste her and hold her.

"Let's not talk about family right now. I don't want my libido to shrivel up and run away," I said.

As predicted, she slid on top of me. "I don't want it to leave either. What should we do to make it stay?"

"Hmm. I can think of a few delicious things."

"Oh, yeah?" She kissed me.

I grabbed her waist and dragged her up me until her knees were on either side of my head. "Definitely this right here." I brought her pussy down onto my mouth. Brook wasn't ashamed or embarrassed to have sex. I tapped her thigh several times when her moans grew loud. She'd quieten but then get loud again. When she finally came, I held her legs down until she rode each wave out. I knew she was loud, and the bed was moving. I just prayed no one heard us.

"That was definitely worth losing sleep over," she said. She crawled off me and stretched out beside me. I pulled her into my arms when she put her head on my shoulder.

"I promise to never disappoint," I said.

I felt her nod, and within seconds, her breathing evened out. I reached for my phone and set the alarm for two hours from now. Hopefully the kids wouldn't get up early.

❖

If I thought Gwen was rude before, she was unbearable this morning. I almost took my cup of coffee upstairs but decided to hang out to find out the day's plans. I was surprised to find luggage by the front door.

"Are you really leaving?" Erica asked Gwen.

"Yes."

"That's it? Just yes?" Erica grabbed Frances and hugged her.

"Ask Brook. She knows why." Gwen huffed and glared at me.

Fuck. She knew. I wonder who else did.

"Where is Brook?" Erica asked.

"She probably needed a nap after her night," Gwen said.

I sputtered out my coffee, spraying some of it on the counter, then apologized and wiped the mess with a napkin. When Camila walked into the kitchen, she didn't look at me.

"Good morning, everyone."

"Good morning," Erica and I said in unison.

"What are the plans for the day?" Erica asked.

"We're going for a sleigh ride tonight before dinner, but the day's free. Cassie, what are you thinking for Griffin and Noah?" Camila asked.

"I guess since I have only them, we can go tubing on one of the steeper hills. Two kids are a lot easier to handle than three," I said.

"Good morning."

Brook breezed into the room, Noah close behind her.

"Hi, Cassie," Noah said.

I ruffled his hair. "What are you hungry for?"

"I already ate."

I looked at my watch. "It's only eight. What time did you get up today?"

He shrugged. "I played on my iPad until Mom found me."

"Were you hiding?" I was a little nervous at his answer. It had never occurred to me that Noah might try to sneak up to my room and want to play on the Switch. What if he'd heard me and Brook? I watched his behavior, but he was acting like himself, not like he'd heard or, worse, seen his mom and me having really good sex.

"What are the plans for today?" Brook asked Camila.

"Just skiing and later going on a sleigh ride after dinner. Cassie, you're more than welcome to join us on the sleigh ride and for dinner since this is our last night," Camila said.

I gave Brook a quick glance to see if she was okay with the plan before I accepted the invitation. She gave me her signature nod.

"That sounds really nice. Thank you."

"Our ride's here," Gwen said.

I shrank in my chair, waiting for her to tear into us. Something had really pissed her off, and I could only imagine it was our activity four hours ago.

"Good-bye, Mother." She kissed Camila on her cheek and whirled by me on her way to air-kiss Erica's. "I'll see you next week." She kissed Noah on his cheek, too, which he promptly wiped off. I turned my head and tried not to smile at his honesty. Lipstick was pretty gross.

"I'll tell your father you said good-bye," Camila said.

And just like that, Gwen and Frances were gone. I looked at Brook, who shrugged at me. I swallowed hard. We were the reason Gwen left. I felt guilty.

"Well, let's hit the slopes, shall we?" Erica asked. She squeezed my waist when she walked by me, which made me smile. "Cassie, come with us. Camila's going to watch the kids until the men get back from their snowshoeing trek."

I looked at Brook to see if she was okay with the idea. Another nod. "Sure, I'd love to." Never mind that I was exhausted, sore in all delicious places, and could have used the two hours wisely. Any chance to spend time with Brook was always going to win out.

I quickly changed into snow pants and piled on layers to avoid a coat. It was cold but not windy, and I tended to sweat a lot when I skied.

"Mom, call me when everyone gets back," Brook said.

"Don't worry about it. I don't get to see the grandkids a lot. You just have fun."

"Thank you, Camila," I said.

We were barely out of the cabin when Erica turned to us. "What's going on? Is what I think happening really happening?"

"What do you mean?" Brook asked.

"Come on. Gwen heard you last night." Erica was whispering very loudly, and Brook hushed her.

"Gwen did not hear anything last night," Brook said.

Okay, so we were going to pretend the last two nights didn't happen.

Erica turned to me. "Tell me the truth. Did you two hook up?"

Brook laughed and pushed Erica away from me. "Quit harassing Cassie. We're here to ski, not fulfill your weird fantasies."

"Hey. I just want you to be happy. You deserve it after the last two years of complete and utter bullshit." She pointed at me. "I approve."

I stood there and acknowledged nothing. I didn't even smile, although I was dying to celebrate this new situation with someone, anyone. Not that I thought Brook was my girlfriend, but I was hoping for some sort of acknowledgment. I held my hands up and shook my head at Erica.

"You both suck." She stomped inside the coffee shop.

Brook tugged on my jacket to get my attention. "Look, I haven't had time to talk to you, but Gwen saw me creeping out of your bedroom this morning."

"Shit." My heart picked up its pace as panic set in. "What happens now?"

She put her hand on my forearm. "It's none of her business what I do. We're consenting adults."

Technically I was an employee of Wellington Enterprises. I had their health insurance and stock options and 401(k) contributions. "Who all did she tell?"

Brook shrugged. "It doesn't matter. My parents know that my business is my business. I'm sure if my mother was concerned, she'd talk to me about it."

"Brook, it just happened like six hours ago. She's probably trying to come up with the right words. I'm kind of freaking out over here."

• 173 •

"Are you sorry we did it?"

"Are you kidding me? You're a dream come true." That was probably too much of a confession, but it came from the heart.

Brook stared at me. I could tell she was struggling to keep her emotions in check. Even though I didn't feel like she was going to confess the same, the swirling emotions in her eyes gave me just a glimmer of hope. A small smile tugged at the corners of her lips. But then the door to the coffee shop busted open, startling us both.

"Hey, are you ladies coming or what? Oh, wait. That already happened." Erica turned just in time to dodge a giant handful of snow from Brook.

Chapter Twenty-one

I was not a patient person. Another reason I didn't want to be a doctor. Brook texted me to let me know that Noah was going to Lauren's for New Year's Eve. Lauren had asked at the last minute, and Brook had accepted. Brook then invited me over to spend the evening with her. I sent Lacy a message telling her I couldn't make her party tonight, but I'd call her tomorrow to get all the details.

My phone rang, and I was slightly disappointed it wasn't Brook. "Nana. How are you?"

"I'm tired. I've been up since five this morning. I don't think I'm going to last until midnight."

"I hope I do," I said.

"Aren't you going to Lacy's party tonight? You were looking forward to that," she said.

"That's still up in the air. I'm exhausted from the ski trip." That was true, but the adrenaline rush from the last three days had kept me going.

"Tell me about your trip," she said.

"It was actually a lot of fun." It was hard to keep the excitement out of my voice.

"Now, you worked six hours a day for five days, right?"

"Yes. I was on my own the rest of the time. The kids were pretty good. I skied and snowboarded every day, and hung out at the lodge at night."

"How was Brook? Was she nice to you? What about the rest of her family? You'd met them before, right?"

"Brook was fine. Completely chill and laid-back. Noah was a lot of fun. I taught him to snowboard. Well, he's kind of a natural. The rest of the family was really cool, except for her sister Gwen. She has to be related to Satan."

Nana was quiet. I looked at the phone to see if our call was still connected and thought for sure that would illicit a snort and a fitting retort from her. "Okay, dear. I'm glad you're home. I'm going to go lie down. Have a fun and safe night. I love you."

"I love you, too, Nana. I'll call you tomorrow, but not early."

"Definitely not early," she said.

I hung up, and the ding from Brook's text message rang loudly in my ear.

Baby bear has left the building.

I smiled. *How's Mama bear doing?*

She's torn. That was followed by a sad face. *I was hoping for a night with just me and my little guy, but my backup plan looks promising.* That was followed by the devil emoji.

My heart skipped, and I took a deep breath to settle my nerves. *What time do you want me?*

I'm surprised you're not here already.

I shivered, then gave myself one last look-over. I was killing the hot, younger girlfriend look. I slipped into the house via the mudroom. Brook greeted me in the kitchen with a glass of wine and a smile that weakened me entirely and spread heat to all the right places.

"Hi."

"Hi." I took the wine from her outstretched hand. "Are you cooking me dinner?"

She smiled. "I don't cook, but I'm having food delivered from Ruby's."

"Sounds delicious."

"I'm pretty tight with the chef. Plus, after everything we've eaten the past few days, I figured we needed simple and easy."

I walked over and pulled her close. "I like simple."

She set her glass on the table and wrapped her arms behind my neck. "Guess what?"

"Um. You missed me?"

"And?"

"You couldn't wait to see me again?"

"And?"

I stopped myself from blurting out anything I couldn't take back. Tonight was another fun night, not a night to express my deepest thoughts and desires. "And we're going to celebrate a new year?"

She thought about it and nodded. "Okay. I can go with that."

"Wait. What did you mean?" I tucked her wrist behind my back so I could bring her closer and I brushed my lips lightly over hers.

"Mmm. I was just going to point out that we are in a twelve-thousand-square-foot house."

"Mansion," I said. Nana lived in a house. This was an estate.

"Twelve-thousand-square-foot house. Just us. Nobody can hear us. We don't have to be quiet." She placed a soft kiss on my neck, then scraped her teeth over the skin. I shivered. "Oh, do you like this?"

"Oh, yes, I do."

"What do you think we should do until the food gets here?" She slid her hands down the shoulders of my neatly pressed shirt and unbuttoned the top three buttons.

I stopped her hands. "Let's wait until the food gets here. I don't want to stop once we get started."

She stepped back. "You're right. We have time. Come on. Let's relax in the living room."

Brook looked incredible. Even though we were staying in, she looked really chic. Cashmere sweater, dark skinny jeans, and suede ankle boots. Her hair was down and wavy, just how I liked it, and her makeup was light and fresh. I was more casual than she in my untucked, button-down fitted shirt and jeans. I'd slipped on loafers, knowing full well I'd kick them off soon. I kept my hair down because Brook liked it that way and treated tonight like it was my first date with her. Instead of showing up with flowers, I showed up with brownies. I baked when I got antsy. Two dozen chocolate-chip cookies and a bundt cake were cooling on the counter in my apartment. Today had been the longest day, but tonight would be the shortest night.

"I should probably tell you that wine isn't my favorite drink."

"What's your poison? I have a full bar and can make you anything at all," Brook said.

"I'll be bartender tonight."

"You'll need the codes to get into the bar. Remember, I have a child."

"He's six. I can't imagine he even knows what alcohol is at this point." I could see the bottle of whiskey I wanted. It didn't look opened, but it was one I was dying to try. "I can have anything in here? Anything at all?"

She smiled at me and nodded. "Anything at all. The code is 6969."

"Seriously?" I laughed.

Single nod with an eyebrow quirk thrown in. I carefully lifted out the bottle of High West A Midwinter Night's Dram and twirled the bottle in my hand to read the label. It was perfect to celebrate the season, the night, and the woman I cared for. "Last chance," I said, my hand ready to pop the cork.

"I'll even put my wine aside and drink a glass with you." I poured two glasses and handed her one. "What should we drink to?" she asked, her glass a few inches from her mouth.

"Let's drink to acoustics," I said.

She tapped her glass against mine. "I can't wait to fuck you."

I almost dropped my drink at her confession. Instead, I took a sip. The spicy warmth nipped at my taste buds. I leaned forward so my face was inches from hers. "I can't wait either."

She licked my bottom lip. "Mmm. You're right. Very tasty."

My desire for her spiked. This Brook was relaxed, knew exactly what she wanted, and was going to get it, too. The gate chimed, breaking our erotic yet playful moment.

"Saved by the bell." She delivered a swift kiss and left the room to collect dinner. I followed with our drinks. "Have a seat. I ordered tapas and dessert."

"That's a lot of food," I said.

"It'll sustain us."

This was the first meal I'd ever had with her where it was just the two of us. I was excited and nervous and knew I wouldn't eat a lot. The last thing I wanted was to fall into a food coma when we only had a small window of time.

"Have you talked to your parents since Christmas?" Brook asked. I shrugged. "My mom texted me Happy New Year, but that was it. I texted back. We're going to have to ease back into a relationship. It's a good thing I have Nana as a referee."

"I'd like to meet her."

I choked on my bite of salad. "Nana has no filter. She speaks her mind and will probably say some very interesting things to you."

"She's a pistol, I'm sure. A real firecracker."

"I love her. Maybe the next time Noah's with Lauren, we can all share a meal."

"I'm in."

It was nice how accommodating Brook was. I wasn't sure of what was happening between us other than really good sex. I don't think either one of us was ready to talk about it. Correction. I was ready, she wasn't. I needed to be careful because we were on shaky ground, but being with her felt so good and right.

"Let's talk about your family. Why are you and Anthony so reserved with each other?"

"Ah, so it's noticeable. Okay. It's a long story. I always knew I was going to work for Wellington Enterprises. All three of us did. We interned during summer breaks and holidays and had a healthy sibling rivalry. He and I both wanted to work export. I liked the travel, and Anthony liked the lifestyle. We both did the job well. My dad picked Anthony over me for the position because he's a man, and international business is still very sexist."

"I'd be concerned if I was your father throwing you into a room of wolves." I tried to be honest without stepping on any toes.

"My father felt the same way. Anthony rubbed his decision in my face and got to do everything I wanted to, while I stayed home and built up Wellington's grocery stores. I was upset with my father and set out to prove him wrong. In the meantime, Anthony started screwing up the export business. We were losing money. My father chased behind him, cleaning up his messes. Finally, he pulled him from the position."

"Is that when he realized he wanted to be a chef?" I asked.

"Ironic, huh? He's all about food and I'm all about business, and my father mixed us up."

I took another bite. "Well, I think you're both doing well, and I'm sorry it took forever to get there."

She shrugged. "I can't get mad over it now, but we'll always have that fracture."

"Why, though? I mean everybody's happy and things are great. And Erica's wonderful. I really like her."

Brook sat back in her chair. "Maybe I'm just too stubborn for my own good."

"I wouldn't say stubborn. I'd say determined."

"You sound like my mother." She laughed and shook her head at me. "I know. It's not mature, but it fractured my life, my marriage, and all because Anthony wanted to prove he could beat me at something."

"How do you feel about things now?"

"Disappointed that I'm responsible for a broken marriage. I didn't give it the time and love it needed. On the other hand, I really love my job. I'm good at it. I've doubled our worth. And I've created some very profitable accounts."

"So, you and Anthony are doing what you both love to do. You can't change the past. You can only learn from it and move on."

She leaned back and crossed her arms. "You're right. About everything. I need to relax about Anthony and focus on my family, my son, my libido."

I looked up from my plate when she said *libido*. She gave me a sly wink. I laughed. "I need to focus on school, saving the planet, and masturbating less."

"Ah, youth," she said.

"Oh, like you don't? You're a passionate woman with very strong needs. I mean, I don't know your dating habits, but I know you like sex." I wasn't fishing for information. I was curious about our relationship, but I wasn't going to press her.

"Cassie."

"Brook."

"I don't date."

"Well, except for the woman at the Pearl."

Brook waved me off. "You're right. That technically was a date, but nothing happened."

I held my hands up at her. "You don't owe me an explanation at all." Jealousy wasn't a trait I was proud of, but it was there.

Brook pressed her palms on the table and stood. She slowly

walked over to me and rested her hip on the table. "What about you? When was your last date?"

I reached for her hips and slid her so she was between my legs. "I don't date."

She smiled and leaned so that her lips hovered over mine. "Liar."

I shrugged. "I go to school, and I have a very demanding job. I don't have time for frivolous things like dinners, movies, and dating." I tried to kiss her, but she playfully pulled back.

"Is your boss a hard-ass?"

I played along but still chose my words carefully. "Oh, most days she bosses me without even looking at me."

"That's horrible." She cupped my chin and tilted my face. "And such a gorgeous face, too. Why would she not want to look at it as much as she could?"

My cheeks warmed at her compliment. "She's very busy running a massively successful business. She doesn't have time to slow down and enjoy life or me. And I recently heard she doesn't date."

"She's a hag. I hate her already."

I ran my hands up the curve of her hips to rest on her waist. Then I brushed my fingertips under her sweater and pressed my lips against her stomach. "Don't hate her. She has good qualities, too."

She wound her fingers in my hair, pulling me closer. "Oh, yeah? Like what?"

I ran my tongue right above her waistband and slowly unbuttoned her pants. She didn't stop me. "She's very smart, and deep down, she's a softie." I looked up at her. "And sexy as fuck."

She answered me by sliding her pants down her hips and kicking them to the side. I wasted no time in touching her all over. I stood and gently pulled her sweater over her head.

"Want to see my bedroom?"

"I've seen it already."

"Want to see it from the inside?"

"Definitely."

She led me up the stairs, kissing and touching me the entire time. By the time we made it to the bed, I was on fire. My shirt was somewhere in the hall, but I couldn't get my jeans off. I tripped and fell on the mattress. "Help me."

Brook smirked and straddled my hips. "I kind of like you tied up and helpless."

"But I still have the use of my hands." I stroked her breasts until her nipples strained against the fabric.

She moved my hands above my head. "Don't move them."

"That's not fair, though."

"I never said it was going to be."

"Tyrant."

She smiled. "You say it like it's a bad thing." She ran her tongue over my lips. The lightness of her touch tickled, but I was too turned on to care. I lifted my head so I could lose myself in her kiss. She indulged me for a few seconds and then pulled away again.

I groaned. "You're killing me. Please let me touch you."

She unlatched her bra and slowly slid it down her arms. It ended up somewhere near the closet. "Not yet."

"At least let me kick off my jeans."

She shook her head. "But I like you at my mercy."

"I'm always that. Maybe we can find a nice silk scarf instead of jeans."

I sighed when she climbed off me and pulled off my jeans. Down to my bra and panties, I sprawled out, giving her quite the view.

"Have you ever been tied up before?"

I shook my head. It was always a fantasy of mine, but one I never voiced or tried. I was always so focused on actually getting laid, I never gave foreplay or role-playing a second thought. I smiled when she resumed her spot straddling my thighs.

"Is it something you're into?"

"I don't know. I mean, I like this, but I don't know if I can handle it. Look at you. I want to touch you everywhere."

"You'll still get to do that."

Her smile sped my already racing heart up. She was so beautiful. "But you told me I had to keep my hands above my head."

"Do you always do everything you're told?" She kissed along the edge of my bra. I gasped when she pulled down the lace to expose my nipple. She rapidly sucked it into her mouth. I hissed with a mixture of pleasure and pain. When her teeth grazed the sensitive, swollen bud, I cried out. She released my nipple. "Did that hurt?"

"Yes, and no. Fuck, I don't know. It felt good, though."

She raised her eyebrow. "Do you want me to stop?"

"God, no. Don't ever stop touching me."

The talk about tying me up ended the second her lips touched mine. Our passion and the newness were entirely too strong to keep playing the game. I wanted Brook. I wanted her unrestricted in my arms. I wanted to hear her come loudly. I flipped her and pressed my hips between her legs. She unhooked my bra while I slid off our panties. We moaned when we touched in the most intimate way.

"You're so wet already," Brook said.

"You've been touching and teasing me for hours and hours. You did this to me. You." I captured her lips for another mind-blowing kiss. Then I ran my tongue down her neck, biting sensitive areas and relieving the ache with my tongue. By the time I reached her navel, her hands were on my shoulders, pushing me down.

"Cassie, I can't wait any longer."

I slid two fingers inside her as far as I could go. Her hips rose and pressed against my hand. Her moans turned me on so much that I started moaning with her. I squirmed with need as her voice got louder and her moans deeper. I slid down so I could finally taste her. Her warmth and slickness surrounded me. My hips gyrated against the mattress. I fucked her with my fingers as I sucked and licked her clit. When she shook, I knew she was close.

"Yes, just like that. Don't stop. Please don't stop."

It wasn't quite a shout, but loud enough to startle me. I remembered nobody could hear us and increased my movements until she came hard against me. I had to pull away to breathe. Her body shook in the aftermath. I pulled her into my arms and wrapped myself around her until her shaking subsided.

"Wow," Brook said.

A surge of adrenaline spiked my heated body and fed my ego. When I first met Brook, I was instantly attracted to her, but no way did I ever believe this could happen. She was everything I wasn't—confident, successful, and sexy. At this moment, though, I felt like her equal.

"Agreed." I couldn't have summed it up better without exposing my heart.

"Your hips are amazing. Have you ever used a strap-on?"

"It's been a long time, but yes." I felt weird talking about sex so cavalierly after we'd just had a very emotional moment. I wanted words of love, not just physical want, even though I was guilty of both.

"Would you ever fuck me that way?"

I stilled. My blood, my heart, my breathing seemed to stop. My head felt heavy when I looked up at her. "If you wanted me to, I would."

She played with a piece of my hair and tucked it behind my ear but didn't say anything. We stared at one another for what felt like hours but was really only about three seconds. She gave me the single nod.

Chapter Twenty-Two

I had a pair of briefs with different sized O-rings. I had no idea why I kept them, but I was thankful I did. "I have a harness I can wear if you have a favorite dildo." I wasn't about to wear briefs somebody else wore to fuck her.
"I have something new I've been waiting to try out."
I almost wept with relief that it was something new. I crawled away from her warm body and slipped on one of the robes she had hanging in her closet.
"I like looking at you," she said.
I tied the sash around my waist and sat next to her. She opened the gap in the silky material and lightly stroked my chest. My nipples were already hard, and I was aching for release, but I still wanted to please her more than I wanted to satisfy my own needs. "I like that you do."
She leaned up, the covers clutched to her chest, barely draped over her breasts, and kissed me deeply. I moaned at how provocative and powerful that kiss was. "Hurry back."
I stood on wobbly legs and, with great effort, walked, not ran, out of her bedroom. I made it to my apartment and tore apart the dresser looking for my black briefs. Of course they were in the back of the bottom drawer. I slipped them on, thankful they still fit. My clit twitched at the tightness and anticipation of being back in action. I grabbed two bottles of water on my way back into the house, eager to get back into bed with Brook.
"It took you a while."
Brook was inside her closet, clad in a tiny robe that barely covered anything.

"What are you doing in there?" I peeked over her shoulder to see. Much to my surprise, Brook had a drawer of new, still-in-the-box, silicone dildos.

"Trying to decide."

I reached in front of her and untied her sash. I ran my hands up to her breasts and squeezed them, playing with her nipples until she moaned and backed into me. She reached up and dug into my hair almost painfully. I slid my hand to the junction of her thighs and massaged her swollen slit.

"Let me help you decide."

She sighed when I pulled my hand away and watched as I held up one that was seven inches long and not quite two inches wide. I couldn't imagine controlling something this size yet. She bit her lip as she stood there.

"What about this one instead?" She picked up a different box.

It was a respectable size for both of us. I nodded. "Open it."

She pried open the package while I massaged her slit from behind. She spread her legs apart for easier access and bent forward. I slipped two fingers inside. She moaned and pressed back against me.

"Give me the toy. I'll get ready and meet you in bed." I fucked her hard for ten more seconds, giving her a taste of what was to come. She turned and kissed me before doing exactly what I told her to. I slipped into the bathroom, washed the dildo in the sink, and harnessed it into the briefs, then looked at myself in the mirror. Christ, I'd missed this. I hoped my stamina was good and that I would please her. Brook seemed insatiable. I tied the robe closed and walked into the bedroom. She was under the covers, her hair splayed out on the pillow, waiting for me. I was beyond excited. And nervous.

"Hi." I stretched out next to her and propped myself up on my elbow to look at her.

"Hi." She touched my face. I caught her hand and placed a soft kiss on her palm. She pulled me to her, and my instincts took over. Within seconds, we were pulling at one another, trying to get closer. I settled between her legs on my knees and ran my fingers up and down her slit. She handed me a bottle of lube. I was shaking with excitement. She moaned when I ran the tip up and down her slit and gasped every time I touched her clit.

"Please, Cassie."

"Please what, Brook?"

"I want you inside me."

I leaned forward and slowly penetrated her. Her mouth opened at the girth as I gently moved forward. When I was all the way in, we both moaned. The base hit my clit, and a jolt of pure pleasure exploded throughout me.

"Yes," she said. She reached up and touched my face. "More."

I kissed her and started to move. She spread her legs and moved her hips against mine. We found a great rhythm until she wanted more. We were both sweating, and I lost count of how many times she came. I held off on my own pleasure until I knew she was completely satisfied. I was almost there. I slowly slipped out of her and flipped her.

"Oh, my God." She held herself on her hands and knees, and I entered her again. She cried out and moved against me. I took a few deep breaths before I moved with her. My knees were raw and I was out of breath, but I was going to give Brook exactly what she wanted. What she needed. After what felt like an eternity, I finally succumbed to my own raging orgasm. I wasn't quiet and neither was she. I pulled out, and she dropped to the mattress, sweaty, gasping for breath. I flopped next to her.

"I can't move." She reached over to touch me.

I curled up behind her and pulled her close. "I can't either." I reached for a water, offered her the first sip, and gulped the rest down.

She turned to face me. "That really was amazing." She ran her thumb along my bottom lip. "You have wonderful lips. I've always admired them. Now I know."

I held her fingertips to my lips and kissed them. "Thank you. I've admired every single part of your body since the day I met you. Literally, since the day I met you."

"Oh, stop."

Even though she was flushed from sex, I could tell she was blushing. I touched her neck and ran my finger down her chest and back up to her cheek. "You're beautiful, Brook. I've always thought that." She didn't answer me so I backed down. I was getting close to a more personal confession, one I didn't want to admit and one she didn't want to hear. "I'm going to take a shower. You should come with me."

I crawled off the bed and padded to the bathroom. I didn't want her to see that I was somewhat upset. I satisfied her, but was it enough?

Was I enough? The nanny. I was a trope. Brook was a single mom, but still. I was the hired help. I wanted to loathe myself, my lack of willpower, but I was hopeless. I wasn't in love with Brook, but I was damn close.

The hot water felt amazing on my sore muscles. I stretched and narrowly missed punching Brook.

"I'm so sorry." I grabbed her head and kissed it before turning to get her under the hot stream.

She laughed. "Mental note, don't sneak up on Cassie in the shower."

I watched as she wet her hair, allowing the water to cascade over her. Her hips flared out just enough from her waist to give her a nice hourglass figure. She was definitely the curvier of the two of us.

"I really like your curves." I washed her back and ran the sponge over her chest and down her legs.

Brook took the loofah from me. "My turn," she said. The soap smelled like oranges and vanilla. I smiled because I'd smelled it on her for weeks. "Holy shit."

"What?"

"Your knees. They're raw." She looked up in surprise.

"I was kind of on them a lot tonight," I said and looked at hers. They, too, were slightly pink.

"No skirts for you for a few days."

She was careful to wash around my knees. By the time we were done, we were wrinkled, laughing, and just being sweet with one another. It was nice. She had terry robes for us on the towel warmer. "Cassie, I owe you. Thank you for a fantastic night. I know that's a weird thing to say, and our dynamic is completely out of the norm, but I really appreciated the time to just lose myself in you."

Her words didn't warm my heart, but I knew what she meant. That was all she could give at the moment, and I relished it.

"Let's go back to bed. We have eight hours before Noah gets home," I said.

She stopped me and pulled me close. "Happy New Year, Cassie."

Before I could say it back, or anything at all, she kissed me, and all the doubt I'd had since we left the bed vanished as I kissed her back.

❖

"Breakfast in bed."

I grumbled when I felt a poke in my back.

"We have only three hours left." Brook handed me a cup of coffee and made me sit up so she could put the tray over my lap.

"Didn't we just go to bed?" I asked.

"You can sleep all day today. I have to wrangle and entertain a six-year-old."

I looked down at the tray. "Wow, you've really outdone yourself. Eggs Benedict?" I lowered my voice. "Oh, my God. Is Patrick downstairs?"

She laughed and took one of the plates off of the tray. "No. It's still just us. I do know how to cook some things. Anthony rubbed off on me, I guess."

I kissed her. "Thank you for fixing me breakfast. That was sweet of you." I tried to figure out how to eat, make love to her, and stretch out the three hours as long as I could. I hated that we fell asleep but was thankful she woke up early and we had this time together.

"Okay, so this is going to sound clingy or whatever, but what happens now? With us, I mean?"

Brook's fork froze midair. Shit. At least I didn't ask her when she had a mouthful of food.

"I'm not really sure. I don't know what the rules are or what happens next. I'm not ready to have a relationship in front of Noah. And I need to be certain that whatever relationship I do have, it's for the right reasons."

My heart landed in my stomach. "So, this was just for fun? I'm confused."

She touched my hand. "No. This wasn't just for fun, but a relationship like this will be hard. I work a lot. I'm fourteen years older. You're still in college with your whole life in front of you. I don't want you to feel any obligation to me. Then there's the added stress of defending our relationship in front of others."

I swallowed hard but didn't look at her. I couldn't. "So, we go back to boss and employee Monday? I just need to know if this was a holiday thing."

She turned so she was facing me. "It wasn't a holiday thing. I don't want to stop, but I don't want you to think that I'm using you for sex. You mean more to me than you can imagine. I just don't think either one of us is in a place for a long-term thing right now."

My heart fluttered back up to my chest and throbbed. Not from excitement but dread. This was not how I wanted to start off the new year. "No, I get it. It's just going to be hard to see you and not want to touch you or lower my guard."

She ran her hand down my cheek and cupped my chin. "It's going to be harder for me. Especially since I know how incredible you are." She sealed that sentiment with a soft kiss. Not a passionate one, but one that hinted of finality. "Let's just have a nice time until Noah gets back. Please?"

I couldn't deny Brook anything. I nodded and ate a bite of toast. It took everything I had to swallow. I sipped my orange juice to get it down. We spent the next hour talking about mundane things like the news and resolutions. She asked me about the rest of my day. I told her I was going to do laundry and see Nana.

"Noah and I will go see my parents. We usually have a dinner over there."

"Sounds like fun. I'm glad Noah has a good relationship with them."

"I love that you genuinely care for him. He's come out of his shell so much this year. I know a lot of it is because of you and the relationship you've carefully built with him. You take the time to listen."

I waved her off. "Some kids are late bloomers. Plus, he's six. And he's quiet and sweet. I couldn't have asked for a better kid. You know the hell I went through with Emma."

I decided it was time to leave this paradise, put on clean clothes, and get my first day of the new year started. Brook was already dressed for the day. "Do you happen to know where my panties are?"

She smiled. "I made a neat little pile for you in the bathroom."

"I'm going to get dressed. Thanks again for the breakfast in bed." I tried to sound chipper, like this final hour wasn't shredding my heart into tiny pieces.

"I'll see you downstairs."

I watched her gather up the dishes and breeze out of the room. How could she be fine? How could she seem so unaffected? I headed to the bathroom and smiled at the folded pile of clothes. My briefs were at the bottom of the pile sans dildo. I wanted to try everything with her.

The tease of wearing it only fueled my desire to fuck her more. I had the emotion and desire to be invested in a relationship. She had a point, though. It was going to be hard with her schedule and mine, but I was willing to try. I went downstairs dressed, my emotions in check.

"Not that I was prying, but you have a ton of missed calls. I kept hearing a buzzing noise in the living room and saw your phone," Brook said.

"Oh, crap. I left it down here last night." For the first time in forever, I didn't care about social media or anything newsworthy. Being cocooned with Brook was the best way to start a new year. I was going to make her notice me, want me, need me. Right then it rang again. "Ugh. It's my mother, probably wanting to wish me a happy new year."

"Maybe you should answer it just in case," Brook said.

"Hello, Mother. What's going on?"

"Cassandra! We've been trying to reach you for hours." My mother's frantic voice was so loud, I had to hold the phone away from my ear. I rolled my eyes at Brook.

"Well, I'm here now."

"Honey, it's Nana. She passed away last night."

I don't remember much after that. My mom said a few more things, but I dropped the phone and slid down the kitchen island until I hit the floor. Brook yelled something at me, but I just shook my head. I watched her pick up my phone and reach for me. I saw nothing after that.

Chapter Twenty-three

When I was in Brook's arms, Nana passed away. They said her heart just gave out. I knew she wasn't feeling well, but I was so eager to be with Brook that I blew her off. That was going to weigh on me the rest of my life.

"Honey, it's not your fault. You talked to her, and she only said she was tired. You have to understand that Nana was just at that age. She wasn't going to last forever," Mom said. She stroked my hair and tried hard to snap me out of my trance.

The funeral was this afternoon. I'd been almost catatonic for three days. After my parents had delivered the horrible news, they'd picked me up from Brook's and taken me home. My father made all the arrangements while my mother consoled me. Her mother had died. I should have been the one consoling her, but my relationship with Nana had helped me in so many ways I never thought she would leave me, voluntarily or not.

"She loved you so much. She always talked about you, even when you and I weren't speaking."

That only made me cry harder. "Why did it have to happen now? We were supposed to have more time together."

"It's unfair. But she wouldn't want you to be sad. You have too much good going on in your life. She would want you to dust yourself off, celebrate her life, and do the best you can with yours."

I cried harder. My mom was right. Nana would be kicking my ass right now if she saw me wallowing in self-pity. I took a deep breath and made myself sit up. Mom handed me a tissue, and I blew my nose. I took another deep breath. "What happens now?"

She took my hands and squeezed them. "Now we go to the funeral, we celebrate Nana, and we get up tomorrow and continue our lives. We never forget though. None of us could forget that sassy woman."

"I'm sorry, Mom. I know you need to mourn, too."

"Nana was an extraordinary woman. I'm just glad she was responsible for raising two strong women." She swayed my hands back and forth with hers until I smiled.

"Okay. Let's go do this. It's time," I said.

We went downstairs, where I sat and ate for the first time in three days. I couldn't eat a lot, but it was enough to appease my family.

"I need to call Brook." It was the first time I'd thought about her as a person and not the reason I missed Nana's death.

"I talked to her. She knows you aren't going to be in all week. She's made other arrangements."

That wasn't the point. I knew she was worried about me. I remembered the look on her face when she talked to my mother. I'd seen concern, fear, sympathy and something I thought was love. "Where's my phone?"

"It's charging in the living room. I turned it off because you were getting a lot of messages and it was distracting."

My mother, the control freak. I took a piece of toast with me and hunted for my phone. I turned it on and waited. I had thirty-eight text messages from friends, but I was most interested in the ten from Brook.

I'm so sorry. I know how important Nana was to you. Are you okay?

And seven more messages of the same. There was a selfie of Noah, who also told me he was sorry and that he missed me. I teared up again. I missed him. I missed them both. It seemed like weeks had passed, but it had been only three nights and four days. I didn't know what to say to Brook, but I needed the connection.

Hi. I'm sorry I haven't responded. It's been crazy over here.

That wasn't entirely true. The last thing I wanted was for Brook to think I was weak or that I was avoiding her. I looked at the time. Shit. Brook was probably in a meeting. I checked my email and gasped when Brook called me twenty seconds later.

"Hi. Are you okay?"

My lip trembled when I heard her voice. It was low and sweet and made the ache in my heart and in my stomach throb. I didn't realize how much I needed her until right then. I took a deep breath to steady myself.

"I decided it was time to get out of bed. The funeral is today."

"I know. We'll be there."

I bit my lip to stop from crying. "You don't have to. Don't pull Noah out of school." I tried to keep the desperation out of my voice. What I wanted to say was yes, be there for me. Let me lean on you.

"I'm really sorry this happened. I know what a strong role model Nana was to you, and I'm just sorry I never got to meet her." She sounded so sincere.

"Thank you. I'm sorry I wasn't able to be there for you and Noah this week. I should be better by Monday."

"Don't even worry about that right now. You just take care of yourself, and we'll figure out things here."

"Thank you, Brook." I hung up before I even gave her a chance to say good-bye. I was too close to tears again and was trying to be strong. I needed to be strong. Mom was right. Nana would have none of this weakness and would scold me if she were here. That made me smile, picturing her scowling at me, her lips pursed, and that judgy "tsk tsk" sound she made. I missed her so much.

"Honey, why don't you take a shower and get ready? I brought some clothes from your place. Brook let me in. I left the bag in your bathroom."

My parents had kept my room the same, even though I hadn't lived there in six years. I was never allowed to have posters or holes in the wall, so it looked like a guest room with a shelf of awards I won in high school for sports and academics. I kept all my photos and cutouts taped to my vanity mirror.

I looked in the bag and found clothes, some makeup, and hair product. It wasn't everything I wanted, but it would work. I was ready to go home. The shock of Nana's death was starting to wear off, and the reality of life without her was setting in. I had to keep going. I peeled off the clothes I'd been in for three days and stood under the water a good five minutes before I even thought about soap.

❖

I stood in the receiving line next to my parents, even though I wanted to sit down and avoid everyone. The more people I saw from Nana's life, the sadder I got. I didn't start crying until I saw Brook, Noah, David, Camila, and Erica enter the church. They made their way down the line, solemnly and respectfully. Brook reached for me, and I melted in her embrace. I tried to be quiet, but it was so hard. She held me tighter and wouldn't let me go. Noah clutched me, clearly confused at my sadness. I held him close while Brook held me. We were delaying the line, but I didn't care. Some guests opted to bypass me to get to my parents, which was fine.

"Be strong, Cassie." She held my face in her hands and looked at me. I saw fierceness. She was protective of me, and that almost made me smile.

I nodded at her, then squatted to see Noah. "Hey, buddy."

He still looked confused. "I miss you, Cassie."

"I miss you, too."

"When are you coming home?"

That innocent question hit me right in the gut. He considered me a part of them. I nodded at him. "Soon. Probably Monday. School starts back up then, right?"

"Yeah, but I want to show you how good I am at *Mario*. Can I come over Sunday?"

"Honey, let's give Cassie some time, okay? She'll let me know when she's home, and when she's ready, you can spend some time with her." Brook gently pulled him back. She gave me a quick nod and moved to give her condolences to my mother and father. Camila hugged me tight, as did David. Erica was dabbing her tears when she got to me and hugged me hard.

"Cass, I'm sorry. I loved the stories you told us about Nana."

She made me smile. One of the nights at the cabin while we were drinking wine around the fire, I'd told them about the time she got us kicked out of the grocery store, their grocery store, because not enough lanes were open. And the time she got banned from the PTA after arguing on my behalf with one of the parents about equality in sports.

"Thanks for coming. It means a lot to me," I said.

She nodded and started crying again. "I'll talk to you later."

My eyes were on Brook the entire time before the funeral started. She looked at me twice, her guarded expression hard to read.

My mom leaned over and whispered, "I can't believe the Wellingtons are here."

"Why not?" I was taken aback.

"I mean, they didn't even know Nana," she said.

"No, but they know me, and I know you don't think they're my friends or that employers and employees can be friends, but we are. The Wellingtons are good people."

She reached for my hand. "I don't mean that in a bad way, sweetie. I just meant it's odd to see them at such a personal event."

"They are wonderful to support me. Us."

"It's time to sit, ladies." If nothing else, my dad's timing was good. My mom and I weren't headed for a fight, but we were in a highly emotional state.

Mom kissed my cheek. "I'm sorry."

I took her hand, and we sat in the first pew before services began. I was heavily armed with tissues in preparation for everyone telling their stories about Nana. I wasn't prepared to give any type of eulogy, but both my parents did. My dad's speech was clever and touched on the happy moments with Nana, but it was my mother's eulogy that broke me.

"My mother not only raised me to be strong, but she helped raise my daughter to be strong, too. I never realized what my mother went through until I became a mother. It's the most challenging and rewarding experience of my life. It was a beautiful thing watching my daughter and my mother create an unbreakable bond. With my mother behind me, supporting me, supporting our family, I was able to make my dreams come true. Late nights and early mornings were tough on the family, but she was always there to lend a hand. She was brave, compassionate, and my true north. I'm going to miss her terribly, but I know she's looking down on us, will always be looking down on us, guiding us in our hearts."

That's when I lost it. I never knew my mother paid attention or understood the relationship I had with Nana, but she did. My father scooted over and held me. I was too exhausted to be strong, so I leaned against his chest and cried. When my mother sat down, she reached for me, and I didn't hesitate. With Nana gone, even though my mother had caused me a lot of heartache, I knew it was time to forgive her. Time was precious.

"That was beautiful, Mom."

I was calm the rest of the service. My parents had a wake afterward, and their house was packed the entire time. I sneaked off to the kitchen for a quiet minute.

"How are you holding up?"

I turned to find Brook standing three feet away from me. Her eyes told me everything. I might never hear the words I wanted to hear, but she was here for me because she cared. My emotions were too raw to have an adult conversation with her.

"This destroyed me," I said.

She reached for me, and I cried in her arms for what felt like forever. People coming into the kitchen turned immediately around to give us privacy.

"I know it did. I'm so sorry, Cassie. I'm sorry I didn't get to meet her or spend time with the both of you," she said.

I pulled back because I really needed to stop. "I'm so tired of crying. I can't possibly have any more tears, you know?" I dabbed at my eyes and nose and tried to smile at her. "Wait, where's Noah?"

"I left him with Mom. She's been spoiling him all week, so there's no rush for you to get back to him. Just take whatever time you need, okay?"

I felt like our night together had been eons ago. "I really need to get back into the swing of things. Next week I need to head to her lawyer's office for a reading of the will, but I don't think it'll interfere with Noah's school."

She held my hands in hers. "Whatever you need, okay?"

I nodded.

She put her forehead against mine and pressed a quick kiss to my lips. "I'm going now. Let me know when you're home again."

"Thank you for coming." I watched Brook slip out the side door. Her support gave me strength to finish the day and deal with all the people who offered their condolences. So many people had loved Nana. She would forever be part of me and always in my heart.

Chapter Twenty-four

I'm *ready to get back to work.*

I almost followed it by saying "Boss," but I was afraid the word would be misconstrued as rude. It was early Sunday evening, and hopefully I wasn't putting a cramp in Brook's alternative plans for daycare. I knew Camila looked after him all last week.

Are you sure? Are you home?

I am—to both. Hi.

Hi. Want to come down for a glass of wine? Noah's working on his homework, and the both of us would love to see you.

It was going to take me a few minutes to try to look normal and get the puffiness out of my eyes. *Give me twenty?*

Take all the time you need. Let yourself in. We'll see you soon.

Instant butterflies. Even through all of the hardships of the last week, my heart still fluttered when Brook gave me attention. My foundation was broken, and Nana's passing had scarred me, but my heart was still beating, and it sped whenever I interacted with Brook.

I decided on a pair of jeans, a loose sweater, and my Ugg booties. I threw my hair up in a bun, added Visine to my burning eyes, and walked into the house. Noah was at the kitchen table finishing his homework, and Brook sat beside him typing away on her laptop.

"Hi," I said. I'd missed her pale-blue eyes and her smile and everything about her.

"Cassie!" Noah raced over to me and hugged me.

"Hey, buddy. I see you're busy with homework."

"It's not bad. Math problems," he said.

I cupped his face and refrained from kissing his cheek. I'd missed them so much.

"Hi. Can I get you a glass of wine?" Brook had stood when I entered the kitchen but allowed me a moment with Noah first. I looked at her red lips and licked my own. I missed tasting her.

"Sure. That'd be nice." I was nervous to be here. So much had happened in the span of a week. I felt like a stranger, yet like I belonged. I didn't know how to act around Brook. I smiled and took the glass from her hand, making sure our fingers didn't touch. I needed to prove to her that I could handle a professional relationship, hell, even a friendship with her.

"How are you doing?"

"I'm okay. Thankful that school doesn't start for another two weeks so I have time to adjust to things." I sat across from them. "Let's see what you're working on."

"I'm almost done. We're learning how to multiply."

"But you're six. Your teacher is assigning multiplication?" I was surprised. When I was six, we concentrated on not eating crayons and paste.

"Do you have math homework at your school?"

I nodded. "I do a lot of algebra to help me figure out how plants breathe."

Noah laughed. "That doesn't make sense. Plants don't have noses or mouths."

I stole a glance at Brook, who wasn't as tense as she was when I first showed up. She was watching Noah and her gaze moved to me. The look was intense, like she had something to say to me but couldn't. It was obvious we had unfinished business. Neither of us moved. Not until Noah repeated himself and nudged me with his elbow.

"What?"

"How do plants breathe if they don't have noses or mouths?"

"It's not really like how you and I breathe, but it's kind of the same process. Leaves have tiny holes that you can't see, and they breathe in bad stuff and breathe out good air. It's called respiration. One day you'll learn about it in science class," I said.

"Oh, okay. I'm done, Mom. Can we play a game real quick before bed?"

Brook quirked her brow at me. "I guess so. What do you want to play?"

"*Mario Kart*. I'll get it set up."

Brook made him put his homework in his backpack before he raced to the living room to start the game. It was just us for a few minutes.

"Your grandmother's service was very nice. She had a lot of friends," Brook said.

I smiled sadly. "Most of them were from bingo and from the neighborhood. She had so much fun with them."

Brook squeezed my hand but pulled away before it meant more than a supportive gesture. I nodded and stood, needing space from her.

"I'm ready, Cassie," Noah shouted.

"On my way."

Noah and I plunged into the game. I was thankful for thirty minutes where I wasn't thinking about Brook, or Nana, or what I was going to do with the rest of my life. At least I'd bridged the gap with my parents, and we were talking again. This morning I'd had a decent conversation with my mom that lasted longer than five minutes.

Brook appeared in the doorway. I hadn't realized she'd left the room. "Okay, Noah. Five more minutes." Her phone rang, taking her from the room again.

"I almost beat you," he said.

I ruffled his hair. "You sure did. Come on. Let's turn this off and get ready for bed."

"Are you staying the night?"

My heart fluttered. What did he know? Did he know what happened at Mountain Ridge? Did Gwen say something? "No. I'll be at my place. Why?"

He shrugged. "I'm not sure. You're sad, and you should be somewhere that makes you happy."

I teared up. He was such an intuitive kid. "Thanks, buddy. But I'll be fine upstairs. Plus, I know where you are, and if I need you, I'll find you."

He hugged me and darted off upstairs. It felt strange to be alone down here. I waited for three long minutes before deciding to leave. I'd see Brook in the morning.

I'm sorry I disappeared. Work. Where'd you go?

My heart skipped at Brook's message.

Upstairs. I figured you had things to do. I'll be down in the morning. I'm ready for structure.

I saw bubbles appear, then disappear, then appear. It was driving me crazy. Two minutes later, I finally got her response.

I understand. Good night, Cassie. Try to get some sleep.

My heart sank. *Okay. Thanks again.*

I turned my phone off, put it on the charger, and decided to binge-watch. I could ignore life for one more day. I could ignore the pinging in my heart, the heaviness in my chest for one more day.

❖

"Good morning, Cassie."

Brook breezed into the kitchen dressed in her black suit and cream-colored blouse. She placed her bag on the counter and fixed a cup of coffee.

"Good morning."

Noah was right behind her, fully dressed and ready to eat.

"Are we going in early today?"

"Yes." Noah and Brook answered in unison.

I couldn't stop myself from smiling at them.

"I have a meeting at eight, but I need to get in early to prep for it," Brook said. She kissed the top of Noah's head and told us to have a good day. She was gone before I even had a chance to tell her to have a good day, too. I sighed.

"Are you hungry?" Noah asked.

"Since it's a new year, let's go to McDonald's."

"I've never been. Do they have breakfast?" he asked.

"They have some of the best breakfast foods. I survived college on McDonald's breakfasts."

"But you're still in college," he said.

"It's like different schools. You know how you're in elementary school now, and in a few years you'll be in middle school? Well, I'm in the middle school of college."

"Whoa. How many schools are there?" He looked so concerned.

"A lot. It depends on how much you need to learn. Like you'll probably go to middle school and high school and college. You can go to special schools after that, like your mom studied business at a special school."

"How long is it going to take?"

"About sixteen years."

"Sixteen years!" He slapped his palm to his forehead and groaned.

"Yes, and you'll do well and love it the entire time. Come on. We'll grab McDonald's, then head to school. What's new and exciting there?"

"Nothing. Same stuff. A lot of kids got gaming systems. Do you know about *Halo*?"

"Yes, and you just be happy you have your gaming system. That's not for you for a long time." I understood Brook's hesitancy, especially with online gaming. But I also understood technology and the importance of advancement. I loved playing online, but I was old enough to know the dangers. Noah was just getting started. "Grab your stuff and let's go. There's an Egg McMuffin with my name on it."

"Do they have milk?"

"Of course. Come on. Let's go."

Noah wanted to eat inside, so I parked and watched him skip ahead of me and wait at the door. How had this kid never been to McDonald's before? The menu proved to be too much for Noah, so I ordered for him. We took our time and hung out eating, talking, and sharing stories about our trip.

"Snowboarding was the best part," he said.

"You're pretty good at it. Like a natural."

"Maybe I'll be in the Olympics or X Games."

That was another little secret we shared. I loved watching the extreme sports, and Noah had gotten hooked on them, too. It wasn't on the banned list, but I wasn't sure Brook would approve. "Maybe so. You'll have to practice a lot. Finish your milk, little man, and let's get to school." I checked the time. We had thirty minutes to get there. That would still give him time with his friends.

I decided to go to Nana's after I dropped Noah off, just so I could start sorting through her things. I didn't want to give stuff away since she had a will, even though I knew she'd want the nursing home she visited to have her craft stuff and the church to have her clothes.

"See you later, Cassie."

"Hey. When do you want me to pick you up?"

"After school. I missed you."

My heart lodged in my throat as I blinked back tears. If he only knew how much I'd missed him, too. I nodded and waved because I was too emotional to talk.

Chapter Twenty-five

McDonald's? Brook texted after Noah went to bed.

Busted. But really? The kid's never been? He's six.

He talked about it all night. During his bath and when I tucked him in.

I know I should have asked, but it was a moment of weakness. Forgive me? That was a little flirtier than I intended.

Okay, but keep the trips to a minimum. Now that we have gaming in our lives, I need to make sure he stays active and doesn't build unhealthy habits.

Patrick keeps him healthy. And the school's lunches are impressive.

Do you have a copy of the school menu?

I had lunch there a while back.

Oh.

I smiled. That was kind of a jealous-girlfriend response. I wanted to push back, but I didn't want her to run away again. I missed her. I missed our intimacy. I wasn't ready to give up, even though she gave me no encouragement.

Have a good night. I'll see you in the morning. No McDonald's.

My phone rang. Perfect timing.

"How are you holding up?" Lacy's voice was a blessing. I was a bit disappointed that it wasn't Brook, but happy to hear a familiar voice.

"I'm okay. I spent time at Nana's today. It's amazing how much stuff she had."

"When's the reading?"

"Tomorrow. Can you believe that?"

"Wow. Well, that's actually good, because then you all can start moving and get her things to the right people and organizations."

"I think Mom's going to help me this week. She had a few things to finish today but has the rest of the week off." I spread out the blanket on my couch and snuggled into its warmth.

"Cassie, I'm so proud of you. I know losing Nana was the worst thing, but I'm happy you made amends with your parents. And we both know Nana would be super happy, too."

"I can't cry any more. I'm out of tears. And if it wasn't for Noah and Patrick, I probably wouldn't have eaten today. I need to do a better job of taking care of myself."

"Do you want some company?"

I knew I should have tried harder, but I was exhausted. "Thanks, but I'm just going to go to bed. I'm back at work this week, so my day starts at seven."

"Let me know if you need anything."

"Maybe I'll stop by the Pearl tomorrow night, and you can feed me and keep me hydrated." I felt like I'd lost five pounds over the last ten days, and my energy was waning. Today was the first day I'd eaten more than one meal in a single day since Nana died.

"You're on, sister."

I hung up, set the alarm, and fell asleep immediately.

❖

"Excuse me, what?" I clearly didn't understand what the lawyer was saying.

"It's all yours, Cassandra. The house and everything inside, her life-insurance policy. She asked that a donation of ten thousand dollars be made to the Nature Conservancy, and she said you would know what to do with all her belongings."

I put my head in my hands and sobbed. Not because she gave me everything, but because everything was final. I had nothing to cling to. I had to move on without her. She was my rock, my best friend, my strength.

"It's okay, honey." Again, my mom was comforting me when I should have been consoling her. Neither of my parents was surprised at the outcome. I wouldn't have been surprised to find out they already knew. Nana had written each of us a letter. Her lawyer passed them out, and I cried even harder. I couldn't read mine. I tucked it into my jacket, thanked my father for his handkerchief, and stepped out of the office to keep myself from embarrassing the family.

One of the lawyers peeked out of the office. "Cassandra, before you leave, you'll have to sign some papers."

After another minute of normal breathing, I went back inside. My parents were discussing their own matters while I signed my name on all the pages flagged with red tabs. The lawyer handed me copies of everything, and twenty minutes later, I was in my car driving with no destination. It was a lot to process. The money would get me through school, even after the sizable donation to the Nature Conservancy. I smiled. Nana did that on purpose. She left me just enough to keep me out of debt, but not enough to make me irresponsible. She was frugal in life and in death.

"Hi, Mom." I answered on the second ring.

"You holding up okay? I know that was hard." She sounded tired.

"I am. How about you?"

"It's been a tough couple of months, that's for sure," she said.

"I'm sorry I caused so much grief for everyone." It seemed so petty now. I was willing to walk away from everything. Now I'd give anything to have all that time back.

"Baby, it's just a part of growing up. Did Nana ever tell you about the time I ran away?"

I laughed. "You? You legit ran away from home?"

"I was seventeen and wanted to go to a concert, and Nana didn't want me to. It wasn't really the band she was against. It was the guy I was dating. He was older and nothing but trouble, but I wouldn't listen to reason. She told me no, so I packed a bag and left for five days."

"Nana didn't hunt you down and drag you back? That amazes me." I pictured her banging on doors and cursing everyone until she found my mom.

"Oh, no. After four days, I was done living in my car. I was desperate for a shower, and I just wanted my simple life back. I walked into the kitchen like I was never gone. Mom fixed me a sandwich and told me the next time, she'd change the locks."

"She definitely was sassy." I pulled into the driveway of what was now my house. The bungalow was small, but so much of her personality was in those walls. She and Papa had downsized when they retired. It was perfect for them. Three bedrooms, two baths, and a backyard full of trees and bushes. Nana liked to garden and had tons of flowerpots on the front porch and on the back deck. It was going to take months to get through all her things.

"I miss her, too. I'll see you tomorrow. Let me know when you want me over." Mom disconnected the call while I sat in my car. It was so quiet here. The neighborhood was a community of older people who looked out for one another. I didn't know where I belonged, but I didn't belong here.

By the end of the week, Mom and I had gone through all Nana's clothes and donated them to her church. I kept an overcoat of hers, a few scarves, and costume jewelry that was so old, it was back in style again. We decided to have an estate sale in a few months for the furniture and things we didn't want to keep. Four days and a full weekend, and Mom and I were spent. I wasn't complaining, though. It allowed me to keep my mind off Brook and spend time with Mom. Talking about times with Nana all week was therapeutic for both of us.

"Are you sure you don't want to come over for dinner?" My mom leaned down to see my face through the car window.

"Thanks, but I need some downtime. I need to go do mindless things and eat greasy cheeseburgers and fries drenched in ketchup and mayo," I said.

"Promise me you'll eat something healthy. I don't need you to wither away." She reached in and tucked my hair behind my ear. I was surprised at the gesture. My mother was never a touchy-feely person.

"I promise. Don't stay late. You have a busy day tomorrow, too." I pulled out of the driveway and headed back to my place, stopping for fast food along the way. Tonight I'd sift through some paperwork, read letters Nana wrote Papa when he was stationed overseas, and play video games.

During the week I was back and forth from Nana's house to the Wellington estate. I took care of Noah in the morning, sifted through Nana's stuff until three, then headed back to school to collect him until seven, then drove back to Nana's until ten or eleven. Nana was a pack rat. The pantry, the closets, the shelves were all stacked with things. Every bit of available space was utilized. I had one more week to get as much done as possible before school started.

Are you home?

I sat up. It was Brook. She had a thing for texting me Sunday evenings.

I just got back from Nana's.

How are things going?

Brook knew I was splitting my time between here and Nana's. I told her it wouldn't be a problem to still do my job and deal with Nana's property. She seemed taken aback when I told her it wouldn't take time away from Noah.

We did a lot this week and weekend and haven't even touched the basement. Mom and I decided to have an estate sale in a few months.

If you need help, I know people.

That made me smile.

Thank you.

About an hour later, Brook texted me again.

What are you doing now?

Trying not to fall asleep. You?

Trying not to miss you as much as I do.

Her words shot me off the couch. I stood there, holding the phone in both hands, and stared at it. There were more bubbles.

I shouldn't have said that. I'm sorry. You have so much going on right now, and I'm being selfish.

I was already racing to the bathroom to take a quick two-minute shower and slip into fresh clothes. I checked my phone but found no other texts from Brook. I raced through the garage and texted her.

Open the door.

Bubbles appeared and disappeared. I waited two minutes by the door, willing to give her five. When I heard the chime of the alarm being disabled, I stood tall.
"I didn't mean for you to come down," she said.
I knew she was lying. I pulled her toward me and kissed her. I missed her mouth, and she pressed herself against me. She was warm and soft and wearing nothing under her robe. I broke the kiss and stepped away from her.
"You're beautiful." I opened the robe completely and ran my fingers over her curves. Goose bumps spread over her skin and her nipples puckered. "And I can't tell you how much I've missed you."
She touched my face. "You scared me when you didn't answer me."
"I had to wash off the day at Nana's. Let's go somewhere warm and private." I led her by the hand up the stairs to her bedroom and locked the door in case Noah wandered in.
I just needed her. I needed to be inside her, lose myself in her touch, forget about everything but her. I pushed back the covers and

slid the robe off her shoulders. She stood naked and proud in front of me. I pulled off my T-shirt while she worked on my sweats. I was wearing only those two articles of clothing and slippers.

"You've lost weight," she said. She ran her hands delicately over my rib cage and across my stomach. I shivered at her touch.

"It's been a really shitty month until now."

"I haven't helped at all," she said.

"That's not true." I didn't want to talk. I wanted to touch her and hold her. I wanted to bury myself in her warmth and forget about time and my problems. I crawled onto the bed and gently pulled her toward me. "Come here. Let's slide under the covers and get warm."

She slipped underneath me and pulled my hips to rest against hers. It took about thirty seconds of kissing before I felt like I was on fire. I rolled my hips against hers and pushed against her wetness. I slipped my hand between us and rubbed the moisture up and down her slit until I reached her clit and gently circled it with my finger. Brook bucked against my hand.

"I need more, Cass. Please don't tease me." Her voice held a note of desperation that empowered me, made me feel like I was the best lover she'd ever had.

I leaned back so I could watch her face as I entered her. Her mouth opened and her breath hitched when I pushed two fingers deep inside. She gave a moan so guttural I stopped, afraid I'd hurt her.

"Don't stop. Please don't stop."

I leaned over her, supported myself on my elbow, and fucked her hard and fast. She spread her knees farther apart and dug her heels into the mattress. Her hips rocked against my hand. We kissed hard, and when she came, she shouted in total abandonment. I quickly put my hand over her mouth, afraid we'd wake Noah.

"You have to be quiet," I whispered.

Her breath was labored, and she still shook with aftershocks, but she nodded. I slowly removed my hand from her mouth to find her smiling at me.

"He's not going to wake up. He sleeps so hard."

"Unlike Gwen, who hears everything," I said.

"She's probably got this place bugged."

We both laughed, and I looked at her. "I missed you, too."

She pulled my forehead down to hers. "What are we going to do?"

She closed her eyes and repeated the question. This was more than just sex. I think she'd wanted it to be simple and easy, but something had happened along the way. We'd both slipped. Not that I thought she would admit it, but she couldn't let me go.

"Why do we have to put a label on this? Why does this have to be explained?" I thought I hid my desperation well, but when she touched my cheek, I knew I'd failed.

"It's not fair to tell you one thing, then invite you up to my bedroom. It's fucked up, I know," she said.

"Brooklyn Wellington."

She looked at me. "Yes, Cassandra Miller. What can I do for you?"

"Go to dinner with me. Like on a date."

She covered her face with her hand. I leaned down and gently kissed her knuckles. "Come on. It'll be low-key, somewhere fun, but we'll have to get a babysitter for Noah. I can't do both."

Her hand still covered her face, but she nodded. Brook Wellington, COO of a multi-million-dollar corporation, smart, beautiful, and so extremely fuckable, had just agreed to go out on a date with me.

"I'll pick you up Friday at eight. That'll give you enough time to find a place for Noah and change from your power suit into something casual," I said.

"Are you leaving?"

"No. Why?"

"Because you asked me for a date for next weekend, and we still have"—she leaned back to look at the clock—"we still have three hours and eighteen minutes before we need to focus on sleep."

"Yes, but I knew we'd be busy for the next three hours and eighteen minutes and wanted to ask you just in case we accidentally fell asleep."

"You're a romantic," she said.

I shrugged. "I wanted to ask you before somebody else did."

She skillfully flipped me and straddled my hips. "There's no one else, Cassie. I promise."

Chapter Twenty-six

To say I was nervous was a giant understatement. Brook got home early and took Noah to Lauren's for the weekend. She gave Patrick the night off. I told Brook our date was going to be casual, but I was having a hard time finding something to wear. I wanted to look beautiful and decided on a V-neck sweater, jeans, and low suede boots. I styled my hair and put on makeup that was a little bolder than I was used to, but I looked hot.

My plans included dinner at a little Mexican restaurant Lacy and I'd discovered as undergrads and ice-skating at a rink that was far enough away from home, but still easy to get to. After that, I planned to suggest a nice glass of wine by the fireplace. Her fireplace. Friday night was a popular date night, but since it snowed, I didn't think places would be crowded. At eight o'clock sharp, I rang the front doorbell.

"Get in here, you goof." Brook pulled me in by the lapels of my coat and kissed me. "Why didn't you come in through the mudroom?"

I handed her a single red rose. "Because this is a first date, and I didn't want to assume anything."

She wrapped her arms around my waist. "Well, we kind of did things backward here."

I put my hand on my heart as if in shock. "What? Whatever do you mean?" I blushed when she whispered exactly what she meant in my ear. "Okay, okay. I'm trying to do the right thing, that's all." I watched as she found a bud vase for her rose. I knew it wasn't much, but I think she appreciated the gesture.

"Would you like to call David Wellington, too? You know, to

really do the right thing?" She winked at me playfully and grabbed her coat. "Come on. Let's get out of here before I decide we're staying in."

"Trust me. Your fireplace comes into play later, but you're right. Let's get out of here and have a different kind of fun." I grabbed her hand and walked her to the garage.

"Let's take the Range Rover. It's four-wheel drive," Brook said.

"Do you still want me to drive it, or do you want to?" I didn't want to assume, especially since it was her car.

"You've driven it more, and you planned the date. You drive it."

She gave me the single nod and walked over to the passenger side. I slipped into the driver's seat and backed out of the garage. I was giddy as fuck but didn't want to seem like a kid on a first date. She looked cool and calm, as if we'd been dating for months. "I like what you're wearing."

"You said casual, so I listened."

Brook Wellington was wearing flannel. It wasn't hipster bro flannel, but form-fitting pink-and-black flannel that accentuated her breasts and small waist. The shirt was tucked into black ankle jeans, and she wore warm winter boots that hit just below her knee. Her hair was loose and curly, the way I liked it, and her makeup light. She smelled like sandalwood. "You're adorable."

"Am I too casual?"

"Not at all. I actually have chainsaw ice sculpting on the agenda. You'll fit right in."

She gaped at me, then playfully punched my shoulder.

"Ow." I rubbed the spot. "Do not impair the driver."

"You're not even out of the driveway yet."

I stopped the car before we reached the gate, put it in park, and kissed her softly on her lips. "Thank you for agreeing to this date. I know this scares you, but I want you to know I'm taking this seriously."

She cupped my cheek. "I know you are. You'll have to bear with me as I deal with everything. Emotionally I'm going to be all over the place. But I promise not to shut down if things get too much. One day at a time, okay?"

I nodded and continued down the drive. I was in heaven. If only I could share this with Nana. Of course, it would have taken me months to tell her, but I think she would have approved. Eventually. Maybe she was smiling down at me. No, probably scolding me.

"Is tonight a surprise, or are you going to tell me?" She reached over and touched my thigh. The muscle twitched under her hand.

"Dinner, ice-skating, and incredible sex by the fireplace."

She laughed at my honesty. "Okay, I'm in, but I'm not the greatest skater. You'll have to massage me if I fall."

"Especially if you fall on your ass."

"Definitely if I do."

After two margaritas, Brook was flirty and relaxed in a way I'd never seen her before. I stopped after one, but when she ordered the second one, I didn't stop her.

"Remember, we have to be on skates in thirty minutes," I said as I watched her drain the last of her glass.

In the middle of the restaurant, in front of a solid crowd, she kissed me. It was so playful, and yet I looked around, worried that somebody had seen. Nobody seemed to care. I took a deep breath and focused all my attention on her.

"Tell me about your dreams when you were a little girl. What did you want to do with your life?" I asked.

"I don't know that I even had dreams."

"Oh, come on. You didn't want to write a best seller, or be a rock star, or be a movie star. You could have been on the runway or had some modeling career."

She held my hand, running her thumb over my fingers. "I'm not that pretty. You're just smitten with me."

"Smitten? Who says smitten?"

Brook covered her mouth with her hand. "You're right. That dated me. Don't forget, I am a lot older than you are."

I leaned forward so my lips were close to hers. "You don't act it, you don't look it, and you certainly don't fuck like it."

"Mmm. I so love a woman in control."

Our waiter walked by, and I asked him for the check. Perfect timing.

Brook leaned back and smiled. "You're buying dinner, too?"

"This is a date. Of course I'm buying. And I'm paying for your skate rental. But the wine in front of the fire will come from your bar," I said. The waiter handed me the check. "Let's get out of here so we can make out in the car. That's mature, right?"

"I'm in." Brook grabbed her jacket and followed me out of the restaurant. "How far away is the rink?"

"About ten minutes away. Are you cold?"

"No. I'm good. It's not too bad out. It's the wind that makes winter bad."

"Agreed."

She kissed me as soon as we slipped into the car. While the makeout session had been my idea, I changed my mind when I realized the car was parked in front of the large restaurant window, where everyone could see us. "We should go. I want you all to myself without an audience." I pointed to the patrons. Brook giggled and sat back in her seat.

"I'll hold you to that," she said.

I backed out of the spot and headed to Holiday Skating Rink, a seasonal outdoor rink that was borderline overdecorated with inflatable snowmen, reindeer, and garland that looped around the entire rink. More people were there than I expected. Brook wasn't as good on skates as she was on skis, but she was still impressive. I whizzed by her, skating backward, showing off. She rolled her eyes and chased me. I wasn't expecting that and lost my balance trying to skirt around a little kid. Falling backward sucked because you inevitably hit your head. Thankfully, my slouchy beanie helped cushion the slam against the ice, but damn, it hurt. Brook fell into me, so we were a heap of tangled arms and legs. She started laughing once she realized I wasn't hurt. I rubbed my head and laughed, too. She kissed me and made me forget about the throbbing ache at the base of my neck, giving me a throbbing ache somewhere else.

"Aunt Brook?"

We both looked up at the little kid who'd accidentally tripped me. It was Frances, Gwen's daughter, wrapped up in a snowsuit, hat, and mittens, completely unidentifiable except for her chubby cheeks and familiar blue eyes.

"Frances. Hi, baby. What are you doing here?" Brook clambered off me, accidentally kicking me with her skate.

I hissed at the pain and tried to get up quickly, too, but slipped and fell down again.

"What's going on here, Brook?" Gwen. My nemesis loomed over both of us.

"Gwen, hi. How are you?" I smiled and nodded, not as afraid of her as I used to be, but I still felt guilty.

"So, it's true. I thought maybe the ski trip was just a quick fuck because she's the nanny and that's what rich people do. But this? Are you two together? Are you dating your nanny?"

Brook put her hands on her hips. "Whatever's going on here, it's none of your business."

"Hi, Cassie." Frances looked down at me.

I found my footing and struggled into a standing position. "Hi, Frances. I didn't know you could ice-skate. You're pretty good."

She smiled at me. "Want to skate with me?" She held her hand out and automatically I reached for it, but Gwen whipped her away from me.

"Don't touch my daughter." I saw so much hatred in the way she looked at me that I actually flinched.

"Settle down, Gwen."

"We'll talk about this later." They skated away.

Brook turned to me. "Well, that was a combination of awkward and total bullshit." She took a deep breath and laughed nervously.

"I'm sorry." I didn't know what else to say.

"You didn't know she lived around here. It's not your fault." She pulled me closer and swung my arms back and forth with hers until I relaxed and smiled. "Come on. Let's get out of here. We'll definitely have more privacy at the house."

"Music to my ears." I followed her to the skate-rental place, and we quickly slipped into our boots. Brook visibly relaxed once we were in the car driving away. We were both quiet. I was worried about the fallout of Gwen seeing us on the ice and how Brook would process it. "Hey, are you okay?"

Brook nodded. "I just hate that she ruined a perfectly good chase."

I played along. "You never would've caught me."

She reached over and squeezed my thigh. "Don't be too sure. I always get what I want." Her fingers sliding up my leg made me shiver with anticipation.

"Always?" I asked.

"Always."

The fifteen-minute drive felt like it took forever. I was trying to pay attention to the roads because there was still a good amount of snow on them, but her hand making its journey up to the soft area between my legs made it almost impossible to concentrate. I jerked under the pressure of her fingers and moaned in appreciation when she tapped her fingertip right on my clit. I spread my legs apart to give her better access. "You're killing me."

She turned in her seat so she was facing me. "Do you want me to stop?"

"Yes, no. I don't know." I was torn. I just wanted to get home safely and then fuck her a thousand different ways, but this foreplay was so erotic and something we shouldn't be doing. When she unbuttoned my jeans, I slowed down. I was driving twenty in a forty zone. The driver behind me wasn't happy.

"You're so warm and wet," she said. She leaned over and kissed my cheek softly. When I felt her teeth tug at my earlobe, my whole body jerked and the car swerved. "Stay in your lane. We're almost home," she whispered.

By the time we got through the gate and into the garage, I was so ready to come. I barely had the car in park before Brook released her seat belt and bent over me. I slid down my jeans and panties and groaned when her tongue touched my clit. I grabbed the steering wheel and the back of the passenger side seat and pushed my head back. I wasn't going to last. I wanted to feel her inside me, but the restrictiveness of the car prevented that. We had all night, and this was a delicious appetizer.

"Yes, Brook, yes." I held her hair back and tried hard not to buck against her mouth. She knew how to please me, and as much as I wanted to draw this out, I really wanted to take this inside. I came hard. The rushing sound of my heartbeat filled my ears as I gasped for air. Brook kissed me firmly and left the car. I waited ten seconds to catch my breath and pull up my pants.

I found her coat on the floor of the mudroom and hung it on the coatrack. Her boots, smack-dab in the middle of the kitchen, almost tripped me. I booted them aside. It wasn't until I found her sweater on the floor that I realized she was stripping. I slipped my sweater over my head and kicked off my boots. By the time I reached the hearth room, she was down to bra and panties. I paused because she took my breath away. "You're so beautiful."

"Get over here. And grab a few blankets."

I fell trying to walk and take my jeans off. My fall wasn't graceful, and I should have been embarrassed, but when I looked up at Brook, she simply smiled and crooked her finger at me. I ripped off my jeans and crawled over. She slowly dropped to her knees and met me in front of the fireplace.

"That was sexy as hell," she said.

I kissed her because she made me feel beautiful and alive and happier than I'd ever been. I was exactly where I wanted to be. "Thank you for saying that."

"I mean it. Let's get this fire started and see how we can entertain ourselves."

I couldn't help myself from touching her skin. She was so soft and hard at the same time. Brook was a solid ten. She was perfection. Aside from our frosty start, I couldn't find anything wrong with her.

I couldn't believe how drastically my life had changed. In a year's time, I'd had my plush life taken away, but I'd landed the perfect job to get me through graduate school. I'd lost someone I loved very much but found Brook, who was helping me piece my heart back together. When I was with her, the sadness was bearable. I was able to focus more on the good memories and not the fact that Nana was no longer in my life.

"You have a faraway look in your eyes. Are you okay?" Brook turned away from the fire she was building to watch me.

Right now, I had Brook's attention, all of it, and our togetherness was perfect. I could only nod. A lump formed in my throat, and I swallowed hard at how important this moment was. I was in love with her. As ridiculous as it sounded, she completed me.

"Ta da! Fire. Now let's get under the blankets and finish what we started back there." She lifted her eyebrow at me.

This wasn't just about sex. She felt something for me, too, whether she showed it or not.

"Yes, Brookie."

She straddled my hips and looked down at me. "Didn't we discuss you never calling me that?"

I pointed to the clock. "But it's after seven, and you aren't my boss at this moment."

"Oh, really?"

She kissed my neck, scraping her teeth along my sensitive skin. She wasn't gentle about it, and I didn't mind one bit.

"Who's in charge here?" She cupped my breasts and pulled down the lace of my bra. My nipple sprang free, and I moaned when she sucked it into her mouth.

"Me."

She moved her mouth away. "Are you sure about that?"

I raised up on my elbows and tugged her bottom lip with my teeth. Once she succumbed to a deep kiss, I flipped her so she was on her back. "I'm a hundred percent sure I'm in charge." I kissed her hard and spread her legs with mine.

She wrapped her arms around my shoulders. "I guess I can give up control for a night."

"Just one little night?"

She kissed me softly, surprising me with her tenderness. "Or a few."

"Or whenever we want."

"Or that."

I kissed her softly to let her know I was serious. That kiss grew into something more emotional and less playful. She unhooked her bra, and I followed her movements as an excuse to touch her. "You're so smooth." I ran my tongue over her breasts and down her stomach until I reached the soft skin right above the waistband of her panties. A gentle tug and she lifted her hips. I was dying to taste her again. I caressed the inside of her thighs until she completely relaxed. We might have rushed in the garage, but I was going to appreciate every minute we had until it was time to rejoin civilization.

"If I fall asleep, it's on you," she said.

"Oh, really?" I ran my tongue over her slit, making her jerk at the unexpected touch.

"Okay, maybe not."

I felt the soft caress of her hand on my head. She didn't want me to leave the apex of her thighs. I adjusted my seduction, spreading her apart and running my tongue up and down her warmth. I belonged here. This wasn't about control or who was the boss. This was about so much more, and even if we weren't going to say the words, the feelings were there. Her touches were softer, longer, and the looks she gave me spoke volumes.

"Roll over," she said.

Without hesitation, I did as she asked and waited. Brook surprised me by turning around so we could taste one another at the same time. I brought her to my mouth while spreading my legs for her. It was perfect. I needed both hands to hold her hips in place. When she slid two fingers inside me, I moaned. How she could use her mouth and fuck me at the same time in this position overwhelmed me. I held off as long as I could. The more I moved my hips, the more she did, too. I dug my fingers into her skin, doing my best to hold her in place, but when Brook did something, she was all in. My mouth was numb, and I was breathing hard, but I refused to stop. We came at the same time, gasping for breath, moaning with pleasure. Perfect, even if she wasn't ready to admit or accept it.

"Fuck." Brook's voice broke. She slid off me and rested in the crook of my arm.

"Well said."

She laughed breathlessly. "You are amazing."

I tilted her chin toward me so I could look into her eyes. "No, Brook. You are." I looked away because I knew she could read my emotions. I made a big production of covering us with the blankets so that she couldn't see my face. I knew my feelings showed. I couldn't hide the fact that I loved her. But as much as I wanted to profess it, she wasn't ready to hear it.

Chapter Twenty-seven

I didn't hear from Brook all day or night. After such a perfect date, I would have expected to. But that morning I woke to a screaming match between her and Gwen. Gwen had taken the liberty of letting herself into Brook's house to tell her I was a gold-digging whore. She was pretty angry when she found us asleep together in front of the fireplace.

Brook said I did a good job defending myself, but I was so stressed I couldn't even eat. I avoided calls from my mother and Lacy, promising Brook I would let her handle things. That meant keeping to myself and trusting her to do the right thing.

Mid-afternoon I got a text from Brook.

Hi Cassie. Can we play Switch?

It was a text from Noah on Brook's phone. While the note was endearing, my heart sank that it wasn't from Brook.

Where's your mom?

Here.

I assumed she knew he'd invited me over, so I primped for a few minutes, grabbed the Switch, and headed downstairs. The door was open, and Noah was sitting at the counter drinking a glass of milk.

"Cassie. Hi."

"Hey, buddy. What are you doing in here?"

"I needed a snack. Yay. You brought your Switch. We can play it on here and then play *Mario* in the living room."

I sat and handed him the system, then casually turned in the chair and looked for Brook. I could hear people talking, but I didn't know if the television was on in the other room or if Brook had somebody over.

"Noah, is somebody here besides your mom?"

"Yeah. Grandma, Grandpa, Aunt Erica, and Aunt Gwen. They're having a meeting."

I stood. "Noah, does your mom know you invited me down?"

He looked at me quizzically. "You're always invited. You're family."

I leaned down to face him. "Honey, you can't just invite me down without your mom knowing. It's just better if you tell her." His eyes started to water, and I immediately backpedaled. "You didn't do anything wrong, buddy. I'm glad you texted me. You know I love playing games with you. It's just on the weekends, you need to check with her first."

"What are you doing here?" The venom in Gwen's voice was unmistakable.

I froze because this was going to be hard to explain, even to Brook. "I was invited."

Gwen scoffed. "Bullshit. Look at you, all comfortable like you belong here. Guess what? You don't."

I pointed at her. "Watch your mouth around Noah. You might be his aunt, but this is his house, and I'm pretty sure Brook doesn't like swearing, aunt or not."

"Cassie, what are you doing here?" Brook walked in and stood between me and Gwen.

"Noah invited me. I thought you were okay with it. I'm so sorry I'm interrupting." I held my hands up and backed away slowly.

"No, stay. I'm glad you're here. We all need to talk." She reached for my hand.

I tentatively took it and allowed her to lead me into the living room. All eyes were on me the second I entered.

"Cassie." Erica hugged me and squeezed my arms when she finally let me go. "It's so good to see you."

Gwen slithered past us to stand next to her parents.

"What's going on?" I asked, even though I was a hundred percent sure this was about me.

"Everyone thinks you're out for our money." Gwen's smile was crooked, borderline evil.

"Shut up, Gwen. That's not even true. Quit trying to speak for us," Erica said.

Looking around the room, I understood why Brook was so good at masking her emotions. With the exception of Erica, I couldn't read the room at all. "I didn't mean to crash your family meeting, but since I'm here, let's talk about it. What do you want to know?"

"Not a word, Gwen," Camila said quickly.

I held my head high and sat in a chair. "It's okay. I know Gwen's opinion." I wanted this relationship to work, but in order to have everyone's support, I was going to have to fight for it.

"Cassie, this is not an inquisition. You don't have to be here." I could hear the discomfort in Camila's voice.

"Oh, I want to. What have I missed so far? Or should I take a stab at it?" I really wanted to get up and pace, but I needed everyone to know I could handle a conversation that involved my reputation, my integrity, and my intentions, so I crossed my ankles and rested my hands in my lap. "I get it. You guys are old-money wealthy. I would be skeptical of everyone, too. Here's the thing, though. I took this job because I needed it. I didn't single Brook out. I didn't demand the job. Hell, I didn't even know she was looking for someone."

"If it wasn't Brook, it was going to be somebody else," Gwen said.

"To nanny for? Definitely. To fall in love with? No. You can't plan that."

"Sweetheart, you're so young. Do you even know what love is at your age?" Camila took a few steps toward me.

"No disrespect, Camila, but weren't you pregnant with Brook when you were my age? I'm not as young as you all make me out to be. I deserve love, too." I had to stand. Too many people looking down on me was hard to take.

"Good point, Cassie." Erica was practically cheerleading.

"I don't need your money. I don't need Brook's money. I'm not sure if Brook told you, but my grandmother left me very comfortable. I don't even need this job anymore, but I love it. I love Brook and I love Noah, and I still want to get my degree and make a difference in their lives and hopefully in the world. Brook and I haven't discussed feelings at all, but she has to know how I feel about her." I glanced at her, but she remained emotionless.

"You've barely started your life, Cassie. How do you know this is what you want?" Camila asked.

"How do you know it's not?"

"Cassie, I'm fourteen years older. When I'm fifty, you'll be thirty-six. That's a big difference. I'd hate to think you gave up anything for me," Brook said.

While I appreciated Brook breaking up the exchange, I hadn't expected her sentiment, or lack thereof. I held my hands up. "Nobody's listening to me." I turned to Erica when she made a small noise. "Except for you, and I love you for it. Every single person here got the chance to love somebody and make a life together when they were my age. None of you had a guarantee it would work out. I'm not saying this will turn into what you all have, but at least give us the chance to try. My intentions are true."

"Okay. I'm done being quiet." Erica stood up and joined our weird little circle in the middle of the room. "Cassie's right. Every single one of us had obstacles, and every single one of us had a chance. This isn't our decision. This is between these two. Cassie's heart is in the right place. We all know her. She's wonderful with the kids. She cares for Brook. Look at her face. Short of tattooing it on her forehead, the message is clear."

Again, all eyes were on me. I was already flushed from anger and defending myself, but I reddened even more.

"I just don't want to see Brook being taken advantage of. You know what happened the last time. Hell, the nanny's already driving her car and living on the property. How long before she's on the bank accounts?"

"That's enough, Gwen," Brook hissed.

"You don't see it because sex is clouding your judgment."

"Don't you wish you were lucky like me," Brook said.

"All right. Listen up. I understand Gwen's concern," David said.

My heart fell. He'd been quiet this whole time, and I hoped his silence was because he was on my side, but I wanted to let his daughters hash it out.

He walked over and put his arm around Brook's shoulders. "But this is none of our business. Erica's right. We know Cassie. And everybody here has had their share of scandal. People are always going to look for a weakness in the Wellingtons. It's our job as a family to stick together and support one another. Gwen, if Brook and Cassie want to date, let them. If people want the scoop on their relationship, then I'm sure you'll defend it or say nothing at all. That's what Wellingtons do. Are we clear?"

And just like that, the tension in the room fizzled. When David Wellington made up his mind, the whole family apparently did.

Camila pulled me to the side. "I know you care for our Brookie, but just know she's had a lot happen in her life, and I don't want to see her hurt. I think you're wonderful, and you might just be what she needs."

"I promise I have no desire to hurt her or Noah. I really care for both of them." I clutched her arm harder than I should have because I wanted her to know that I was serious.

She patted my hand until I released the pressure and apologized. "I know, dear. My heart is telling me to trust you."

"I really appreciate your support."

"Cassie? Are we going to play?"

Noah's little voice silenced the room. Even Gwen stopped scowling.

I reached for his hand and smiled when his little fingers slipped into mine. "Hey, buddy. We sure can. Why don't you set it up, and we'll play?"

"That's our cue," David said. He motioned for everyone to leave, hugging Brook and ruffling Noah's hair on the way out. He gave me a wink. It was enough to make me smile.

"I expect to hear from you in the very near future. Let's do dinner at Ruby's this week, okay?" Erica said. She moved in closer so that only I could hear her. "Bring Brook, or not."

I laughed and nodded. "You're on. Hey, and thank you for believing in me."

Ten minutes later, Noah and I were in an otherwise empty living room playing a game. I was desperate to find Brook, but she had to finish up with her family.

"I'm beating you," he said, enthusiastically.

"You are. You really are." By the time I paid attention, it was too late. I'd lost. He jumped up and whooped.

"Yes! I finally beat you. I won!"

I applauded his victory dance and didn't blame him one bit.

"That's not good sportsmanship, Noah. You know better." Brook walked into the room and sat beside me. Her warm fingertips pressed into my neck, giving me a soft massage.

"I'm sorry. Good game, Cassie."

I shook his tiny hand and challenged him to another. He wasn't going to be happy playing for only ten minutes. Brook knew, though. She was patient and cheered for both of us as she watched us battle for control of the road. An hour later, she told Noah game time was up and he had to go upstairs and read.

"But, Mom. It's the weekend. I can read later."

"You're the one who signed up for extra reading. You want to win the prize at the end of the school year, don't you?"

"What's the prize? A car? A motorcycle? A puppy? Oh, say it's a puppy."

Brook nudged me with her foot. Oops.

Noah laughed. "No. It's a limo ride for me and three friends. And they rent out a theater, and we see a movie. Just us."

"Oh, I wonder if I can go?" I said. Noah shrugged. "Well, you'd better go read so you can win it."

He jumped up and raced out of the room. We waited until we heard his feet on the stairs.

"So, that was something, huh?" Brook touched my arm.

I grabbed her fingers and laced them with mine. "First of all, I truly thought you knew I was coming down. I'm sorry for interrupting your family meeting, but at the same time, I'm glad I did."

Brook scooted closer to me and rubbed her thumb on my bottom lip. "We should talk about what all was said."

I sat up straighter. "I really want to try this, Brook. I know you're worried about the age gap, but I'm not."

"You say that now, but what's it going to be like in ten, twenty years?"

I pulled her closer and looked into her beautiful eyes, momentarily forgetting my train of thought. "You're so beautiful."

She smiled. "Focus, Cass."

"Right. In ten years, we'll be ten times better than we are now. In twenty years, we'll be unstoppable."

"You're such a romantic." She looked away, seeming to listen to the sounds in the house, then leaned back to kiss me. "Let's talk about what else you said."

I froze. "What did I say? I mean, I said a lot of things all at once. A lot of really powerful people were just grilling me in this very room."

She softly kissed me and rested her forehead against mine. I felt her hand at the base of my neck, holding me next to her. "You told everyone in this room that you love me, except you never told me."

My heart fluttered. Shit. I'd come in guns blazing and rescued the princess before I professed my undying love to her. I tried to pull away, but she held me in place. "Yeah, I wanted to tell you before all of this with your family happened, but I never got the chance. Plus, I knew you were hesitant, and I didn't want to scare you."

"You still haven't told me."

I didn't hesitate again. "I love you. I have for a long time, and I hope you give me the chance to show you."

She tucked my hair behind my ear and rubbed my cheek. "You're the beautiful one, Cassie. I'm sorry I'm so guarded, but as you know, I have good reason to be."

"I promise I won't hurt you. I have no reason to. I understand you have Noah and want to protect him. We can go at whatever pace you want. Please just give us a chance." She nodded and my heart swelled. I couldn't sit any longer. I stood and pulled her into my arms. "Tell me you feel something for me. Maybe it's not love, but I know something's there."

She put her fingers to my lips. "Stop talking. Of course I love you. You've brought so much happiness to my life and to Noah's. You put up with my attitude and directness with ease. You see through all of it. You see and love me. Me."

"I wish you knew how perfect you are. For me. For Noah."

"What do we do now?" she asked.

"Well, we can keep this private until Noah finds out or we tell him. I'll continue to be the nanny from seven to seven and your doting girlfriend before and after hours. You can text me, call me, sext me, whatever you want."

Brook looped her arms around my waist. "Such a temptress you are." She kissed me quietly, but within seconds, we had to pull apart before we got carried away.

"You've got it all wrong. You, Brooklyn Addison Wellington, were always my perfect temptation."

Epilogue

We managed to hide our relationship from Noah for three months. Even then, he probably knew.

"Cassie. Are you awake? Want to play a game?"

I blinked awake and thought for sure I was dreaming. Noah was a foot from my face. I turned over and reached for Brook. Her warm, soft body was close. She snuggled back against me when she felt my touch.

Somebody was shaking my shoulder. "Cassie, I know you're awake. Come on."

My eyes flew open. Holy shit. I wasn't dreaming. "Um, Brook. Brook. Wake up." I gently shook her.

She rolled over and snuggled against me, a slight purr of contentment escaping her lips.

"Mom, can Cassie come down and play with me?"

Brook opened her eyes immediately, and we stared at one another for several seconds.

"Noah, did you knock before you came into my bedroom?" Brook propped herself up on her elbow to see his face, directly over my shoulder. He had crawled up onto the bed so he was almost leaning over us. Thank God the blankets were covering our nakedness.

"I did, but it was unlocked so I came in."

Brook looked at the clock. "Noah, it's not even seven. Let's have a rule where you don't wake us up until eight on the weekends. Give us time to sleep in. Go downstairs and eat a bowl of cereal if you can't wait for me to cook breakfast. We'll be down later."

He jumped off the bed. "Okay. See you later."

"Close the door behind you," I yelled. He returned, smiled, and closed it. And just like that, we were outed.

"That didn't last long," I said. I turned to Brook. "How are you with this? You good?"

She snuggled deeper under the covers and rubbed her hands over me. "He seems completely unfazed. Almost as if he already knew."

"I didn't tell him."

Her laugh was low and throaty. "I'm sure you didn't. He's just a smart kid."

I rubbed her back and placed little kisses on her forehead. "Are you okay with this?"

"Stop talking. I'm still sleeping."

That was her way of telling me she was good. Once we decided to go forward with our relationship, it was almost flawless. I was the nanny until seven, but I ate dinner with them every night. Sometimes I brought my homework and sat with Noah at the table. Sometimes the three of us played board games.

Once the school year was over, I planned to give up my position as nanny. Brook wanted me to apply to intern at Wellington's Green Alliance Organization this summer. Because I was keeping the apartment, I told her I'd still be available to work with Noah when school started in the fall. I wasn't keen on the idea of Noah getting a new nanny, but she didn't want me to be her girlfriend and his nanny. I told her we'd revisit the discussion at the end of Noah's summer.

"Maybe I should go downstairs and check on him. Just to see how he's doing." I was nervous about how he'd taken what he saw and knew he'd probably have questions.

"Close the door behind you. And put on some clothes."

"Yes, Boss." I kissed her cheek and slipped out from the warm covers, then found lounge pants and a T-shirt in Brook's closet. I had finals next week and needed the time to study, so getting up early was a necessity. This semester wasn't going to be all As like the last one, but I was close and had way more important things to think about than perfect grades.

"Cassie, want to make breakfast?" Noah was sitting at the counter playing on my Switch.

"Do I want to? I suppose I could make bacon and eggs and cinnamon toast. How's that sound? Better than cereal?"

He nodded. "I can help."

His little face was so bright and beautiful I couldn't help but squeeze his cheeks. "You can make the toast. How do you want your eggs?" He watched me sauté mushrooms and offered to add cheese when I started scrambling the eggs. "Maybe you'll be a chef when you grow up." He shrugged. "Okay, champ. What do you want to be when you get older?"

"A pilot. Or a superhero. Or a truck driver."

"Well, I think your mom will be proud of whatever you decide to do." I was sure Brook was out on the truck driver job, but she also wasn't going to force him into something he didn't want to do. We'd already had that talk. Given her history, Noah was being given a clean slate. And he had all the money he'd ever need to live comfortably, even if he wanted to be a surfer in Australia.

"You two are so loud." Brook slipped into the chair next to Noah. My heart thudded every time she walked into a room. She kissed Noah's cheek and winked at me.

"Art. Being creative cannot be done quietly." I waved the spatula at her. "I hope scrambled eggs are fine."

"Just don't burn my bacon."

"Shit," I said and flipped the pieces over in the pan. I cringed. "Sorry, Noah."

He giggled. "It's okay."

"I think we're ready for the toast." I pointed at the bread, and he jumped up to put slices in the toaster. I looked at Brook. "He's very helpful. He might end up being a chef like his Uncle Anthony or Patrick."

"Or a truck driver," Noah said.

Brook gave me an eyebrow raise.

"He's six."

"I'll be seven in ten days," Noah said.

Brook had planned a birthday party that was out of this world. He was at the age where it was expected to invite his whole class to his party. Even though it was May, the weather was iffy, so Brook was having it at the country club. She thought the house was too small and also didn't want a ton of people traipsing on the grounds, especially after the pool incident.

"Your party's going to be off the hook," I said.

I fixed three plates and sat on the other side of Noah. I tried not to read too much into this moment, all of us together doing a normal family thing, but I had to look away because I was choking up. I had lost and gained so much in less than a year. Who knew I would end up here, so much in love with an instant family? I knew it wouldn't always be perfect, but right here, right now, it was my everything.

"You better eat your food before I do," Noah said.

I turned back around to face them, knowing they would see the tears in my eyes even though I tried hard to hide them. "I can always make more."

"We have everything we need right here. Thank you for making us breakfast," Brook said.

"Thanks for having me over. You know how much I love you both."

"We love you, too, Cassie," Noah said. He munched on his toast like nothing major had happened this morning, like us sitting at the counter eating breakfast was normal.

Brook brushed away a tear off her own cheek. "I couldn't have said it any better."

"You still good with everything?" I was still worried about Noah finding out and how Brook would handle it.

She leaned back, winked, and gave me her signature single nod.

About the Author

Award-winning author Kris Bryant lives in Kansas City. She received her BA in English from the University of Missouri. She enjoys reading, writing, binge-watching TV shows, photography, spending time with her family, and being the faithful sidekick to her famous dog, Molly. Reach her at krisbryantbooks@gmail.com, www.krisbryant.net, or @krisbryant14.

Books Available From Bold Strokes Books

Flight to the Horizon by Julie Tizard. Airline captain Kerri Sullivan and flight attendant Janine Case struggle to survive an emergency water landing and overcome dark secrets to give love a chance to fly. (978-1-63555-331-4)

In Helen's Hands by Nanisi Barrett D'Arnuk. As her mistress, Helen pushes Mickey to her sensual limits, delivering the pleasure only a BDSM lifestyle can provide her. (978-1-63555-639-1)

Jamis Bachman, Ghost Hunter by Jen Jensen. In Sage Creek, Utah, a poltergeist stirs to life and past secrets emerge.(978-1-63555-605-6)

Moon Shadow by Suzie Clarke. Add betrayal, season with survival, then serve revenge smokin' hot with a sharp knife. (978-1-63555-584-4)

Spellbound by Jean Copeland and Jackie D. When the supernatural worlds of good and evil face off, love might be what saves them all. (978-1-63555-564-6)

Temptation by Kris Bryant. Can experienced nanny Cassie Miller deny her growing attraction and keep her relationship with her boss professional? Or will they sidestep propriety and give in to temptation? (978-1-63555-508-0)

The Inheritance by Ali Vali. Family ties bring Tucker Delacroix and Willow Vernon together, but they could also tear them, and any chance they have at love, apart. (978-1-63555-303-1)

Thief of the Heart by MJ Williamz. Kit Hanson makes a living seducing rich women in casinos and relieving them of the expensive jewelry most won't even miss. But her streak ends when she meets beautiful FBI agent Savannah Brown. (978-1-63555-572-1)

Face Off by PJ Trebelhorn. Hockey player Savannah Wells rarely spends more than a night with any one woman, but when photographer Madison Scott buys the house next door, she's forced to rethink what she expects out of life. (978-1-63555-480-9)

Hot Ice by Aurora Rey, Elle Spencer, and Erin Zak. Can falling in love melt the hearts of the iciest ice queens? Join Aurora Rey, Elle Spencer, and Erin Zak to find out! A contemporary romance novella collection. (978-1-63555-513-4)

Line of Duty by VK Powell. Dr. Dylan Carlyle's professional and personal life is turned upside down when a tragic event at Fairview Station pits her against ambitious, handsome police officer Finley Masters. ((978-1-63555-486-1)

London Undone by Nan Higgins. London Craft reinvents her life after reading a childhood letter to her future self and, in doing so, finds the love she truly wants. (978-1-63555-562-2)

Lunar Eclipse by Gun Brooke. Moon De Cruz lives alone on an uninhabited planet after being shipwrecked in space. Her life changes forever when Captain Beaux Lestarion's arrival threatens the planet and Moon's freedom. (978-1-63555-460-1)

One Small Step by MA Binfield. In this contemporary romance, Iris and Cam discover the meaning of taking chances and following your heart, even if it means getting hurt. (978-1-63555-596-7)

Shadows of a Dream by Nicole Disney. Rainn has the talent to take her rock band all the way, but falling in love is a powerful distraction, and her new girlfriend's meth addiction might just take them both down. 978-1-63555-598-1)

Someone to Love by Jenny Frame. When Davina Trent is given an unexpected family, can she let nanny Wendy Darling teach her to open her heart to the children and to Wendy? (978-1-63555-468-7)

Uncharted by Robyn Nyx. As Rayne Marcellus and Chase Stinsen track the legendary Golden Trinity, they must learn to put their differences aside and depend on one another to survive. (978-1-63555-325-3)

Where We Are by Annie McDonald. A sensual account of two women who discover a way to walk on the same path together with the help of an Indigenous tale, a Canadian art movement, and the mysterious appearance of dimes. (978-1-63555-581-3)

A Moment in Time by Lisa Moreau. A longstanding family feud separates two women who unexpectedly fall in love at an antique clock shop in a small Louisiana town. (978-1-63555-419-9)

Aspen in Moonlight by Kelly Wacker. When art historian Melissa Warren meets Sula Johansen, director of a local bear conservancy, she discovers that love can come in unexpected and unusual forms. (978-1-63555-470-0)

Back to September by Melissa Brayden. Small bookshop owner Hannah Shepard and famous romance novelist Parker Bristow maneuver the landscape of their two very different worlds to find out if love can win out in the end. (978-1-63555-576-9)

Changing Course by Brey Willows. When the woman of her dreams falls from the sky, intergalactic space captain Jessa Arbelle had better be ready to catch her. (978-1-63555-335-2)

Cost of Honor by Radclyffe. First Daughter Blair Powell and Homeland Security Director Cameron Roberts face adversity when their enemies stop at nothing to prevent President Andrew Powell's reelection. Book 11 in the Honor series. (978-1-63555-582-0)

Fearless by Tina Michele. Determined to overcome her debilitating fear through exposure therapy, Laura Carter all but fails before she's even begun until dolphin trainer Jillian Marshall dedicates herself to helping Laura defeat the nightmares of her past. (978-1-63555-495-3)

Not Dead Enough by J.M. Redmann. In the tenth book of the Micky Knight mystery series, a woman who may or may not be dead drags Micky into a messy con game. (978-1-63555-543-1)

Not Since You by Fiona Riley. When Charlotte boards her honeymoon cruise single and comes face-to-face with Lexi, the high school love she left behind, she questions every decision she has ever made. (978-1-63555-474-8)

Tennessee Whiskey by Donna K. Ford. After losing her job, Dane Foster starts spiraling out of control. She wants to put her life on pause and ask for a redo, a chance for something that matters. Emma Reynolds is that chance. (978-1-63555-556-1)

BOLDSTROKESBOOKS.COM

Looking for your next great read?

Visit BOLDSTROKESBOOKS.COM
to browse our entire catalog of paperbacks, ebooks,
and audiobooks.

**Want the first word on what's new?
Visit our website for event info,
author interviews, and blogs.**

Subscribe to our free newsletter for sneak peeks,
new releases, plus first notice of promos
and daily bargains.

SIGN UP AT
BOLDSTROKESBOOKS.COM/signup

Quality and Diversity in LGBTQ Literature

*Bold Strokes Books is an award-winning publisher
committed to quality and diversity in LGBTQ fiction.*

Lightning Source UK Ltd.
Milton Keynes UK
UKHW031345190221
379065UK00001BA/100